Outlaw's Obsession

Grizzlies MC Romance

Nicole Snow

Content copyright © Nicole Snow. All rights reserved.
Published in the United States of America.
First published in March, 2015.

Disclaimer: The following book is a work of fiction. Any resemblance characters in this story may have to real people is only coincidental.

Description

AN OUTLAW'S OBSESSION RUNS FURIOUS, DEEP, AND FOREVER...

CHRISTA

Hell always screams into my life on two wheels – so why the *hell* does he look like heaven? Rabid's nothing like the other vicious thugs in the Grizzlies Motorcycle Club. When I see the dark ink dancing on his stunning body, I almost believe he's here to save me, instead of just seduce me.

But I won't be fooled again. All the club brings is ruin, and they're back to give me more.

Sure, Rabid saved me once. Doesn't mean I'll get closer and dig my grave deeper, no matter how nice his rough hands would feel locked around my waist. Angels never kiss like devils, right?

RABID

I can't get her outta my skull. My brothers say she's like broken glass, but they don't know she's already lodged in my heart.

She's tense, suspicious, and totally scared. I'm gonna find

out why. Secrets don't mean a damned thing if she's in danger.

Christa's mine. I don't care if my patch makes her flip, or even if she keeps breathing fire my way every second we're together. I'm the best thing that ever walked into her life, and I'm not walking out.

I'll bleed rivers to get my brand on this woman. She's gonna wear it and get used to calling me her old man. I'll have my lips all over this redhead knockout if it's the last thing I do...

The Outlaw Love books are stand alone romance novels featuring unique lovers and happy endings. No cliffhangers! This is Rabid and Christa's story in the Grizzlies MC series.

I: Some Wounds Don't Fade (Christa)

It was hard to say goodbye to the kid because I knew what was waiting for me up the street.

Martin made tutoring easy. Only eight years old and obsessed with Napoleon, he wouldn't have needed me at all if the schools did a better job kindling his interests.

"His grades are already coming up! I dunno how you do it, lady, but you earned this. Here." His mother, Shirley, gushed all over me, pushing the check in my hands.

"Thanks." I was careful to make sure she didn't see how hard I pinched the scrap of paper when I stuffed it into my purse.

I didn't even take a second look to verify the right amount. There was no point when every single cent was going to an utter bastard who'd have me by the throat for the next ten years, no matter how much I earned.

Shirley gave me one last wave and I headed for my crappy old beater parked near the curb.

I got in my car and tried to collect my wits. It wasn't easy with the evening sun setting over Redding, casting its light across the dashboard. If there was one thing I hated as much as getting paid and forking it over to Big Ed, it was seeing my face in the rear view mirror.

The scars were still there. Visible reminders that the Grizzlies Motorcycle Club had wrecked my whole life, and it wasn't going to let up anytime soon.

Sure, they'd healed about as much as they were going to after a couple months, but my skin would never be the same. Fang robbed away what little beauty I had, torturing me in the back room of their clubhouse, all over an internal war I didn't even know about until he began to slice into my face and whisper death threats in my ear.

I pulled away from the curb and set off toward the nursing home, trying not to let my scars summon old ghosts. I'd survived Fang. Hell, I'd helped his own men kill him.

Missy, Brass, and that other man I didn't dare think about saved me from an agonizing end. And I returned the favor by marching out with them as living, breathing proof of everything the Grizzlies MC's old President had done.

Half his men couldn't take seeing me standing with Brass and his buddy, cut to pieces. They turned on the devil and his flock of demons. Rabid barely had time to escort me to safety when the shots started going off.

When it was all over, the man who pressed the knife into my face was dead. The Grizzlies MC chapter here in Redding began to change with new guys in charge.

Maybe their lives changed – I didn't care to know.

Mine didn't. Fang's death didn't change a thing. I was still knee deep in the same old shit that began long before the monster pressed his blade to my cheeks.

Big Ed answered to Redding, but he obviously wasn't interested in listening to the new crew leading their mother charter. He had his own agenda. All the bastards in the Klamath charter did, and they were going to make me pay until I was destitute and bloodless.

His bike was already parked outside the nursing home when I got there. A quick stop at the bank turned my hundred dollar check into cold cash, the only thing he'd accept. I added it to a couple hundred more I had waiting for him, hoping it'd be enough to make up for the payments I'd missed last month.

I parked and headed inside. Walking up those stairs was like going into hell. Without Ed, it would've been hard enough seeing my dad screwed up.

With the nasty looking biker hovering in the room like a total thug, it was much worse.

How bad would it be today? Would I have to listen to dad ask me who I was for the thousandth time while Ed stood by, cold and calculating, a grim reminder that there worse things waiting for my dad than early onset Alzheimer's if I didn't pay up?

They sat in their usual spots when I opened the door to my father's room. There was dad, staring out the window in his wheelchair. Big Ed was sprawled out on the bed. He bounced up with a muscular jerk. His large gut got in the way, and his trademark handlebar mustache twitched angrily, the only thing drawing attention away from his dark eyes.

"What the fuck took so long? I got another run to make before I head home to Klamath tonight. Fucking bitch." He spat on the floor. "You've been keeping me here all evening."

I stepped over his spit and reached into my purse, digging for the money as quickly as I could. He watched me while I pulled out the little stash and tore off the money clip. I shoved it into his face, trying not to shake.

"Here. Count it. Everything I promised."

He flipped through the twenties, letting out a loud snort when he finished counting. "That's it? Babe, you'd better start coughing up a whole lot more if you ever wanna skip these little visits. You're about one dollar over the threshold that keeps me from knocking his fucking teeth out. One."

Ed growled, pointing to my father. Dad stayed mercifully oblivious, muttering to himself as a little bird landed on a tree branch outside.

"It's everything I have this week," I whispered, trying to stay calm for my father's sake. "Don't know how I'm even going to make rent, to be honest. I'll have more for you later."

Big Ed shot up, grabbed me by the shoulders. His hot breath reeked tobacco, sour whiskey, and something else I could never quite identify. It stank plenty.

I was scared for dad, but not for me. Not anymore.

Surviving Fang's torture drove away the terror I used to feel when he got up in my face or slammed me against the nearest wall.

"Stop being such an ungrateful cunt! You know I'm doing you a big fucking favor, right? Because we could do things much differently, babe. Trust me."

"Ed, please." I pushed against his fat chest, but he only tightened his grip.

Bastard. I pushed harder, the way he always made me struggle, before he finally cut me loose. Too bad it never shut him up.

"I could shut the door behind you, cut his fucking throat, and take you for a ride north on my bike. Shit, we'd probably be doing the old fart a favor. It's not like he knows who the fuck either of us are or what we're up to." He paused.

My eyelids fluttered shut. I quietly prayed he'd stop. He never did.

"You're a little worn to be a good whore, Christa, but there are plenty brothers in Oregon who'd love to use that firecracker cunt between your legs. A redhead's still a redhead. Doesn't matter if she's got a few scrapes and scratches." He licked his lips, eyeing the shameful lines on my face.

I shook my head. I was used to crude comments about my natural hair forever, but hearing about the scars was new. Hearing it from Ed's foul mouth was the worse.

"Tell me I'm being a good guy, Chrissy. I wanna hear you say it. You know how fucking easy I'm letting you off?

I'm not even asking you to pay for the gas it takes to get down here just to put your tits into a vise. My bros would kick my ass if they knew what a softie I'm being."

My head snapped up, and we locked eyes. Was he fucking serious? As if this wasn't humiliating enough...

Sigh. I had to spit it out, if only to make him leave sooner.

"You're doing me a favor. You're playing nice. You're the best debt collector a girl could ask for." I could barely force the words through my clenched teeth.

There. Is that what you wanted, you fucking asshole? I hated when my brain felt like burning coal. Every thought hurt, hot and fierce as moving fire.

Big Ed laughed. He walked past me through, moving through the narrow space between dad's bed and the TV stand. His arm went out and gave me a rough shove on his way out.

"Don't you fucking forget it, bitch!" I steadied myself against the wall, hoping I wouldn't have to turn around before he was finally gone. Then he opened his fat mouth again, and I knew luck wasn't on my side today.

"Oh, and don't you dare think about going to any of the Redding boys with this. It won't help your ass – it'll just be more trouble. Rip's never backing down. He doesn't give a fucking shit what Blackjack or any of those other cocksuckers say. We don't take our orders from this town. We're free men. And if you stir up trouble, you'll just cause a damned war on your doorstep. Your job's easy. Fucking remember it."

Easy? Easy?!

Now, I had to turn around. I wanted to throw myself at him, scream, jab my fingernails into his eyeballs and tear his stupid mustache off.

But it wouldn't do any good.

If I somehow survived and got him arrested, his brothers would come to town. They'd know who did it. And everything I'd heard said the bastard was right – the new Grizzlies leadership in Redding was too busy finding its footing.

My problems weren't theirs, if they even cared. Besides, I wouldn't dare drag Rabid and his brothers into this, though he'd jump at the chance. They saved me once. I'd already screwed over my dad, and I'd rather die than see anybody else get killed for my screw ups, my debt.

"Ed – we're done. Please." He wanted me to beg him, so I did.

The asshole stopped, stood up straight, pulled on his cut. He was coming toward me again.

No, no, no...

"What'sa matter, Chrissy? Seriously?" His voice was so soft, but the way he grabbed my chin and tilted my head revealed his inner demon. "You ought to work your little ass off and go on a retreat. You're so fuckin' stressed. It's no good for your heart, you know."

He thumped his chest. The sound was the first thing to really make me shake. It reminded me how huge, dangerous, and ruthless these men really were.

"Life gives do overs if you play your cards right. Keep

coughing up the dough. Keep doing everything I say. The old fuck over there'll get to live out his days in peace. You'll get to live another week without my boys running a train on your sweet ass, wearing nothing but their cuts. God, I bet you fuck *good* – even if you look like you stuck your fucking face into a cat fight."

Laughing, he reached for my ass, pulled me to him. I had to fight to make sure his disgusting tongue never contacted my skin.

Ass. Hole.

He let me go at just the right time. I went spinning toward the wall and crashed, hit the TV hard with my hip. Big Ed roared, stomping past me again, this time ripping open the door to the hall.

"You take care of yourself, Chrissy. Who the fuck knows. The universe works in mysterious ways. You keep working with a fire under your ass, maybe you'll get to have a little biker bar up by Crater Lake again one of these days. We'd *love* to give you the fucking money to get it off the ground again, soon as you pay this shit off."

I closed my eyes. Finally, he was gone, leaving the thunderous echo of the door slamming behind him in his wake. Just before he disappeared, I caught the roaring grizzly bear on his back, hateful symbol of all my terrible mistakes.

Christ. Seriously. He'd gotten to me again, even though it took a lot these days. My hand was squeezing my purse for dear life, and that made me realize how fucking empty it was. Just then, dad chose to turn around and look at me with his vacant eyes.

"You lost, lady? Can I help you?"

I stopped and stared up at the ceiling for a full minute. There was one more thing in my purse, something I'd bought with a couple bucks I hadn't forked over to Big Ed.

"Here, dad. Your favorite candy." It was a dark chocolate bar I'd gotten at the gas station, something he always liked in better times when he could still fish and ride his bike.

With any luck, it might slow the weight melting off him too. Dad didn't look like the man who raised me anymore. He used to be big and strong and muscular, ready to lift the world. Now, he couldn't even lift his own legs to walk.

He sniffed, gave me the look that hurt the most – the vacant one that reminded me he really had no clue who I was, and probably never would again. The lucid moments were so rare these days. It wasn't fair, damn it.

He wasn't even sixty. Four or five years ago, he'd been enjoying his first year of early retirement, and now everything he'd scrimped and saved was being used to support him while every last light went out in his head forever.

"Hm." He unwrapped the chocolate slowly, something that had become our ritual for the last six months. "Oh, yeah. Hell yeah. Tastes good."

He chewed a square and looked up at me, wonder in his eyes. I sniffed back more tears. He didn't remember his daughter, but I'd managed to make him truly happy with this little thing.

That counted for something wherever my worldly karma was being tallied up, right?

"What was your name again, dear?"

"Christa. Christa Kimmel. You can count on me to be here next week, dad, same as always." I leaned down and gave him a quick peck on the forehead as his lips formed a confused smile. "I don't care how hard anybody makes it. I'm never going to stop loving you."

That night, I stared into my empty refrigerator. My stomach growled, pissed that I hadn't fed it anything since the roast beef sandwich Shirley gave me. I turned away in disgust, gulping two big cups of water to take the edge off.

Dad was safe for another week, the only thing that really mattered. But I couldn't stop wondering how *I* was going to keep living like this.

Something had to give. It always did. Bad luck caught up to me with trouble right by its side, always wearing a Grizzlies MC cut.

I'd been in deep before I got into trouble with the Redding club. Fang and his monstrous brothers tortured me because I'd been tutoring this teenager, Jackie, younger sister to Missy, who'd been claimed by Brass. He was the VP now, but he'd been one of the main traitors then, leader among the men who ended up destroying Fang and taking over the club.

Well, at least there was one less demon in the world.

Not that it did me much good.

The awful memories weren't the only thing that kept haunting me. Every few weeks, Rabid came by, quite possibly the only man I didn't mind seeing with the murderous bear patch on his leather. His club sent him around to make sure I wasn't going to go to the cops about anything that happened during Fang's overthrow.

They didn't have a clue I'd been avoiding pigs since I was fifteen. I'd been wild, and I'd made dad's life a living hell for the next few years. Guess it went with the territory growing up a biker's daughter without a mother to straighten me out.

The stupid shit I'd gotten into wouldn't have wrapped around my neck like a noose if it didn't keep compounding. At eighteen, I hitchhiked my way up to Klamath Falls and made the greatest mistake of my life.

I was young and stupid. I thought I understood outlaw motorcycle clubs since dad was in one, but I didn't really know crap. My teenage brain couldn't even compute borrowing six figures from one with double digit interest.

I thought I was tough and wild. Thought I could run a bar without letting the Grizzlies MC walk all over me. I completely wilted the first time they wanted me to launder money through them.

Their President, Rip, got in my face, close enough to feel his beard's tangled bristles. He reminded me exactly what I was – their bitch, not a real businesswoman.

I had to get out. I ran, and ran the bar into the ground, leaving a real accounting mess behind. The whole thing fell apart within a year, but the debt remained.

I should've seen it coming. I'd been a smart girl, a trophy winner and a gifted kid before I flushed my brains down the toilet for adventure. I'd still managed a perfect score on the SAT even when I was fucking off.

I should've seen it coming, but I was too young, too naïve. Too strung out on hope and smarts. I didn't realize I was missing the magic ingredient – bravado – until it was too late. Some lessons have to be learned on the streets instead of in schools, I guess.

My head knew it. My heart refused to listen.

The years after Klamath went by in a blur of failures and intimidation, and there I was at twenty-three, slaving away for these savages I'd never escape.

God, what I would've done for a good drink to knock me on my ass. The gifted brain I'd never done anything good with sure loved to think. It never shut up unless it was doused in poison. And so, I suffered another evening alone, resisting the urge to pick up my cheap pay-as-you-go phone and call up Rabid.

I still had his number – he'd insisted on me taking it, the same way he made me promise to call him if anything came up between his visits.

He tempted me to pour my heart out. Maybe more than that too.

The boy – no, the *man* – was handsome. Six feet tall, broad shoulders, short dark hair and pristine hazel eyes to match. Lickable was too weak a word for how his clothes clung to the sculpted muscle underneath, the kinda hard, rugged strength a man gets with violence, rather than pumping iron.

He couldn't have been much older than me, but his face had experience and wisdom. He wore a confidence that said he'd avoided all the stupid things I'd done in my youth.

When I let it all lay out, Rabid was a fucking conundrum.

He excited me as much as he scared the hell out of me.

I hated being attracted to a brother in the Grizzlies MC at all. Too bad loathing the dark men behind the bear patch hadn't stopped me from admiring anything dark, masculine, and heavily tattooed.

That was Rabid to a tee. Rabid the brave, Rabid the biker bastard, Rabid the enigma who got into my head during dark hours like these, nudging me to learn more about him.

Thank God he wasn't perfect.

It didn't take hanging around him long to realize he was a crazy, womanizing biker who partied, drank, and fucked as hard as the rest of them. I had a pretty good idea what men like him did behind closed doors after the bar, and what happened in outlaw clubhouses was ten times worse.

I didn't care if Rabid melted my panties off. I wouldn't let myself get an inch deeper into his wicked world. And even if he wanted me, scarred cheeks and all, there was no way in *hell* I'd end up in his bed and become one more notch on the bedpost.

There were bigger problems to deal with than a silly cat-and-mouse crush. There always were.

Welcome to my life.

II: Playing With Fire (Rabid)

Red was riding my cock like a champ, but for some fucked up reason it was taking ages to blow. My nuts didn't want to give up their fire.

Before Christa, this bitch rocking her hips into mine, screaming as she sank down to my balls, absolutely slayed me. Now? Fuck, I was lucky to stop thinking about the chick outta my reach just long enough to bust inside this slut's tight cunt.

And I really needed that shit. Anything to sandblast the edges off my stress, everything Doctor Jack couldn't reach.

"God, baby! Rabid!" Red growled, grinding her pussy on my dick, staring down at me through half-narrowed eyes. "I'm going to pop my spine out of place if you don't give it up. Don't you want to come for me?"

Her long fingernails raked down my chest. They were painted bright red. What fucking else?

The slut was a knockout, and she was all mine. I hogged her to myself, never letting other brothers have this pussy while I was using it, which was all the fucking time when we didn't have some shit to deal with outside these walls.

Greedy bastard. Hard not to be when this chick was hot, horny, and just a little crazy.

I should've been satisfied with her sucking and fucking me dry. So, why the hell was it so hard to let go and float away on Red's pretty skin?

"Get off," I snarled, giving her ass a sharp whack. I always loved the way a chick's butt bounces when I smack it around. "On your hands and knees. Stuff that fucking pillow into your mouth and swallow your screams. Roman gave me shit about us keeping brothers up last night."

She rolled and flipped over, waiting for me with her fine ass up, nice and submissive. It wasn't just an act. She really loved the way I fucked her. The girl never complained about the way I kept her away from all the other brothers. She'd do any dirty, nasty, fucked up thing I commanded.

Had a feeling she was holding out to be somebody's old lady like a lot of sluts. Shame the chick was too dumb to realize that barely ever happened.

Whores were for fucking. Old ladies were for loving, and a man in this club never went back to skanks after putting his brand on some worthy chick.

I looked at the clock. Fuck.

Already past three in the morning, and we had club business tomorrow. The brothers had every reason in the world to knock down this door and beat my ass if I didn't let them get some shuteye.

Easier said than done when I mounted Red's pussy

from behind. The whore had a mouth like a siren on her. She was drooling and shrieking like a wild animal just three strokes in. I stopped, reached between her legs, and gave her clit a rough pinch.

"Baby! Why'd you fucking stop?" she moaned, desperate as all hell.

"You gotta keep it down. Either stuff that goddamned thing in your mouth like a good girl, or I'll finish myself in the shower."

She loved to be bossed around. I helped shove one corner of my pillow into her mouth before I started thrusting again. I didn't need to follow her gurgles and rasps to know she'd started coming.

Her whole fucking body seized up. That soft, warm silk around my cock turned molten hot, gushed and locked onto my dick. Her skin heated just as much under my fingertips.

I was frustrated as fuck I wasn't there yet. Seriously, what was this shit?

I pinched the whore's nipple 'til her moans went silent, rubbing her clit furiously to start them all over again, never letting up on the bone shaking thrusts. I'd fuck her right through the goddamned mattress if this kept up.

I knew why it felt like a chore. Knew it, and didn't want to fucking admit it.

Red couldn't get me off anymore because she wasn't the one I wanted. Ever since I got my hands on a hotter redhead a couple months ago, I'd been fucked in the head, like the chick cast some kinda hex or something.

Trying not to think about Christa was like that fucking kid's game where you're not supposed to imagine a pink rhino.

In my screwed up head, it wasn't the club slut thrashing and screaming her throat raw underneath me. It was demure Christa, her nice full ass shaking on my cock, full figure tits bouncing in my hand. The hips on that woman were built to suck a man dry, and I'd bet every dollar I'd ever earned her pussy's like a fucking virgin's compared to this slut's.

Shit! Hellfire churned in my balls, ready to burn a hole through my sack if it couldn't get out.

Grabbing Red's hair, I snarled, pushed her face first into the pillow stuffed in her ruby lips. Christa's locks were brighter, softer, gold to this bitch's bronze. My brain wouldn't shut the fuck off once it fixed on her image, and I slammed my cock up to the whore's womb, imagining I was having somebody better.

This fuck was all hate. Envy.

I hated myself for not being able to get over that chick who wouldn't even look at my dick, let alone let it between her legs. I'd given her plenty of opportunities too. I had good pussy – at least by any club whore's standards – but I still wanted more.

I wanted the absolute fucking best.

The rickety bed snapped like it was going to collapse when I finally came. The seed pouring out in thick jets set Red off all over again. Her spasms went fucking nuclear around my dick and I threw my head back, growling out a long curse, aching each time I imagined Christa's sweet cunt wringing the come from my body instead.

"Fuuuuck!" I worked my hips into her, hate fucking, not stopping 'til everything below my waist went numb.

When it was over, the disgust set in. I pulled out, reached for the bottle of Jack on the floor, and took a long pull. Thank fuck it was still half-full.

"Rabid? What's wrong, baby?" Red wasn't totally stupid. She could sense the change coming over me the last few weeks, ever since we offed Fang and started to clean up the shithole this club had become.

"Nothing this venom won't solve." I rolled over after another good swig, forcing the bottle into her painted fingers. "You're not my fucking shrink. You're fun for me and any other brother who wants your ass. Drink your fill and go the fuck to sleep."

"Okay."

Good girl. Smart girl. Any other answer would've stirred up the bitter, crazy shit churning in my guts, and I'd have thrown her outta the room so fast she'd be lucky to pick her skimpy clothing off the floor.

Red knocked herself out long before I did. I drained every last drop in that bottle, praying it'd be enough to put me down 'til morning.

Luck wasn't kind tonight.

It took forever to feel Doctor Jack work his magic. Christa didn't want to leave my brain. Worst of all, my dick was hard again before I nodded off, jealous and hungry for everything I couldn't have, and that *really* pissed me right the fuck off.

Two Months Earlier...

I'd never forget the first time I saw her.

She was broken, scared, and just barely made it into the van in time before Fang's goons came after us. Brass' old lady, Missy, had barely gotten her outta the clubhouse in time before Fang and his loyal bastards closed in.

We'd snagged Christa at the last second, yeah, but shit hadn't gone according to plan. Both women were supposed to come with us, but Missy was too late. I had to watch her get dragged back into the clubhouse while I floored it. She'd be a goner 'til the final showdown.

The first good look I got at the redhead was in the rear view mirror. I saw right away they had her long enough to do some serious damage.

I knew she was hurt, but I didn't realize how bad 'til I helped clean her cuts later. The angry red imperfections our fucked up Prez carved barely registered. I was too lost in those eyes and the smooth creamy skin contrasting with the fire in her hair.

Imperfections? Fuck that.

The first time she looked up into my eyes, bright green eyes glowing, my dick beat like a second heart in my pants. My eyes didn't give a fuck that she was hurt. They were greedy sons of bitches, and they went all over her body, studying her curves while I cleaned her face with a warm washcloth, offering her sips of water from a canteen.

The swollen blotches on her face and the scratches left

by the bastard Prez's knife didn't hide a fucking thing. The girl was *hot*, a full figured hourglass with ample tits and ass. She was a natural too. Hotter than Red or any other whore the club had – fuck, maybe hotter than any it would ever have.

I knew I was fucked for wanting to bed her when she was so hurt. The last thing she needed was a wolf like me breathing down her neck, pawing at her, hungry to shove my tongue between her legs.

I had to restrain myself. Tying down my instinct was the hardest thing I'd learned in twenty-four years on this earth, but I managed. I let her rest, guarded her in the backroom while the boys in the front plotted one last hit.

The whole destiny of our club was changing, and I knew I might end up dead. One wrong move was a fatal one in a motorcycle club's civil war.

But just then, staring at the red haired beauty, I didn't give a single shit.

She gave me something more to fight for. Brotherhood should've been enough, but dammit, I wasn't sure what it meant anymore with Fang and half the old crew showing their true demon faces. Everything I wanted was right there in the room with me, and I wanted revenge.

I wanted to tear Fang and his boys to pieces, almost as bad as I wanted to pull Christa into my arms and tear her clothes away. I was used to hauling tail into my bed or the nearest ditch on demand. Holding back was new to me, and watching her sit still and breathe, shaking every supple part, just caused lava to rush through my veins.

I had to splash water in one palm and wipe it over my face several times. Wondering if I was dreaming, wondering if I'd melt from the inside out – fuck!

Worst timing ever too. Blackjack, Brass, and the Prairie Devils who'd come down from Montana to help us out were all riding my ass to focus on the mission.

Brass came up with the fake surrender idea – a trick to get us one last meeting with Fang beneath Mount Shasta. He also had the balls to think up using Christa to hit any of the brothers with a heart where it hurt, make them see with their own two eyes what kinda sick shit Fang and his cronies were up to.

When I heard about the plan, I nearly lost my shit. I wouldn't have hesitated to punch my best friend and closest brother right in his fucking face for putting her in danger – but Christa refused.

She insisted on playing her part. Fuck, she *agreed* with facing down the heavily armed sadist who'd left those scars on her sweet cheeks.

I tried like hell to talk her outta it, but she was determined.

I knew right then the chick was either batshit crazy, or she'd already seen some serious shit before. Later, when the moment came, she stepped up with Brass, facing the armed bastards Fang had called in from other charters face-to-face. Brass made a pretty speech, showing off the girl, making every brother decide right there if this was the club they wanted.

When the shots started going off, I went absolutely

ape. I grabbed her, forced her to the ground, and covered her with my body while the shots exploded all around us. My brothers were in the thick of it, pushing the fuckers back, killing anybody who didn't surrender and give us Fang's head on a pike.

"Stay down, baby. You move with me. If I get hit, you stay down too. Ignore whatever happens to me. Don't move 'til the gunfire stops."

"Rabid, it's fine. We're almost –"

Fuck. She was trying to crawl out from under me. Damn if I didn't grab her, slam her down to the ground, and hold her rough in the California dirt. Just in time too. Some asshole's bullet buzzed right over my head. A couple inches to the right, and it'd have gone through us both.

That did it. She flinched underneath me, yelped, and still I held on, waiting for more shots to come. I was ready for anything to keep this girl safe. I'd let the lead rip right through me and bleed all over her if I had to.

Anything to keep her safe.

Fang and his assholes put her through hell once. I wasn't gonna let them put her through any more. Not just because she was the hottest thing I'd ever had wriggling underneath me, but because it was *right*.

The cancer in the MC had us all fucked up about right and wrong. It took Blackjack and Brass leading the charge to remind me what this club was supposed to be about.

We were Grizzlies. We were bikers. We were warriors.

We were a shield to everybody under our protection, especially folks like Christa, who'd done us a huge fucking favor while we were busy cleaning house.

A few weeks ago, I'd been too scared to vote for Fang's removal when we had the chance to oust him peacefully. Well, more peacefully than this – I still doubted the old dog would step aside without a fight. Now, I was hellbent on making sure all the evil shit he'd done – hell, the fucked up things I'd done by default – were undone.

This wasn't about some high minded flowery crap. This was about becoming real men who defended their family, the righteous blood and brotherhood the club was supposed to represent. And God willing, soon would again.

"Go." I pressed my lips to Christa's ear and said it, hot and insistent.

She crawled forward. I moved with her, grateful the anarchy behind us was quieting down. Somebody had gotten the upper hand.

I turned, looked behind me, and let relief pour out my lungs. I didn't see an army of Fang's bastards descending on us. Instead, our boys were rounding up the assholes who'd surrendered, and the ones who hadn't were bleeding out next to the trees.

It was gonna be hell to clean up later. Right now, all I cared about was putting more distance between her and the battlefield. I headed for our bikes, and didn't let her move a single limb outside my shadow 'til we had vehicles between us.

Blackjack, our de facto Prez, came staggering toward the van with a couple other brothers helping him. Poor bastard had a fresh hole in his leg, staining his jeans dark red. Fuck.

The battle wasn't bloodless, but it had to be close to over. We'd won. Fang would be finished soon, if he wasn't already.

I got on my feet and gently pulled Christa up with both hands. "You did good, baby. Seriously. You've done more for this club through this whole thing than anybody could've asked."

She shrugged. "Common enemy. I'm not the type to let a man torture me and then walk away. He's still got Missy."

"Not for long," I growled. "Brass'll find her. She's his old lady. A man in this life never lets his woman down. Never."

"If you say so." There wasn't much feeling in her voice.

That caused my eyes to shift and lock onto her. What the fuck? Did she really believe any of us would leave a brother's old lady MIA, resigned to whatever evil shit was waiting for her?

Maybe she wasn't as smart as I thought. I'd cut her some slack, seeing how she'd just done us a massive favor. Coming outta any meat grinder can do fucked up things to a person's mind.

"Walk with me." I reached out, grabbed her hand.

One of the brothers tending Blackjack looked up and nodded, a stern faced dude with a shaved head and lightning bolts on his temples named Asphalt. He confirmed what I knew: we were done here, and I was free to take her home, away from this place with burned flesh and blood curdling the air.

I led her to my bike and helped her on it, fixing her helmet. She winced once when my hand accidentally brushed the long cut flowing from the corner of her mouth to her ear. My heart beat hellfire all over again, enraged that the bastard we'd all followed had marked her this way.

"Sorry," I grunted, strapping her in.

"It's okay. Just take me home. I need rest."

Christa gave me directions to her place, and soon we were heading south toward Redding, ahead of the rest of the crew. Thank fuck I'd get a break from the cleanup duty. It was gonna take a lot of hands and some heavy bribes to any cops to hide all those bodies and broken vehicles.

On the open road, with her on my back, the shit seemed a million miles away, though. A cool spring breeze coursed through her hair, sticking out the helmet around the edges. I watched it flow in my mirrors and suppressed a smile.

This was living.

If I ever needed proof we'd both survived and gotten away intact, it was right there on the back of my bike. Beautiful, radiant, and alive.

No, it wasn't just her fingers hanging tight around my waist, driving my dick up harder than the steel rod it became in the thick of battle. Having her so fucking close, pressed up to me like this, did awesome things to the heart. This gal was a feast for all the senses.

Something about her made me feel alive without having to hit the bottle or jackhammer between her legs. Oh, you'd better believe I wanted to shake her to fucking pieces. Bite her, claim her, and mark her as mine. I wanted to pump my seed in every hot wet hole she had, having her like nobody ever had, like nobody ever would again.

But there was more to this shit. Something I couldn't pin down. I'd never been big into philosophy and true love bullshit, so I switched off my brain and rode, enjoying her warmth amid the breeze.

Shit was getting ridiculous. I wasn't about to shelve the partying I was used to, all for some chick I barely knew who just wanted a ride home.

God damn. Maybe it's time you start fucking some variety to get off this redhead fixation...

Easier said than done. The minute we pulled up to her apartment and she hopped off my bike, I was gawking like a moron at her long legs and firm ripe tits again.

"Thanks for the ride. Guess I should thank you for saving my butt too," she said, reaching up to undo her helmet. "I should've said something sooner. I think you'll understand if I'm a little out of it today."

"You got every right to be," I said, standing up and putting her helmet away. "There's nothing you need to apologize for, baby. It's gonna take this club some time to sort out all the shit that happened today. When the dust settles, everybody with a brain's gonna agree we owe you big time."

"Rabid, no." She held up her hands, closing her eyes like she was sick at the thought. "I don't want any favors or anyone to owe me anything. I just want to be done with this. I'm trying to live a normal life here."

Fuck! My heart sank at about the same rate my dick deflated. She didn't want to see me again, or any other brother wearing the bear patch.

Not like I could blame her.

On the other hand, *so fucking what?* Why the hell was I so disappointed? The chances of ever having this girl were next to nil, but fuck if that ever stopped me before. It was just gonna take some work.

I nodded, trying to look as understanding as possible. "I gotcha. I'll be by for the next month or so to check on you. If you change your mind about anything, just shout."

I revved my bike, ready to peel outta there and leave her to chew on what I said. But she stopped, put her boot on mine, and tugged on my cut. Her emerald eyes were just like a jaded cat's.

"You heard what I said. I know you're a smart guy, Rabid. Look, I'm not going to go to any authorities about what happened if that's what you're worried about."

Damn it. She knew us too well.

I wondered how, narrowing my eyes as I looked at her. "Not my call, babe. All the brothers feel sorry as shit for what happened. We're making the bastards who did it pay, and that's the best we can offer. If it were up to me, I'd cut you loose and never come knocking on your door again."

I snorted in my head. *Yeah fucking right.*

"Sounds a little too easy," she said, a snarky smile tugging at her lips.

"Fuck yeah, it is. The club's gonna have a metric fuck-ton on its plate when our leadership's done playing musical chairs. Plus we got the Mexican cartel cutting us to pieces further south. Those fucks aren't gonna go for a truce just because Fang's out. They're not easy like the Devils MC up north."

Christa nodded, almost like she understood. The girl might be wise as she was beautiful, but fuck if I was gonna leave it at that.

"I trust you, Christa, but the club won't 'til some time passes. You're a civilian. Blackjack and the rest need to make sure we've got an understanding. It's not every day somebody like you stumbles into our world, and I wish to hell it never happened like this."

"Oh?" She folded her arms, reaching one finger to the bright red cut on her face. "Doesn't this say anything? Our understanding's written in blood on my fucking face."

Ouch. Those earthy green eyes turned ice cold. I didn't blink. I shook my head, hoping she'd get it if I just worded shit differently.

"It's not like that. Look, we don't know you from Eve. We gotta look out for ourselves too, especially with rival charters who won't be happy to see Fang go. We can't risk any run-ins with the Feds here in Redding. I can't turn you loose with just your word. I gotta make sure our understanding's really as clear as the hurt on your face."

"Whatever. Once a week. Five minutes. That's all I'm giving you, Rabid. I don't owe you anything. If I was some weak little thing built to go running to the cops at the first sign of trouble, I wouldn't have asked you to drive me home. I'd have asked for a phone and dialed 9-1-1 instead."

Christ. It's like she caught my balls and gave 'em a twist. Just *who* the fuck was this chick?

I'd never heard of a part-time tutor who held her ground like this. If I didn't know any better, I'd have guessed she had experience in the MC world before. Maybe a brother, or a father in some club?

"Trust me, baby, five minutes is all I fucking need."

Oh, yeah. I said it. Didn't even disguise the lust thudding in my chest.

Never mind the fact that I'd love to spend five hours minimum making her howl and dig her nails into my back. The dagger tongue on this chick just fanned the flames, made me shift my legs to hide the massive wood jerking in my pants.

"Good. I'll see you around, then." She turned, flashed me one last glimpse of that brilliant red hair, and headed for the door.

"Hey!" I yelled to her before she took the handle. "What's your last name?"

She hesitated. I squeezed the handlebars, wondering how I could be so fucking stupid. *Think fast.*

"You know, so the club can keep tabs. Make sure your property's all protected from any fucks who wanna retaliate over Fang. We won't dig into anything we shouldn't. Promise."

I did a quick X over my heart. Crossing my chest meant more than any civilian doing it. My Grizzlies MC patch was inked on my chest underneath the shirt and the leather. When anybody wearing the bear made a promise like this, it fucking meant something.

"Kimmel," she said, flinging open the door.

I watched her disappear. Question time was over. Fine by me because that last piece was all I needed.

Bike purring, I headed for the highway, ready to rejoin my brothers to clean up the battlefield and then lock down our clubhouse. Ours, not Fang's.

For now, I had everything I needed.

Christa was gonna be a challenge, all right. I could feel it in my bones. Taming her was gonna be as big and bad and beautiful a task as remaking our whole MC after all the dark times.

Fuck if I didn't love the chase. It wasn't a question of *if* I'd find out what kinda panties she wore to compliment that blazing hair.

It was when, where, and the answer was *fucking soon.*

Two months later, on a bright summer day, something hit me in the face. Shit kept coming like a heavy rain, pungent and bitter as napalm.

I snorted out Jack. Somebody dropped the bottle that was splashing me in the face.

I jerked awake, listening to Red yelp next to me. My

fists were up, ready to punch whoever the fuck was rousing me like this. The big shape I aimed for caught my hand like a wall with fingers, squeezed, and crunched my knuckles.

"Ah, fuck! Let go! What the hell's wrong with you?" My eyes fought to adjust.

Not like they needed to. I knew who it was before I even saw him. Only one asshole in the clubhouse with a grip like that, the big bastard Blackjack appointed to be our new Enforcer, Roman.

"You already know." He reached to the silver watch attached to the wrist about to break my hand and tapped it. "Three minutes."

"Shit! Fuck!" I kicked my legs against his knees.

Roman never smiled. The fuck rarely showed any expression at all, but I could tell he was enjoying this. He let me squirm for another twenty seconds before he finally let go. I went flying back, fell all over Red, shaking out my hand to bring the blood flow back.

Goddamn it. I'd been chewed out by Brass and Blackjack for being late to church the last couple times, but I was used to their shit. The new guy was something else. He was already gone by the time I was up, grabbing my clothes off the ground and throwing the whore's on the bed.

"Rabid, baby, what's going on?"

"You're gonna get the fuck out and shake your ass elsewhere. Club business."

I'd said everything I needed to. I dressed quickly, not

stopping to give her another look. If it hadn't taken me so damned long to fall asleep last night, I wouldn't be rushing around like this.

By the time I got into the meeting room, all the brothers were waiting. I took my usual spot next to Brass, who shot me a *come-the-fuck-on* look. All the more serious now that he was my friend, my brother, and the VP of the whole club.

"Glad you could drag yourself in here late, son." Blackjack looked like a scorned emperor, his long gray hair flowing down his shoulders. "Pull up a fucking chair and stay awhile."

"It won't happen again, Prez. Late night." Fuck. I sounded like a goddamned kid coming in after curfew.

"Yeah, make sure it doesn't," he growled. "One more time and I'll sit you down for a heart-to-heart with Roman."

The bulldog Enforcer across the table flattened his hands on the wood. All the brothers laughed.

He was a good choice for scaring the pants off any asshole outside the club, but I wasn't intimidated. I'd hit bigger fucks before and won. Never mind the fact this guy was in prison while all the drama in the club was going down.

Bastard probably had about a hundred special ways to tear my head off on Blackjack's order. Fuck it. The officers had good reason to bust my balls, and it was up to me to make sure I never found myself at the receiving end of the gorilla's fists.

"Okay, now that all the jigsaws are in place, let's talk business." Blackjack slapped the bear claw he'd inherited from Fang down on the table, a kind of symbolic gavel. "Brass – you want to deliver the latest on the cartel?"

He nodded, stood up, aiming a laser pointer at the big map of California pinned to the board behind the Prez. "We're holding the line in Sacramento. The heavy shit the Devils sent from Montana gave 'em a few surprises they didn't expect. If all goes well, we might be able to call it our territory and mean it by autumn."

I would've laughed if it weren't so damned serious. It was surreal to see my bro treating this shit like an honest-to-God business meeting. Of course, no boardroom outside the military ever let the pins and flags stuck to their board represent human lives.

Blackjack turned to face us. "Listen well, boys. Every one of you are gonna be helping on the runs to SoCal as soon as we've got our old charter in the capitol locked down. We're not fucking letting up when the Mexicans are on the run."

A couple guys flinched, turned their heads down. Mainly the prospects, who were new to this war business.

Not me. Shit, tearing down the open road and chasing those terrorist, head chopping fucks sounded pretty good right about now. They'd given us hell for the past couple years, creeping north into our territory like weeds.

"I'm ready, Prez." I didn't hide my enthusiasm as my fist hit the table.

Blackjack grinned and chuckled. "Keep it in your

damned pants, son. You heard Brass. We won't be ready for the runs 'til autumn. Maybe September, if we're lucky."

Fuck. That meant I'd have to find some other way to take my mind off Christa and whip my ass into line before then.

"Yeah, don't get too excited, brother." Brass smiled at me. "This isn't gonna be as easy as getting Twinkie's lips on your dick after a couple shots."

More bawdy laughter. I glowered. Didn't he realize I hadn't taken that blonde bitch for weeks? Last time I did, I had Red's face between her legs while I fucked my favorite from behind, and I was *still* thinking about Christa.

Even two moaning whores under me couldn't wipe that chick outta my skull.

Fuck you, brother, I wanted to growl back. But showing them they were getting under my skin would only make it worse.

"Seriously. Without the guns and guys from the Devils, we'd be fucked right about now," Brass continued. "We're working on getting our own house in order, and it's slow going."

Several guys growled, lowered their eyes. "Fucking Prairie Pussies," Asphalt whispered.

Blackjack's fist banged the table, and everybody fell silent. "Don't make me come down there, brother. I told you all last week that term's banned at church. The Devils proved themselves, helped us pull our nuts off the stove before they caught fire. Without those 'pussies,' we'd be sitting in Portland, listening to Fang's bullshit, because the cartel would own everything up through Klamath."

I wanted to whack Asphalt on his bald head. Once for being a dumbass, twice for being a bro and taking the heat off me.

"Oregon," Roman growled out a trademark one-liner. "They still giving the Devils trouble getting down here, or what?"

The Prez looked at us like he'd just swallowed horse piss in his glass instead of coffee. "Rip's a difficult asshole to get in touch with these days. I'm thinking about sending a couple prospects up there with Roman to deliver a message next week."

The big man nodded slowly. He never turned down a chance to throw his weight around. Hell, you could say the same about half the guys in the room, but visiting our brothers in Klamath was almost like going into enemy territory these days.

"What about the Portland crew?" I asked. "They're closer than we are, and we know those boys are loyal."

"Klamath's not on talking terms with them either. I tried going through their channels last week." Blackjack picked up the bear claw and sighed, his frustration adding depth to his natural wrinkles. "We haven't seen the last bad blood spilling between brothers in this MC. I'd love to have Rip come to his fucking senses and talk to me, man-on-man, accept the new national charter like everybody else."

"Bullshit!" Brass spoke up. "You know that's not gonna

happen, Prez. We can't have our routes choked off by a bunch of fucking turncoats between us and our buddies further north. The cartel will be all over us if they find out. If Rip and his men won't stop being bitches, then we'll replace them with somebody else."

The room went quiet. Blackjack was never more severe, deep in contemplation, staring at that fucking bear claw with the full weight of the President patch on his chest. He looked up.

"You're right, Brass. That's why you're wearing the VP patch. Everybody here has their place. A good crew in Redding doesn't cut it. We've got the best, with the biggest balls, and I'm not afraid to let them swing loose. If it hits another charter in the face, then it's for a damned good reason."

Shit. Nobody could even breathe. We were seriously mulling more war within the MC. And going after the Klamath Grizzlies, justified or not, was bound to have serious ripple effects through the whole organization. You don't just smoke an entire chapter without putting your neck under the axe.

A lot of the charters downstate and beyond were happy to go along with whoever was in charge. But some of them were sure to be missing Fang's ways, even if they didn't spit in our faces, openly defying us like the bastards just north.

"One week, brothers. That's what I'll allow before we send some guys up there to send them a message that'll make their fucking ears ring." He held up the bear claw.

"Do we need to vote on this?"

The darkness in everybody's eyes said no. I knew mine had the same killer shit swirling around. We were ready for blood, ready for war, ready for whatever was coming. Letting this club slip back into its old evil ways wasn't an option. It would mean the absolute death of us.

"All right then. Church is adjourned. Stay on your toes. I'll be calling your asses back here if there's any word." The bear claw hit the table, and brothers began to get up.

We all froze when somebody started pounding on the door. Roman moved first, walked over, and ripped it open. An older guy with a big beard and a pot belly I'd never seen before came strutting in, our two prospects standing helplessly behind him.

Useless fucks. They only got guard duty when all the full patch members were occupied. Or maybe not so useless – the patches on the stranger identified him as a brother right away, and when he turned, I saw the big OREGON bottom rocker on the backside. Another turn revealed the name patch on his front, right about a V. PRESIDENT tag – Big Ed.

"You're Blackjack?" He headed for the Prez and stuck out his hand. "Our Prez, Rip, sends his regards."

The new silence in the room was like a volcano getting ready to blow. I stood with Brass, trying not to grind my teeth. Roman's posture said one wrong move would place the Oregon fuck's head between his fists, and he wouldn't stop 'til it fractured.

"What? No fucking notice before you dropped in?" Blackjack snapped. "You realize we're at war down here, right? You should've told my crew you were coming. There could've been a nasty accident if you were mistaken for a cartel infiltrator."

Big Ed laughed. Loud and arrogant, the same way some of the dirty old bastards who served Fang used to sound. That shit instantly set me on edge.

"Come on! I'm here, aren't I? Prez says you've been wanting to get in touch. We're all brothers here."

Brass was closer. I watched my brother's face as his VP counterpart threw an arm around him. Brass staggered back against me as he worked himself outta the other man's headlock. I was ready to grab his wrists and hold them so he wouldn't clock the motherfucker and start the all-out war between charters we'd been dreading right here in the meeting room.

"What?" Big Ed looked genuinely shocked that Brass threw him off. "Do I look like some fucking Pedro smuggling coke up my ass? You boys are way too jumpy. Fang was never afraid of a little hello from your outstate brothers. There's more to this world than fucking California, you know."

That did it. Blackjacked stepped up, his fists flexed at his sides. He was older than the rest of us, but he was wiser too. I wouldn't have counted him down any day, even against a big man like Ed.

"This club's under new leadership now. *Mine.* My patch trumps yours, and it trumps Rip's too. I know damned well what Fang did. He also didn't tolerate any disrespect, and neither do I." Blackjack's fist went flying.

It collided with Big Ed's jaw. The dumb bastard lunged for the Prez a second later, and everybody piled on him. I held one fist while Roman got him in a headlock, squeezing off the fucker's windpipe 'til he started to go limp. I swore the big man was smiling behind his expressionless mask, ready to hold on until the Oregon VP's lights went out and never returned.

"Prez!" Brass looked at Blackjack with panicked eyes. "This fucker's a disrespectful, deviant piece of shit – but isn't it a little early to kill him? We need find out why he's here."

Blackjack stared a moment longer. Big Ed's hand was starting to go limp in mine, ready to fall over with the rest of him. Finally, the Prez nodded.

"Let him up."

Ed tumbled to the ground, coughing and spluttering. He winced when his knees hit the floor. Blackjack stepped up, stabbed his boot on one hand. The fat man roared as his fingers crunched beneath it.

"You want to be our brother? Then show me we can trust you and the rest of your crew. Get Rip on the line *right fucking now,* and we'll forget this disgrace ever happened." Prez flashed his angry eyes at the rest of us. "Everybody out! This is high level business. I'll call if our friend here wants to try anything stupid again."

Brass and I exchanged wide-eyed looks. If some crazy shit wasn't a weekly occurrence here, we'd have needed to pinch each other to believe it was really happening.

"You found the right pussy to take your mind off the redhead yet, or what?" Brass knocked back his second shot of whiskey at the bar.

I'd barely touched mine, knowing the bullshit questions would start. Good thing I came prepared.

"Hey, man. At least I can still pick and choose my chicks as I please – one of the many advantages of not being strapped down with an old lady."

He laughed. "Brother, I get the *only* pussy I'll ever need whenever I want it. Fuck, Missy's become insatiable since I put my brand on her. I'm lucky to get a few nights with more than five hours of shut eye with all the fucking we've been doing. And I still manage to drag my ass in here on time."

Low blow. Bastard. Who was I gonna have to punch to get them off my ass?

"Come on. Don't be pissed. Drink your medicine." Grinning, Brass slid a shot into my hand. "You know I'm just fucking around. Prez is gonna be pissed if you fuck off duty again, though."

"I told you, it's not gonna happen another time. I've learned my lesson. I'll kick the whore outta my bed the night before we have church next time."

"You? Sober up and keep your dick dry?" He smoothed a tense hand through his hair. "Who the fuck am I talking to? That's not the Rabid I know."

"And you're not the same junkie asshole I first met

when you transferred down here," I growled.

That shut him up. Brass really was a different man now. He'd cleaned up, grown a conscience, and turned his fucked up life around. He'd even reconciled with his sister, Saffron. Amazingly, the fact that she'd married the head of the Prairie Devils MC Montana, Blaze, hadn't even stood in the way.

He also liked to pretend the times he was pumping shit into his veins never happened.

"I'm trying to help your ass out, Rabid. You've got your head screwed loose, ever since we rescued that scarred chick from Fang. Let her go. The whole fucking club knows she's not gonna talk. You don't have keep checking in on her and stroking this…whatever the fuck this thing you have is."

"Gotta make sure she's okay. Every time we talk, I can tell something's eating her. Don't think it's related to our old Prez slicing up her face neither."

Brass shrugged. "Your time to piss away, brother. She's not into you. Fuck, you ran her name through our intel like a fucking creep and you still didn't turn up anything."

Fucker. The Jack was starting to kiss my blood hot, and my fingers hummed like they were filled with shrapnel.

I'd show him who the fucking creep was…

Before I got a chance, the meeting room's door swung open. A stern faced Blackjack held it and watched Big Ed limp away, heading for the bar. He kept his distance, and the bartender handed him some ice for the new bruise he undoubtedly had blossoming beneath his bushy beard.

"Huh. Least we know they didn't kill each other in there," Brass growled.

We both followed the asshole with our eyes, and so did several guys hanging further back in the clubhouse. When Ed was done collecting his ice, he grabbed a bottle of Jack, popped it open, and chugged at least a third of the shit right down his gullet.

Jackoff. That meant he was going to stick around for awhile, oblivious to the fact nobody wanted him here, or else wreck his Harley on the return trip to Klamath.

Either way, I wasn't gonna wait around for it. I guzzled some water and slammed my glass down, ready to hit the road. Glad I'd only downed a little bit of liquor and wouldn't have to wait to drive.

Brass reached out and caught me by the shoulder as I was sliding off the stool.

"You're going to see her again, aren't you?"

"None of your fucking business, bro. You told me whatever happens isn't club business anymore, so I'm not sure why you care."

Brass furrowed his brow. He hated it when I crammed his own words down his throat.

"You can't keep this shit up forever," he snapped. "I don't wanna see you go through the wringer because you're so drunk on this pussy you can't even have. If she wants you gone, then go. It's fucking miserable watching you self-destruct over something this stupid, brother."

"Christa's *not* stupid. She needs my help."

I practically ripped my cut tearing outta his grasp. Whatever. I wasn't letting Brass or anybody else stop me from a date with destiny. If shit finally went my way, then maybe the sassy redhead would give me a proper date too.

Fuck, I'd sit through all the wine and movies she could handle for one night with her. Whatever happened after that was anybody's guess. I wasn't gonna force it. I was looking for a good raw fuck I'd never forget, one perfect moment interfacing with her like no man ever had.

Of course, I wasn't stupid neither. Something told me if I got her panties off and twisted that bright red hair in my hands, I'd never settle for anything less again.

True love? I didn't fucking believe it. True lust was definitely on the radar, though, a desire hissing in my veins, turning me into a total feral animal 'til I had her.

On the way out, I was disgusted to see Big Ed. He had his bike parked just outside our open garage. The crazy bastard was strapping himself in for a drunken ride to God only knew where after all.

Fuck. I didn't have time for this. I got on my Harley and fixed my helmet, letting her familiar growl roll through me.

"Hey!" I barely pulled out a couple feet when Big Ed yelled, unsure why I was stopping for this asshole. "You're Rabid, aren't you?"

I nodded, wondering how the sack of shit knew my name. "Why do you care?"

That nasty laugh came again. "So, you're the guy babying Chrissy. Good to know in case it comes down to fists. One-on-one this time. You're like a hundred pounds lighter. I can handle that."

My heart did a flip. What the hell was he talking about? I was about to get off my bike and demand answers, but he moved surprisingly fast once he was on his bike. He took off, tearing down the narrow lot, straight toward the gate a prospect opened for us.

Shit! I was originally paying Christa a visit to clear the fucked up fog in my head. Now, I *had* to see her. I had to find out what the hell was going on.

Brass and everybody else could fuck off with their stand down bullshit. I'd get to the bottom of what was really going on with this chick, and I wasn't leaving her alone 'til I did.

III: Sweet Pursuit (Christa)

I was finishing up a tutoring session with Jackie Thomas when I heard the motorcycle's growl.

"What's Brass doing here?" The fourteen year old blinked at me, relieved to have a distraction from the tough math problem we were wrapping up.

Who could blame her? The way the schools were teaching this crap required a PhD to figure out.

"Probably looking for your sis," I said. Her sister, Missy, was Brass' old lady. I expected her to come by any minute to pick the girl up, but maybe she'd sent her old man to do it instead.

I rubbed my nose. Ugh. I definitely wasn't in the mood to see anyone else from the MC after Big Ed's recent visit.

"You know, here's a good place to call it done for today. We can pick up on this stuff next session. The summer classes move slow, don't they?"

"Yes! God, I keep telling them I know all this. I can figure out the right answers. It's showing my work that's the problem. Just a couple more weeks." No surprise, smart girls like her reacted the worst to this remedial summer crap, purely because she'd missed a few weeks earlier this year.

I was the same way.

"You're getting it!" I smiled. "It's all political, Jackie. They just want you to show your work *their* way. Welcome to the real world. Unfortunately, we've all got to deal with its crap."

The teenager puckered sourly. "Don't I know it, Christa."

I dropped my eyes, helping her gather up her things. She wasn't kidding. Both her and the big sister Brass claimed as his girl had been through hell after their father died. When Missy first hired me to tutor the kid, they were keeping their distance from him, and he was the only thing protecting them from the Grizzlies' wrath.

Something about their dead father's troubles and some money that was owed to the club. Seemed eerily familiar.

Of course, the club got off their throats as soon as Brass stepped in. He remedied everything, and in the process, Missy had fallen for him. She happily wore her old lady jacket nearly every time I saw her. PROPERTY OF BRASS, branded on the back like she was some kinda pet.

I shook my head. No way. I wasn't the submissive type. That thing would never be for me, no matter how hot some of the guys were on their wheels.

I'd tasted the sour side of MC life, and it stuck with me. If there was a sweet side, I wasn't interested in jumping through hoops to find it.

I wanted to make my money, pay my debt, and move

onto bigger and better things. *Someday,* I told myself. *Someday.*

"Hey! It's not Brass." Jackie was peeking through the blinds. They snapped shut when she pulled her hand away. "That's Rabid."

Shit! I got up as calmly as I could, deafened by the alarm bells blaring in my head. Seriously, why couldn't he just leave me alone?

I'd be okay. I could take care of myself. He bailed me out once, and I was grateful, but I didn't need him looking in on me like a kid.

"I sure hope your sis shows up soon," I said. "Come on. Let's wait outside."

And let me find out what this asshole wants now, I thought. *It never ends, does it?*

Jackie stayed on the porch, sipping passion fruit tea from a glass bottle, giving me some much needed space. Brass stopped and slowly took off the shades he was wearing to block the evening sun. My hopes he'd be ready to catch hell vanished when the sunglasses came off.

His dark eyes shined bright, angry, and full of accusations. Damn! I didn't need his shit today – and I *definitely* didn't need a pissed off biker on my doorstep.

"What's going on?" I said, praying we'd get this over with quick. "Didn't know it was time for my weekly parole talk with the club."

"Not today, babe. Cut the shit," he growled. "I wanna know what's really going on with you, and I need to know before the sun goes down."

"What's that supposed to mean?" The ferocity in his tone surprised me. It also set me on edge. "And why is my life any of your fucking business?"

"Because this ugly fucker from Oregon who just came by our clubhouse mentioned you by name. We're not on good terms with him and his brothers. If you're in some sorta trouble with a fucked up charter at our throats, that's something I need to know about. Your business is my business, and it's club business too when it gets tangled up together like that."

"Oh? So it's not just you trying to play white knight?"

He bared his teeth. "Of course *I* care what's going on here. You know I'm not interested in letting the rotten parts of our club hurt you again. I'm here to help, Christa, and maybe you'd figure it out if you'd lay off the venom for a few seconds."

I shrugged. "I need to wait for my student to leave before we can talk. Will you at least give me that?"

He looked at Jackie, and then did a double take. "Shit. Figures every fuckin' thing I do gets back to Brass one way or another…all right! Just get on my bike and we'll make sure she gets home okay."

He wasn't asking. Something about the raw, possessive needles in his voice infuriated me as much as it made me curious. He'd always been super polite before, every time except the day we were getting shot at. He was so powerful, so protective when he held me down in the dirt, edging me to safety.

He would've taken a bullet for me. I guess that counted

for something. Just not enough to make me grin and drop to my knees when he stepped into my life uninvited.

I couldn't be blind to this, to him.

Rabid was a bastard. No, I couldn't deny he was good at what he did. But the good guy mask he wore other times was just an act. The leather hanging on his shoulders with the growling bear's blood red insignia told me what he really was – an unrelenting bastard as harsh as men like Ed – even if his heart was in a better place.

Like him or not, there was no saying no today if I wanted to avoid more crap. I took the passenger helmet from him and strapped it on while we sat.

Missy's car pulled up about a minute later. Jackie came running and hopped into the passenger seat. Couldn't blame the girl for running away from this drama when she had the chance. Just then, I would've killed for some good old fashioned teenage drama instead of being mixed up with this biker.

I watched Missy emerge from the driver's side and come toward us, fishing through her purse on the way. Her transformation was incredible.

The plain, shy, scared woman I'd first met was totally gone. She stabbed the heels of her new boots into the ground like she owned it, and her chestnut locks caught the setting sun. She radiated pure confidence, breaking into a wide, amused grin when she reached us.

"Here's the cash!" Missy winked, pushing several crisp twenties into my hands. Great. Food money for the next week.

"Thanks."

"Since when are you going for rides with Rabid?" Her eyes flitted to the stone faced biker, who grunted a response, all he could do to hide the fact that he wasn't just asking me out for a joy ride. "We need to catch up one day soon, girl! It's good to see you expanding your circle beyond my little sis."

"Something like that," I said. "I've always wanted to ride. I thought Rabid would be the perfect man to show me how."

His shoulder jerked when I laid my hand on it. His eyes caught mine through the mirror, and I smiled when I saw his eyebrows were up. Guess he never expected me to be a good girl and play along.

Whatever. It was kinda fun to screw with him. Least I could do to get back a little of the frustration he gave me.

"I'd appreciate it if you keep this mum between the three of us," Rabid said to her. "Brass is really cracking the fucking whip lately. Every minute I'm spending outside the clubhouse isn't a good one."

Missy laughed and stuck her tongue out. "Tell me about it! I'm about to head home for another evening trying to calm his ass down. He's so wound up anymore. I'm *glad* you're getting out and enjoying yourself, Rabid. Both of you. Your secret's safe with me."

She smiled and pushed an imaginary zipper across her lips. I nodded, mouthed a thanks. Incredibly, I'd be spared the embarrassment.

It was amazing to think the tension between us was

truly invisible to everybody else. Right now, it felt like we were sharing the same noose, ready to swing tight around our throats and suffocate us.

"Use some of that to buy yourself something fun," Missy said, pointing to the wad in my hands.

"I'm sure I'll find something." I tucked the bills into my pocket. "Don't let Jackie waste too many of these summer evenings on her math. We're only young once. She's a smart girl, and it's all coming to her bit by bit. She'll have the rest figured out in no time."

Missy rolled her eyes. "I'm pretty sure your lessons are the only thing she's studying at all. It's hard to keep her in most nights. You know how teen girls are. Stir crazy. I'm kinda glad Brass isn't allowing any boys in, though!"

I plastered on another big fake smile as Rabid revved the engine. "We're all just looking for some fun. I'll see you both next week!"

No more waiting around. The bike jerked forward, shooting along the asphalt, ready to take us wherever the hell he wanted for this talk.

I had to keep my hands on him the entire time. Not knowing what he was really feeling was the hard part. His other courtesy visits were so much easier to brush off than this, and I could read him like a clock.

Now, I barely recognized the demon gripping the handlebars and taking us outside Redding's city limits, sending us north while the sun slipped below the horizon. He was so warm, so hard, so omnipotent guiding this rocket on wheels into the country darkness.

The less sure I was about him, the harder I clung to his waist. I saw my face in the rear view mirror, trying to keep it together.

He wanted me. I wasn't blind to it. What I couldn't figure out was *why*.

I'd seen the kind of women outlaw bikers hung around when I had the bar, the same women dad had flings with when he used to ride. Most of these guys only wanted trashy looking whores with big boobs and gumball butts, their lips painted every pornographic shade I could imagine, and several I couldn't until I actually saw them.

The old ladies were sweet – at least for the good, lucky men. They stood by their guys with their knockout looks and hearts like nails, ready for an endless power dance, treating their brands as seriously as wedding rings when the love was really special.

It was beautiful when it was done right. I didn't know what Rabid was looking for – maybe more than a hard night of fucking – but I couldn't get over *why*.

What the hell did he see in me? Big Ed and the other bastards in Klamath shredded my confidence, and their dead national President stole my looks. It was gone before they ruined my beauty. I barely cried and screamed when Fang slid the blade across my face.

Somehow, I knew I was destined to suffer. Call it bad karma for getting too deep into a lifestyle that was never meant for me.

I thought I was tough, ready to grab the world by the throat, when I went north to start my bar. The world had showed me instead, and now it was slowly choking my life away, piece by brutal piece.

Of course, some of these biker dudes were twisted. It took more than balloon tits and sugary lipstick to turn their crank. Maybe Rabid was one of them.. Maybe he got a hard-on for scarred chicks, and I was supposed to be his latest fetish conquest.

To hell with that! I wasn't anybody's conquest, whore, slut, or girl. I wasn't desperate. I was perfectly content to live out my days all alone, maybe see what the world had to offer in the way of nice, boring dudes who worked in cubicles and left the stink of motor oil to their mechanics.

Badasses were fun to look at, and even more fun to ride. But they weren't good for me. I'd never be anything more than a toy for a man like Rabid, and an intact heart was all I had left to my name.

I swore I'd keep it that way too, temptation be damned.

The bike slowed as we approached an old dirt road. It coiled around to an abandoned ranch, some place he was clearly familiar with.

"Jesus, Rabid. I knew you wanted privacy, but I didn't think we'd be going so remote." Staring up at the stars beginning to sparkle in the sky made me want to eat my words.

The middle of nowhere could sure be beautiful.

"Thought it'd be calming. It's easy not to get pissed and talk like rational people when the scenery's pretty." He got off the bike, unfastening his helmet, and then taking my own.

I grudgingly took the hand he extended to help me off his Harley. We walked toward one of the old buildings, a storage shed that had seen better days, judging by the holes ripped in the sheet metal.

"This bench is still good. We won't fall through it." He pointed to an old wooden loveseat near the back.

It was the kind that had a little swing to it when you sat down. The hinges creaked, but not nearly as bad as I expected based on the age.

"Okay. So, tell me, what is it I need to say to convince you I'm a big girl who can take care of herself?"

"Start by telling me the truth, Christa. Nobody thought you had any connections to this club before Big Ed showed up. Shit, even Fang's old goons who turned to our side acted like they didn't have a clue who you were. There's history here. Don't bullshit me about it."

"Yeah, history. Not with the Redding charter. You're wrong about that," I said, locking eyes with him. "I spent a few years north of here. I wanted to be free and wild, get away from living with my father. I had some cash saved up, so I started up a biker bar outside Klamath Falls. Always thought it'd be a stepping stone to bigger and better things."

"Shit." His eyebrows quirked up. "I never would've guessed you for a biker chick."

"Born and raised. Dad spent twenty years in the Klondike Killers. He rode with them all the time when he wasn't out fishing Alaska's short summers. He retired his colors as soon as he came to Grizzlies territory, though." I didn't mention the Alzheimer's.

I wasn't going to lay all my cards out for him. Only the ones that were relevant to get him off my back.

"Holy fuck, baby. Those guys were badasses. Grizzlies used to do business with them outta Seattle and Bellingham before everything went to pieces. Damn good thing the crazy fucks never expanded past the Yukon." He shook his head, then fixed those bright honey colored eyes on me again. "That still doesn't explain why the fuck you're tangled up with a motherfucker like Ed."

"Ew." I wrinkled my nose. "That's not an image I want. It's not like I ever fucked him."

"Come the fuck on," Rabid growled, something like jealousy lining his face. "You know what I mean. How does he know you?"

"Well, when I ran the bar, I couldn't do it with what I scrimped and saved as a teen. Even dad's contribution couldn't do the job. No bank was going to loan money to a nineteen year old kid with no business experience and no degree. I went to the only ones who could."

He slapped his forehead. "Fuck. Of course. I always heard the crew up there was looking for new fronts to help launder their shit."

"And I wouldn't let them," I said, remembering the blowout arguments with Ed, Rip, and the other Klamath boys who'd nearly cost me my life. "They gave me the loan in the first place because they thought I'd be easy to control. Who better than some little girl they could push around? Except I wouldn't roll over. The money dried up. The bar wasn't bringing in the kinda business it needed to survive, let alone thrive. I couldn't make the payments and my booze dried up. I walked away owing the city a few hundred in licensing fees, plus a little over a hundred thousand to your brothers north of the border."

Rabid stood up, his nostrils flaring. "Sonofabitch. This is bad, baby. Real fucking bad. I have to tell the club. We can get those assholes off your back."

"No!" I reached out and grabbed his hand. His fist was so hard he could've beaten down the old, rickety farmhouse on the hill in front of us. "I'm taking care of it. Look, we'll both agree Big Ed's a piece of shit. He's a fat, crude bully. I hate dealing with him. He only comes and gives me crap when I've fallen behind on my payments."

Rabid spun, pinching my fingers tight in his. "Then let me."

"I can't do that...I know about the bad blood in Redding right now. Your club's still going through major changes. I'm not blind, Rabid. I can see you're on edge, a heartbeat away from tearing into them."

"Damned straight," he growled, jerking me out of the seat. "Those fuckers haven't listened to the new officers since we wasted Fang. They fucking spat in Blackjack's face, and now they're not following the protocol for club debts. Redding's *our* territory. That means everything in it dealing with club biz is our goddamned business first – including anything you owe, babe."

No, no, no. This wasn't turning out the way I wanted.

The bright, mad spark in eyes was way too seductive. He gave me hope I never asked for.

I wanted his protection. I wanted him.

Hell, I wanted to throw myself at him, scars and all. I wanted to feel his massive arms wrapped around me, savor his energy, his belief in a world that still had black and white without endless, suffocating gray.

This was dangerous. Very, *very* bad. If I let him pull me into the dark ink coiling up his arms, I'd never want to leave until I let him drag me bed. Naked, whimpering, and – worst of all – *wanting.*

I couldn't indulge this attraction, no matter how tempting he looked, or how many ways his powerful arms promised to smash Big Ed's ugly face. Sending him and his brothers after Ed would only end in more bloodshed. I couldn't risk their lives, and I *definitely* couldn't risk dad's when Klamath retaliated.

I took a deep breath. *Please, please listen this time. Please.*

"Rabid, look, I can handle this. I've been paying these creeps for years. Ed only shows up to collect when I start to fall behind, like I said. If I keep the money coming, he leaves me alone."

"You can't. Shit, babe, I saw the way you're struggling when Missy handed you that cash when she came for her sis. You fucking needed it bad." He paused, and I lowered my eyes.

Shameful. Was I that easy to read, or was this man just that tuned into me?

"Besides, no club gives debtors an extension without a damned good reason. We're outlaws. When we loan money, there's interest in blood and broken bones. Defaulting's a fucking death sentence," he said, shaking his head. "Baby, you're smart and I'm not gonna treat you like a damned fool. But you're playing with fire here. I'm telling you straight up, this shit's more than you can handle. You're gonna get burned sooner or later if you piss these guys off."

"Don't you think I know that?" I snapped, jerking away from him.

Rabid wasn't taking any shit. He grabbed me by the waist and pulled me close. My face burned. I couldn't tell if the blush in my cheeks was hotter, or if it was the pulse pounding in my temples.

He sure had a knack for making me angry, ashamed, and totally aroused all at once. Three big As crashing through my system simultaneously, hurtling toward overload.

"Of course you do," he thundered in my ear, low and dangerous and so damned close. "You held up like a serious hardass after what Fang did to you. Fuck, after that ordeal, we're the ones who owe you. Granted, it's hard as hell to make the fucks up in Oregon listen to anything right now. I'm talking to Blackjack tomorrow. I'm gonna demand he twists those fuckers' balls 'til your debt's wiped clear. Every charter might have its own business, but you're in our territory. We're the mother charter, dammit, and we run the whole show now."

No amount of determination in his voice meant this was any less insane. The reality was something different. The MC was still at war with itself and the Mexican cartels. Rabid's men needed help from their old rivals, the Prairie Devils, just to topple Fang once and for all. They were in no position to wish my six figure debt away without some serious consequences.

I shook my head so hard it was dizzying. "I'm the one who made the mistakes that landed me in debt. *Me,* Rabid, nobody else. I'm the only one who should pay." My scars were burning. It always happened when I forced back tears, leaving me to wonder if my skin would ever totally heal. "You saw what kind of man Ed is. He won't just drop it. He won't be bossed around, and neither will the other men up north. I met them all when they came to my bar. Jesus, if I could take it all back, I would! I never would've run off and acted like a stupid kid!"

"That's life, baby. We all fuck up sometimes. That doesn't mean you gotta let the past eat you alive. This shit's not like filing Chapter Seven, and you know it. The Klamath fucks won't let you have a second chance 'til you're so worn and beaten, it's no chance at all. That's the fucking problem, and that's why I'm not gonna let them get away with it."

He paused. I gasped and shuddered when I felt the hardness between his legs. I'd been leaning into him, and he was like a rock, crazy with desire. We were so alone and isolated out here. *Anything* could happen if I let it.

I turned to face him, wishing my face didn't look like a

scratched up tomato. He was even more insane than I thought if he was seriously attracted to this. I had nothing to offer him but trouble, a damaged body and a rotten past I hadn't figured out how to reconcile.

And I hadn't even told him about poor dad.

Jesus, he was so hard. The thick, throbbing lump in Rabid's pants was a terrible distraction. I should've spit in his face for inserting himself into my life like this, totally uninvited, but all I really wanted to do was drop to my knees and feel his cock in my mouth.

His eyes burned fiercer than the stars overhead. When my eyes caressed his body, I imagined what his tattoos looked like underneath his clothes. Those big black stripes on his arms probably rolled all the way up, lining the fearsome icons on his chest like all the other bikers I'd seen shirtless.

This body invited questions, filthy curiosities and wonders, and bathed my brain in fire.

Would he look more ferocious than the roaring bear inked on his chest when he fucked me? Would I suck his tattooed skin into my mouth and bite down hard when I came? Jesus, would I ever stand up again if I gave in to one night with this dark Adonis pretending to be a man?

Half the guys in the Redding Grizzlies charter were younger, harder, and hotter than most of the old bastards and greasy criminals who'd visited my bar in Klamath. Without the leather cut and a few less scars on his arms, the man with his hands sliding up my back would've looked like an underwear model.

But no pretty boy modeling ever smelled like this. I couldn't stop inhaling him, and that only made my breaths more erratic, betraying the insane desire I was desperate to hide.

No! I couldn't actually let him see how hot he made me. But I couldn't stop myself from shaking when I pushed my face into his chest and inhaled, filling my lungs with badly needed oxygen.

Pure masculinity caressed my nose. His feel, his smell, his everything burned deep, melting me from the inside-out.

My body understood, even if my mind didn't. This was a warrior man right down to every molecule. Loyal to his club, comrade to his brothers, ready to serve and protect me when I wanted none of it. Also, more than ready to slip inside me, making my body shake and scream in ways I'd never even heard of.

Fuck.

"What? What the fuck is it?" he growled, his hot breath pouring across my neck and up my ear again.

Too much. I pushed against his chest, stumbling backward in the night. The jerky motion combined with the sudden breeze blowing in behind me, forcing me to realize how tingly and wet I'd become.

Holy, holy shit. I hadn't been this soaked for a man since…I couldn't even remember. Probably ever.

"I need to go home, Rabid. It's getting late." My words were so weak. "Can't we be done here?"

He straightened up, turned toward his bike – a little

too fast for my liking. I couldn't tell if he was disappointed I hadn't broken the tension with a kiss, or if he was just trying to hide the wicked hard-on pounding in his denim.

"Sure. Let's go. We're finished as far as I'm concerned." Without looking back, he headed for the bike.

I took one last look at all the old buildings. Seriously, what was this place? It's like he knew this abandoned farm.

"Rabid..." I whispered his name a couple more times as he handed me my helmet. Great, now I was feeling bad about acting like such a bitch.

"Don't, baby. This shit's not about wounded egos or who's right – hell, or even who's been wrong in the past. You told me the truth. That's what I really wanted tonight. The rest is up to me."

The last part was unmistakably sincere. Ouch. The fact I'd told him enough without coming completely clean about Ed's threats, my dad, and so much more just drove a stake through my heart. For a second, I considered coughing up the rest – but what good would it do?

He knew I was hurting and in danger. If he knew Ed threatened my helpless father too, Rabid was just as likely to go off alone, ready to kill without any backup.

The future was dark with certainty now. Rabid and his brothers were going to clash with the assholes blackmailing me. It was bound to end in blood. All I could do was watch, and try to keep myself, and the tiny collection of people I still cared about, safe.

"You don't have to do anything," I said. God, I

sounded so feeble.

It was all I had. One last desperate attempt to convince him not to fight my battles. Too bad I couldn't convince myself I'd ever be able to fight them on my own. Big Ed had a cannon pointed at my face, and I was holding a slingshot.

"I said *thanks*. Now, get the fuck on so I can drive you home. It's a beautiful night." He was staring up at the sky, a serene look on his handsome face that didn't match the frustration in his voice. "Everything's gonna be okay, baby, because I'm gonna make it that way. You just worry about being the best damned tutor in the city limits and figure out what else you wanna do with your life. I'll make sure the shits up in Oregon leave you the fuck alone so you can have that chance."

Awkward. Brutal. That was the return trip to Redding.

The bitter, gnawing sensation in the pit of my stomach just wouldn't go away. I'd just unleashed pure hell, and there was no putting it back in its box.

And that was only half the problem. I couldn't stop thinking about the lost opportunity beneath the stars to taste his lips, if only once. My hands clung tight to his waist, harder than I really needed to keep myself steady on the highway.

We were parked next to my apartment when I ripped the helmet off. Rabid waited for me to go, no doubt eager to be done with this miserable night. Instinct had something else in mind.

Emotions broke loose in a torrent. I couldn't control

myself anymore as I climbed off the Harley, and then threw my arms around his neck before he could pull away. Smashing my lips against his caused such a raw surge in every nerve I almost passed out.

Time stopped, lost to the fire consuming us. It only took him half a second to react. He grabbed me, jerked my red locks tight in one fist, securing my face for his kiss. The full force of his lips swept me away like a lightning strike.

For one sweet second, there was total clarity. I couldn't move, couldn't think, couldn't do anything except taste him. I became the thudding beat in my chest and the molten desire in my veins. Desire opened up like a bottomless pit and swallowed my ego whole.

His tongue pushed past my lips, opening me, exploring the rampant desire we shared to go deeper.

Deeper.

The very word set off an earthquake in my head, and it spread through my body. I was tingling and starting to shake all over as my blown out senses came back. God, he tasted good. I could've stayed locked to him forever, hands splayed on his chest, scratching with need to find out how those sculpted muscles really felt underneath my palms.

More questions. More curiosities. More dirty, nasty want.

Would he growl into my mouth like this while I straddled him, riding his cock? How hard would he shame every boy I'd ever been with? Would I forget about the ugly scars on my face and all the fucked up insecurities with my clit burning against his skin, sending me to sheer ecstasy, where nothing else mattered?

"Baby. Fuck." He snarled his words, lust incarnate, when I tore my head away from his, breaking the kiss.

I had to move faster to shatter his grasp. The wildfire in my body broke inside my brain, silenced by the questions and confusion raging through me.

What the fuck was I doing? The inevitable freak out came.

Panic, fierce and relentless as the desire I'd had a second ago.

I broke and ran. He called after me, but even the fire in his voice couldn't stop me.

I turned my pocket inside-out pulling at my keys. Shoving them into the lock, I flipped open the door, and pressed myself flat against the wall inside. About a minute later, I heard his motorcycle's explosive roar, growling into the distance with as much feral disappointment as I had shaking me to pieces.

I pushed past an idiot with a basket full of clothes, wet shame running down my cheeks, and collapsed inside my apartment. I was too fried to think. What happened at the abandoned ranch blew all my fuses, and the kiss outside ruined them for good.

Tomorrow, I told myself I'd make one last ditch effort at moving my father downstate and disappearing for good. He had enough left in his pension and savings to make sure he was taken care of. I didn't care if I ended up homeless.

At least no one would die thanks to my poisonous debt. And I'd never have to think about waking up to Rabid some morning and seeing the disappointment on his face as he realized how fucked up I really was.

He'd never get anything but a fling with a crazy, pockmarked bitch like me. And I wouldn't even do that to either of us. I'd rather run like a fucking coward, leaving everything behind.

It was all the mercy I could offer this man who'd tried his damnedest to help me. I wouldn't infect him with the same toxic regret I lived every day – just like I wouldn't open my heart to this big, demanding, tattooed sledgehammer.

Ruin was his nature. Mine was making sure I didn't absorb any more savagery from anyone on a Harley. It didn't matter if hurt came wrapped in fierce commands and the most lickable skin I'd ever seen mounted to two wheels.

He was all pain, and I was too fucked up to absorb it. I couldn't. I had to go.

The next day, I woke with a pounding headache. Going through two hours of run around at the nursing home didn't help.

The bitchy administrators did everything in their power to stonewall my questions about moving him. Wasn't hard to see they were hellbent on keeping him there forever, anything to bleed what little remained dry.

Around noon, I stormed out. It was visiting time

anyway, and for once I was looking forward to sitting down with my father after dealing with this shit. It might take my mind off the fact we were both in serious danger as soon as Rabid's promises got to Big Ed.

Dad slumped in his wheelchair near the usual window when I found him. He woke up groggy, irritated, just as confused as ever. I reached for his hand, warming his cold skin with mine.

"We're going to take a nice trip soon, dad. Somewhere warmer, better," I purred, trying to soothe him as much as myself. "I just have to work out the nitty-gritty. I promise, I'm going to keep you safe."

His eyes lit up. For a second, I swore he knew exactly who I was, and he sat up straight in his chair, reaching for my face.

"Why do you go through so much trouble for an old man? This place's downright tropical, girl. You know how fucking cold it got hauling salmon and crab into Anchorage?"

I laughed. I remembered *exactly* how brutal Alaska used to be during the cold months. Yeah, something had definitely given him back his wits today.

"Those were great times, dad. Sometimes, I wish we never left. I wish we hadn't moved here. Alaska might've kept me grounded. I wouldn't have run off and gotten into trouble because there was nowhere to run off to."

He blinked. "You kill trouble. Me and my brothers used to raise pure hell in the Killers. This one time, the Prez asked us to do in this fat little bully. Bastard was a fisherman like me, he brought his crap north from the west coast to sell, ice and heroin. Nothing our crew wanted anything to do with. He liked to beat his wife too."

I swallowed, wondering if he'd plug the last few holes in his memories. Jesus, I hadn't thought of this story myself for several years. I hoped nobody heard him, or if they did, it was just crazy enough to chalk up to the ramblings of an old man out of his mind.

Dad blinked again, and a knowing smile spread across his lips. "We never enjoyed putting the sickos down like hogs. This one, I did, because he led me to the woman who changed my whole damned life. Did you ever meet my wife, Aida?"

"Maybe a couple times," I whispered. "You know we go way back."

"Yeah…I thought you looked familiar. My memory's not what it used to be." He cocked his head, seriously trying to remember who I was for a minute before giving up. "Anyway, my Aida was just a bruised, beat up, shaken little thing when I first met her. Didn't have a damned clue she'd end up becoming the best old lady a man could ever have – the *best* wife. She gave me a little girl before the sea took her home to heaven."

My breaths were slower, shallower. That stupid headache hit its apex and finally began to wane, draining in the emotional climax this conversation was bringing. Why did his best days have to correspond to my worst?

"You don't worry about taking me anywhere, nurse."

He reached over, gingerly patting my hand. "You can't run from what life gives ya. You gotta take it by the horns – the good, the bad, everything. Moving me out of this place won't bring me any closer to my girl. She's waiting for me when it's my time. And my Christa's out there too. She's such a restless girl." He stopped, taking a good long look at me. "You look a lot like her, you know that? Gorgeous red hair – just like hers."

I turned away. My head was spinning, and the tears were coming. I wiped them, refusing to face him, trying to focus on his words. It was better than thinking about the hell, the disappointment, the wall I'd thrown up against Rabid.

"I don't deserve to look like anyone you love. I've made too many fucking mistakes for that." It all came rolling out. "I wish I could be the girl you're imagining."

I shouldn't have expected him to have any clue what I was getting at. But when he squeezed my hand and I met his eyes, I believed he knew I was his daughter. There was dear old dad, the headstrong badass, always ready to support me against the worst the world had to offer.

I still hadn't gotten over the fact that I'd taken his money too for that stupid bar.

"You can't keep living your life with regrets, girl. I beat myself up for a long time over the shipwreck that took my wife. If I'd called off our anniversary surprise and hadn't sailed into that fucking storm, my little girl wouldn't have lost her mother before she could even know her." He sighed. "I did some seriously reckless shit. I drank myself stupid. I rode long and hard up the Dalton Highway north of Fairbanks. My brothers in the MC knocked me down and drove some sense into my head before it was too late. Realized I had my daughter, and Aida in my heart. When it finally sunk in, I couldn't do anything but live without looking behind me."

Wise words. Wise, and obscenely painful just now. It wasn't just the disease in his brain talking either. The dad I knew always looked forward, never at the darkness in his wake.

That was why we'd come to Redding. He was too old to work in fishing anymore, and his old MC mostly dissolved. Too many good men lost, strong men I'd called uncles growing up.

We wanted to experience the world beyond pitch black winters and bitter cold. He wanted to give me a better life, a chance at college, a place to settle down and build something.

Maybe the fact that I'd blown it all to shit didn't really matter. I still appreciated everything he'd done, and damn it, he was right.

So was Rabid.

I couldn't keep living in constant fear. Terror sat heavy on my shoulders now that the Grizzles were about to butt heads over my debt, but something was always bound to give sooner or later.

"Hey. You feeling better, girl? Don't tell me you're going to go out and waste another summer day on me. I'm an old man. It's your turn to have your place in the sun while you're young and pretty. I won't be responsible for wasting it. Time's more precious than you know. You understand me, Christa?"

My jaw practically hit the floor. My hands were shaking as they wrapped around his, and it took a long time to force down the lump in my throat. Too long.

"Dad…you know who I am?"

He paused, his eyes darkening a little more than I liked. "Of course I do! You're that nice new hire they transferred in from Sacramento, aren't you?"

Over and done. Just like that. Slowly, I pulled my hands back, and then gave him one last pat on the shoulder as I rose.

"We'll visit next week. Same time. Same place."

He laughed, shaking his head. "I sure hope so. Tell them to get me a new razor on your way out, dear. Fucking things never last more than a month or two."

"I can do that." Smiling, I headed out, into the waiting sun.

Dad went through electric razors like nobody's business. He'd lost his mind and a lot of muscle, but his hands were still strong. The cheap blades wore down with how hard he pressed them to his face. Soon, it probably wouldn't be an issue, whenever he reached the point where he couldn't shave anymore.

He'd done the same thing sometimes at home, especially the older he got. Thick hair, he said, from too many years living a hard life in the cold. I believed he ran them too long because the whir of the blades reminded him of his motorcycle's growl.

IV: So Bad It Hurts (Rabid)

I was just sober enough to remember how fucking incredible her lips were on mine, how hot and eager and sweet her little mouth tasted. But I was also too fucked up to care, stumbling around like an idiot while Asphalt and I took turns at the dartboard next to the bar.

"Fucking shit, Rabid!" he yelled. "Our colors aren't the frigging bullzeye!"

I laughed as he sped over to the wall where I'd planted my latest shot, at least two feet from the actual board. I'd hit the corner of the clubhouse's old Grizzlies MC flag. Another foot over, anywhere on the bear's snarling face, and I'd have gotten a well deserved beat down from the brothers.

Had a feeling I was fucked. I'd reached the point where inviting trouble sounded good. A few blows to the face might blast some sorely needed sense into my skull, or else make me forget all about Miss Hard-To-Fucking-Get.

Asphalt walked back to me, shaking his bald head. "One more miss like that and you're done, brother. I'm not gonna take the fall if any of the officers walk in on this shit."

I grabbed the half-depleted bottle of Jack off the counter and swung it to my lips. Hot relief poured down my throat, harsh as lightning. Shit hit my guts and exploded, the next best thing to being pinned to the ground while Roman's fist plowed my face.

I had to forget. Needed to. I'd flown way too close to that beautiful redheaded sun, and she'd scorched me for the last fucking time.

Why the fuck was she so caught up on her goddamned face anyway? I knew those scars made her think she was ugly. But, seriously, it's like the girl didn't own a fucking mirror.

If she did, there should've been no doubt she was the hottest piece of ass who ever called this city home.

Shit.

There she was again, rooted deep in my brain, making me wonder how those soft red locks I'd held would contrast with the pert pink nipples I'd felt hardening against my chest.

Missed. Fucking. Opportunities.

My motor skills were too far gone to drink and walk at the same time. I drained another three shots in one big gulp, and slammed into Asphalt's shoulder.

"Sonofabitch!" He screamed. "Hey, lady! Look out!"

Some blonde chick I'd never seen before was walking through the bar. My heart pinched shut as the dart sailed right next to her face and slapped the wall.

Uh-oh.

Asphalt spun, slammed his palms into my chest. I took a swing at my very pissed off brother and missed, dropping to the floor and landing right on my drunken face. Thank fuck it was numb.

"Asshole! What the fuck is wrong with you? Are you trying to get somebody *killed?*" His boot connected with my ribs. The hot crack rippled through my chest.

I rolled, tasting blood, laughing just the same. Christ. I was totally, completely fucked, twisting on the floor like a dumb kid who'd just had his first good joint.

Asphalt was still screaming at me, stooped over, roaring in my face so loud and hard his words were almost incomprehensible. I felt his spit mist my face, and reached up to wipe it off, trying to decide whether I should spring up and bust his jaw.

Why should you? A disapproving voice piped up in my head. *You're drunk off your ass, bro. But not so drunk you're blind to acting like a total asswipe – and not fucking drunk enough to forget her!*

Her.

Christa Sexy Kimmel, part medusa, hot as she was stone cold. She couldn't be all woman. There had to be snakes hiding in her sweet red hair somewhere. This chick was turning me to dirt – or was it rock? Fuck if Greek mythology had ever been my strong point.

Another kick landed in my side. I heaved, sucking smoky air, trying to get the fuck up, when I realized Asphalt was gone. He'd gone over to apologize profusely to the woman who'd walked in.

I was on my hands and knees, staggering up with some help from the bar's counter, when I looked up and had my heart lodge right in my throat. Roman was heading toward me after leaving Blackjack's office, and he looked set on putting me outta my misery.

"Shit! I'm fucking sorry, bro. Me and Asphalt were drinking, we got a little carried away, and I –" My mindless banter was broken by a hiccup. He was only a couple feet away now, close enough to smell the whiskey seeping from my pores.

"Get the fuck outta my way." Roman shoved me aside, heading for the leggy blonde.

I held myself against the counter, only breathing easy when it was totally clear he wasn't gonna split my skull in two. No, he was after the chick. They knew each other.

Whatever was going on, it wasn't a happy reunion. The giant walked her over to a quiet corner, where she disappeared in his shadow.

Had to hand it to her. The mystery girl clearly wasn't intimidated, judging by the look on her face. Meanwhile, I was halfway sprawled across the bar top, ready to piss my pants when I thought our Sergeant-at-Arms was heading for me.

Idiot. Thank fuck the clubhouse was sparse tonight, or I'd never live it down.

"Here!" Asphalt's fist came down next to my face. The darts in his hand hit the counter hard. "Clean this shit up, and then take care of yourself. Seriously, brother. This is the only fucking break I'm cutting your ass if you keep wrecking shit tonight. I'm not your buddy Brass."

We shared an icy look and then he was gone. Bastard was still shaking his wide cue ball head on his way outta the clubhouse.

It took fucking forever to get the darts back by the board. Fine movements and motor control were a crazy dream. Crossing into Roman's line of sight, I tried not to draw attention to myself.

Wasn't difficult with his eyes anchored to the strange chick, speaking to her in low, hushed words. I couldn't quite make out what he was saying, but it was more than I'd heard him talk since he was patched into our charter.

I was about to head back when exploding glass vibrated through the air. Flattening myself against the wall, I spun as quickly as I could without falling to the ground to find out where the fuck it came from.

A bottle lay in pieces at the blonde chick's heels. Her fingers twitched – wasn't sure if she'd dropped it or thrown it. Her bright red face beamed fire at Roman as he stomped away, walking past me, heading for the clubhouse's depths.

"Go ahead and walk the fuck away again, you coward!" she screamed. "At least this time I know it's not the prisons and the courts holding you back! You're not man enough to handle us."

Roman just kept going. The girl was playing with fucking fire, and she'd actually gotten away with it unscratched. I fully expected him to turn around and make her say that again, this time with his massive hand wrapped around her throat.

No, the giant kept going. He was fucking outta there. Who the hell knew retreat was in his vocabulary?

"Hey!" I blocked her path as she tried to follow him. "What the fuck's going on here, lady? Who are you?"

"Out of my face!" She collided with my chest and tried to push me aside.

The girl had fight, but I was much bigger than her. Heavy and stupid as an anchor in my fucked up state too. She squealed as we spun together, and I flattened her against the wall.

"Jesus Christ! Calm the fuck down. I thought I was the only asshole in this bar making messes tonight..."

Her dark blue eyes flashed at me. Next thing I knew, her hands wrapped around my neck. Her fingernails sunk into my skin like little daggers, and she pulled me forward with all her might, trying to get my lips on hers.

What the fuck!?

I broke free and went crashing against the bar. Gave me a minute to study her. Yeah, she was sexy on the eyes and freakishly willing – I knew that look in a woman's eyes – but I wasn't gonna twine tongues with this weirdo who'd just been up close and personal with Roman.

She wasn't the one I wanted. Didn't much fancy the beat down I'd narrowly escaped from the Enforcer either.

"What's eating you?" she demanded. "I'm not pretty enough for you? Or are all the guys in this club just a buncha pussies with mean tats and big muscles?"

"It's not like that." I didn't owe her a damned

explanation, but I gave it to her anyway, hoping it'd get this shit off my back. "There's somebody else on my mind, babe. I might be sauced to the gills with Jack, but I'm not blind. I know you're not her."

"Whatever." The woman shrugged, wiping at her eyes. "I'm Sally."

She walked toward me, holding out her hand. I took it cautiously, gave it a quick shake. Did a quick look over my shoulder to make sure this wasn't some kinda bullshit trap set by Roman. Not that anybody needed much cause to punch my ass out cold tonight.

"Rabid." I turned away from her, jumped onto the bar counter, and reached for my bottle. "You want to sit and have a nip of this, or what?"

Sally took the invitation. I pulled out a glass and poured her a sloppy shot, cursed when the whiskey overflowed. She laughed.

At least I was making somebody happy. I welcomed her company, mostly because she was giving me a way to dispose of this shit instead of pouring it down my throat, where it'd make me do even more damage.

"Seriously, how do you know Roman? I've never seen him so pissed."

"Old flame. We had a good thing before he went behind bars. I heard the club changed, and I thought that meant he'd gotten over his crap too. I was an idiot to come back here."

I stared at the bottle, contemplating another shot. The idea made my bile churn, and I was man enough to realize

I'd embarrassed my ass enough for one evening.

"No, Sally. No you're not," I growled. "If he doesn't appreciate what you tried to do, fuck him!"

My fist hit the table, and she jumped. I refilled her glass, sloshing Jack all over the counter. I was on a fucking roll, and I wasn't slowing down now.

"Drink up. Be proud of what you did. You're a sucker for love." Shit – did I really say the L-word? "There's no shame in that. You don't need to feel stupid for tearing out your heart and offering it to this clown. Roman's a slow guy. It takes time for shit to sink in. Must be all that fucking iron he pumps when Blackjack's not having him chase us down. Too much testosterone clouds the brain, that boy bleeds it. The club's been under a lotta stress lately…"

She gave me a weak smile. "What's your story? Are you just a natural at making girls you barely know feel better, or do you know a Roman too? Uh, a female one, I mean."

"Just another lonely heart." I shrugged. "Better off drinking to it than spilling tears, right?" Fuck it. I could stand one more shot.

I grabbed what was left in the bottle, clinked it against her little shot glass. She laughed again, and we downed our drinks together.

We sat for a long while after, making small talk, mostly saying nothing at all. It was nice to have a companion in misery for a change. Course, I wasn't gonna tell her I'd created some of my own shit.

Hell, I was still creating it chasing the one chick who

wanted nothing to do with me. Fuck if I could let go knowing what the Klamath boys had over her, even if she hated my guts.

"Good luck, baby. Hope to see you again sometime. Try coming by in a few weeks. Maybe by then we'll have sorted through some of our shit."

"I hope so," she said. "Thanks, Rabid. I've got a feeling you'll sort whatever's got you by the balls just fine."

Yeah. Imagine that.

I wasn't gonna say it to her face, but blondie was right. It was time to take my own advice. I wouldn't let her give up on the bruiser who'd turned her away – shit, getting him laid to blow off some steam would be good for all of us.

No contest. I wasn't giving up on Christa – not 'til I had her soft red hair in my fist and my tongue jammed down on hers. I'd claim this chick one way or another, slap my brand on her the minute I was done slapping her sweet round ass.

Fuck – *that ass.*

She had a butt that was nice and full, begging to be spanked every time it rippled while she walked.

I was a goner just thinking about it. There was no way, no how, no fucking chance I was giving up on squeezing it 'til she squealed. Didn't give a shit how many times she turned it toward me and walked away.

One day soon, I'd have it grinding on my lap, teasing my dick awake for the roughest, purest fuck of my whole damned life. Then I'd grab her little ass so hard my knuckles went white, shove it up and down where it belonged, jacking myself off in her tight, wet cunt.

Quitting wasn't in my nature. I always got what I wanted. Every single time.

I couldn't stop thinking about having her naked, pressed up against me, moaning sin in my ear while I made her body shake like heaven. Her tits, her ass, every wild inch of her wound me up like the tightest spring the world had ever seen.

On second thought, fuck the spring. That shit was too weak.

No, dammit, I was more like a ticking time bomb, and when I went off, the whole fucking world would know, and so would she. That's how I got my name.

I've always been that way, dead set on getting my way first, second, and third. And God willing, I always would be. I'd spit fire and foam at the fucking mouth, psycho and rabid as all shit, before I *ever* let something I set my sights on slip away. And I'd already let Christa walk about one mile too many outta my grasp.

When I reeled her in, I was gonna pin her down and fuck her 'til my heart stopped. Just one night having her in my shadow was all I needed. Soon as I got her under me, that sexy, infuriating woman was never, ever going anywhere else as long as she lived.

Standing up, it was easier to head for my room. My boots crunched over the mess of glass and whiskey dribbled all over the floor. Whatever prospect cleaned this shit up had his work cut out for him.

A small hand slapped my chest in the hall, and next thing I knew, someone with a sugary perfume was hanging around my neck.

Red.

Everything I didn't fucking need was summed up in that word.

"Where've you been hiding, baby? Don't tell me you're into blondes now." She tugged my shirt down and started to stamp her lips on my chest, heading toward my face, fast and aggressive how I liked.

Took all my might to turn away from the temptation. But whatever the hell Christa planted in my skull was starting to sprout. Fucking anybody but her was settling for less – and I wasn't gonna surrender to that shame.

"Get the fuck off. I need my sleep. Go find another brother to ride tonight." Growling, I pushed her away, trying not to hurt her as I shoved her to the wall. Bitch held on awfully tight.

Red's mouth dropped open. She shook her head. "Don't do this, Rabid! It's her, isn't it? I've heard the rumors going around the club – you're chasing that bitch with the busted face like a baby!"

Busted face? You're goddamned lucky I don't give you one for saying that, I thought, all my evil senses sparking to life.

Rage throttled my heart. I flexed my fists, forced myself to hold them down, despite how bad the Jack in my veins wanted me to wrap them around her fucking throat and squeeze 'til she thought twice about insulting my woman.

"You don't know shit. How many times we need to go

through this? My business – none of yours! If I want your sloppy fucking cunt, I'll ask for it. That's *all* I ever wanted from you, Red. You're a club whore. You're nobody's old lady unless they fucking say so – and you'll never be mine."

Pure hurt swelled in her eyes. Anguish. Heartbreak.

Too harsh? Maybe. But I had to get her off my ass, get her the hell away before I did something stupid, something that would cost me Christa for good if it kept up.

Her lips quivered, and she covered her breasts, suddenly ashamed of the see-through nightie I liked her to wear when we'd fucked. Shit, I couldn't even stand seeing it now without being disgusted, imagining how much better it'd be draped over Christa's big round tits.

"So, it's true..." She shook her head, horror shining in her round face. "I hate this club! I hate all the fucking changes since Fang died. It's making you stupid, Rabid, you and everybody else. It's making you soft. There you go, just like Brass, chasing some bitch who doesn't give a shit about you or this MC. She doesn't even fucking love you! Why can't you see it? Why!?"

Red flew forward, slapped both hands on my chest. Good thing my motor skills were coming back. I grabbed her wrists and shoved her against the wall, pinned her down 'til I saw the jealous rage in her eyes turn to fear.

"You fucking hit me again, I'll tear that flimsy top off and kick your ass out on the street. You can call a cab with your tits hanging out. You and me – we're fucking done,

Red. Deal with it. Find someone else who wants your skank pussy or leave this clubhouse for good. You're lucky it's me." I clenched my teeth, getting up in her face. "Any other full patch brother would've picked you up and thrown you in the fucking dumpster by now."

I let go, listening to her sobs in the distance as she crumpled to the floor. Several doors swung open to see the commotion. I never looked back.

Let them deal with that shit. I was gonna bury myself in bed and sleep off the hangover. Tomorrow, I'd wake up a new man. I'd sit down with the Prez and tell him everything about Christa's debt.

Then, when the Oregon fuckers were dealt with, I'd ride back to her apartment. Whatever happened next, I couldn't say.

Damned good chance it involved kicking down the fucking door and giving her a kiss she couldn't ignore, clenching her hot ass 'til there was absolutely, positively no goddamned doubt in her head about who she belonged to. This time, I wasn't taking no for an answer, and I sure as *fuck* wasn't gonna let her run from me again.

Blackjack called church early the next morning. I was up and moving, listening to the commotion in the halls, before Roman could get on my ass.

I caught Brass in the hallway, grabbing for his cut before he could fly by. "Hey, bro, what the hell's going on out here?"

He spun around and looked at me. Next thing I knew,

he held up a blood stained patch attached to a piece of fabric, about the size of a palm. No bear on it – it wasn't ours. The furious looking eagle was strangling a serpent on a desert backdrop. I couldn't place the symbol with any known MC.

"Uh, am I supposed to recognize this thing?"

Brass smiled and slapped my shoulder. "Not unless you've been fucking around south of the border. This shit used to be attached to a living, breathing cartel boss. Just got word this morning – one of the Oregon boys killed the motherfucker yesterday and took this off him as a little trophy. Beheaded the sick sonofabitch, same thing they've done to plenty of our guys in the old charters south. Our brothers up north caught those sneaky bitches trying to creep into Klamath, and then circle around and hit us in the soft spot, all the warehouses we've got north."

I didn't say a damned thing. My bro didn't wait for me to either. He took off, marching into the meeting room. Several loud roars broke out when I heard him slap it down on the table.

Dragging myself in, I was totally fucking numb. There was a ringing in my ears like a magnum firing next to my head.

When Blackjack started talking later, it just confirmed my worst suspicions. Everything he said was like a dagger driving into my guts. I had to fold my arms just to make sure I wasn't really bleeding out all over the goddamned floor.

"They fucking did it, Prez. Oregon reeled us a fish we

haven't been able to snag for months. Believe me, I'm just as surprised as anyone." Brass looked more uncertain than when I'd seen him in the hall, his voice low and dark as he looked at our leader. "Where do we go from here? Is this a sign we can trust Klamath again?"

"It's a sign, all right. We'll treat them like our brothers unless there's a good reason not to." Blackjack spoke after a long pause, deep in thought. "I'll be straight: I didn't expect shit after the phone call to Rip – especially not after we roughed up their VP. Only question on my mind was when the bullets would start flying in this club again. Rip's a disrespectful little cocksucker, don't get me wrong. But until this morning, when Brass brought us the news, I was ready for war to bring this club into line."

I looked up, my fists balled like iron. "And now? You're telling me we're not shredding those asses for carrying on Fang's fucked up legacy?"

Blackjack shook his head. Shit happened in slow motion, driving the dagger in my guts deeper, harder. I wanted to fucking puke.

"We can't kill them when they're giving us their full cooperation," he said. "It's not perfect. Rip's playing phone tag again. The jackass won't give me the specifics I'd like about how exactly they ambushed the high ranking asshole that patch right there represents." He pointed to the bloody patch, and everybody stared at it. "Shit's not important. I'll get the truth soon. What's important is what that thing there means. We took down an Ace in the cartel. One down, four to go. Intel says trying to decapitate their leadership's the best way to finish the fuckers off. The boys who'll take over if we kill the rest are so young and dumb they'll run back to Mexico with their tails between their legs."

Blackjack paused. A couple guys coughed, and the prospects shuffled nervously in the corner. Everybody was weighing the heavy shit settling on our shoulders. But unlike the other guys, I was being crushed, held under, and drowned by my own club doing this about-face.

"I can't ask Klamath to submit or die over their cat-and-mouse bullshit when they've given us this," Blackjack continued. "Obviously, I don't trust them – not completely – but I'd be a damned fool if I didn't consider the possibility I was wrong."

My heart dropped like an elevator. Shit. Fuck.

If Redding was about to kiss and make up with southern Oregon, then that meant Ed was off limits. Blackjack wouldn't do shit to rock the boat. The best I could hope for was a slow, half-assed attempt at getting Christa's debt forgiven, if he'd hear me out at all.

Rage shot through me. The stabbing sensation in my guts turned to fire, and I was ready to try lighting up the room like a goddamned dragon.

I wanted to turn the fucking table over. My muscles flexed, tingling with the same adrenaline I'd felt every time I risked my life facing bullets for these colors.

"What's going on over there, Rabid? You look like you got something to say. Lay it out. You know we don't hide bad blood between brothers anymore." Brass folded his arms. He'd been studying me the entire time.

Fuck, fuck, fuck. Just then, I hated my best friend for calling me out.

I stood up. Blackjack's full, dark eyes beamed over me like floodlights, and all the brothers waited to hear what the fuck I had to say.

"You want the truth? I think letting Klamath off the hook's a serious fucking mistake. Unless that deceitful shithead they call their Prez is gonna tell us every last bit about how they magically captured a cartel boss and killed him, we're making a lotta fucking assumptions here." My throat was so fucking tight I had to fight like hell to keep from shouting. "Look, I'm happy as anybody about this damned thing. Wherever it came from, it means progress for every brother in this room."

I reached for the blood stained patch, picked it up, and gave it a good shake before letting it fall back to the table like a soiled leaf. "Thing is, I think we were desperate to score a big win when we've been tangling with these fucks for more than a year. We're so shocked and surprised, so stupid with relief, we're letting our guard down. We can't do that. Not 'til we're sure the Oregon crew's full of real brothers instead of crafty fucking wolves."

"He's right," a voice boomed. Turning my head, my eyeballs almost popped out like a fucking cartoon when I saw it belonged to Roman. "This shit's too convenient, Prez. Don't fucking like it. Don't trust it. They knew we were about to make demands or go for the throat. That's why Ed was here in the first place, and now he drops this off for our Veep with a piss poor explanation? Doesn't add up worth a damn, and you know it."

"Yeah? You two really wanna have an out-and-out fight in this club after we just got done killing each other over Fang? Fuck that!" Asphalt shot up, his face lined with anger. "We're goddamned lucky it's a dead cartel boss' patch and not a bomb showing up on our doorstep! If the Oregon crew really wanted our asses dead, there's way easier traps they could set besides this. I'm willing to give these guys the benefit of the doubt. It's not like anybody at this table has any proof to call their story bullshit."

Blackjack leaned back in his chair, gray hair folded around him like a lion's mane. Roman and I locked eyes. There was a brotherly understanding, coupled with a desire to knock Asphalt's dumb bald head against the wall.

Brother or not, I was sick of his cowardly, endlessly contrary shit.

"Rip, Ed, and his boys aren't the men I want in this MC," the Prez said slowly. "They're the club's past. Brutal. Fucked up. Selfish. But if there's a chance, I don't need to spill more Grizzlies blood when the bastards are cooperating, I'm taking it. We have a chance to reset things here before more brothers get hurt. If we start executing every asshole walking on the dark side, right after they did us a big favor, we'll be on our way out like Fang's crew. This is the mother charter now. It's up to us to grab national by the balls and lead by example."

"You boys hear that?" Asphalt grinned, looking to me and then Roman. "Thank fuck the Prez has a brain in his head. If you guys had your way, we'd be letting the cartel walk all over us while we fucking kill each other."

Smug motherfucker! That shitty, arrogant grin on his face reminded me of everything I was losing with this sick new truce – everything threatening my girl! And no, I didn't give a single fuck that she wasn't officially mine yet.

She would be. *Mark my fucking words.*

And I was gonna mark them in blood too.

I hopped on the table and went right for Asphalt. He saw me coming when we collided. Hell opened up and yawned.

Soon, the room was filled with crashing, fighting, screaming brothers. I swung for the fucker's face, must've busted his lip a couple times over before he finally got his senses back and kicked me off him. I hit the wall, fell, and rolled. Saw Roman on the floor next to me, two full patch brothers, and three prospects trying to hold the giant down while he roared every vulgar name in the dictionary.

Asphalt swung his bloody knuckles at my face. Would've been a direct hit if Brass hadn't ripped me off the ground and slammed me into the nearest wall.

I struggled against him. He put his fucking hand over my face and squeezed, grunting as I drove my fist into his abs. Fuck. It was too hard to do any serious damage to him. I cared too much, even when he was choking me.

"Let me the fuck up!" I screamed. "I'll fucking kill him!"

Brass' hand disappeared. Something hard and furry smashed me across the face. When the stars stopped spinning in my eyes, I saw Blackjack had replaced Brass next to me, holding up the club's bear claw gavel with murder in his eyes.

"You're going to cut the shit right now, son, or you'll be losing a few teeth next." He lifted the claw over his head, ready to swing like a bonafide caveman.

I blinked when I thought he'd hit me across the face again, but the claw hit the wall instead. Hard. Left a fucking hole in the old wood.

The commotion slowed, just in time for Blackjack to get on the table. He climbed faster than I expected for someone who'd taken a bullet to the leg just weeks ago during the final battle with Fang.

"Brothers! Shut your fucking mouths and put your fists down. Take a deep breath. Fill your lungs until they're going to burst. This isn't us. This shit all around you isn't brotherhood."

Several men lowered their eyes in shame. Asphalt glared at me over Brass' shoulder. My friend had strategically positioned himself between us with the prospects to break up new fights. Even Roman stopped struggling on the floor, grunting through his teeth.

"You're welcome to disagree. You're welcome to call a vote on anything that's club biz. That's what the charter says. And it also says you're never supposed to come to blows with anybody else wearing this patch unless there's a damned good reason."

He did a slow turn, making sure we could see the bear roaring on his cut. It was the same thing that bound us all together, our common bond. Kept me from beating fuckers like Asphalt to a bloodless pulp when they weren't being so brotherly.

"Rabid and Roman," he spoke our names, leaning down and looking at us with both hands on his knees. "You're entitled to have this club vote if you want. You're clearly outnumbered, but we'll do it anyway if it'll help you settle the fucking rocks in your heads. Is that what you boys need to be sane, or what?"

There was a long pause. I shook my head. No fucking point. We were totally outnumbered. The Enforcer was right behind me, refusing to meet the Prez's eyes.

"Look at me. That's an order," Blackjack growled.

Roman did. "No. No vote," he said, climbing on his feet as his handlers released him.

"All right. Then it seems we're fucking done here. If anybody wants to start a fight again," he said, looking straight at me. "They'll be answering to me and all their brothers for fucking up this club. We move as one. All we've got in this life is each other, understand? You can shake your head, you can rage, you can vote fuck no. But as long as nobody's spilling his brother's blood or draining his wallet, torturing innocents with no good reason like the man with this gavel before me, then you keep your goddamned hands to yourselves! If you've got a question about any of that, you bring it to *me*." He thumped his chest.

Brass nodded, looked at me, hoping I understood. I did.

I also knew this crazy fucking thing with Christa had just gotten a hundred times harder. Going after Ed for her was gonna be going against Blackjack, against the club, against my brothers.

The Prez didn't fucking understand. None of them did. I couldn't abandon her. Didn't give a shit if the Oregon bastards were showering us in gold coins and perfect pussy. They'd bribed their asses out of trouble – for now.

Only with the club. Not with me.

I'd wait as long as I possibly could for the blowout with Ed, but it was fucking coming. Sure as the storm in Blackjack's eyes when he looked over us like knights in his kingdom.

Later that evening, I was tuning up my bike, trying to stay the fuck away from everybody else. Church ended not long after Blackjack's high and mighty proclamation: we were supposed to grin through our teeth and work with the Oregon boys as long as they were killing the cartel. No matter how much anybody mistrusted them.

Couldn't fucking believe it. *Couldn't.* The Prez was either desperate, fooled, or he'd gone off the goddamned deep end.

I wasn't about to start a riot against Blackjack like we all did with Fang. If this was a mistake – and it sure as hell was – then it was an honest one. The Prez wasn't maliciously blind, even if the decision he'd made caused me to wonder if he was going senile. No, it was obvious –

the Klamath crew pulled the wool over the Blackjack's eyes, but they hadn't corrupted him.

My hands were covered in grease and oil. When I went to pull my wrench outta the crevice in my bike, it slipped in my fingers and pinched my skin tight. Gave myself a nice long scratch pulling out.

"Fuck!" I banged the wrench down, snarling, sucking engine oil and blood through my teeth.

The bike was good to go, and I'd reached my fucking limit. If anybody walked in on me right now, I'd find their head and start smashing it in the ground like a maniac. I had to get the fuck outta here before I got myself killed for defying the Prez.

I had to see her, the only chick in the world who stood a chance at calming my ass down. Even when she was sassing me, screaming at me, or giving me the cold fucking shoulder, it was something. Christa reminded me I still had a pulse. She let me enjoy all the nuances between numbness and hot outrage, things I couldn't find anymore inside this clubhouse.

The killer body attached to her perfect flaming hair didn't hurt neither. My dick ballooned and strained in my pants the instant I thought about her. Hungry, yearning, losing its little mind right along with me.

Lust turned my blood molten when I traced her curves in my brain. Goddamn. The woman barely had a clue what she did to me, and I had to make her understand.

Tonight.

The psycho games had to end, and so did this

obsession. I'd ride this bike to her place, and I wouldn't hop on it again 'til I mounted her like a wild animal. We were fucking tonight one way or another.

Fucking to restore my sanity. Fucking so I didn't leave a crater in the ground with all this pent up need. Fucking so hard I'd feel her pussy clenching on my dick for weeks, taste her on my lips with every new breath, and remember how hard my eyes rolled back when I filled her cunt to overflowing...

Christ. It took a full minute to remember how to move my body after being lost in sexual la-la land.

Reaching for my phone, I flipped it open, ready to dial her number. She was coming out with me tonight one way or another, even if I had to drag her. Didn't expect to see four missed calls. All from her number.

Fuck.

I was on my bike, roaring outta the garage and through the gate, before I had the phone pressed to my ear, listening to the voicemail.

V: Off the Chain (Christa)

Two Hours Earlier

Where the hell was Rabid? Why hadn't he called?

I was seriously starting to wonder if my bitch act had scared him away for good. For once, I truly missed his smug, sexy face, especially now that I'd come to terms with him offering me more than eye candy. Dad's words helped with that. It's funny how much wisdom he still had, despite his memory being shot to hell.

I couldn't believe how wrong I'd been. I hadn't even given him a chance. No, I wasn't ready to jump his sexy bones and let him come crashing into my heart, but he deserved a hearing. I couldn't deny the *possibilities* he offered anymore.

Rabid was redemption. A way to get rid of Ed and save my father without forking everything over to the bully who wanted to drag me deeper into permanent slavery.

I was lost in my thoughts. It took a little boy's shaky voice to bring me back.

"Christa? It says here the Emperor died on St. Helena

after Waterloo. Not Elba." Martin and I exchanged a stupefied blink.

The kid looked at me like I'd grown a second head, his finger pointed to the right spot in the history book. Crap.

"Jeez! It's a good thing you were paying attention today." Smiling, I ruffled his hair with my fingers. "Grown ups make mistakes too. Better you learn that today, along with this French history."

The boy was growing up fast. I missed his innocence, the same thing I'd once had on those long days in Alaska when dad's mind was there, and I didn't have a care in the world.

"Great work today, Martin. Keep working on your report and I'll look it over next lesson. Let's call the day done right here."

He watched me as I scribbled on a few sticky notes and posted them in his book. I marked the most important chapters in the Napoleon biography he'd picked out. When I'd finished, his mother, Shirley, came into the kitchen where we'd set up to study.

"Bad news, lady," I said, working the longest face I could manage. "I think you've got a historian on your hands."

She burst into a grin and laughed. "Seriously, he's doing an amazing job. Pretty soon you won't be paying me at all. He'll be presenting his papers to academics in their ivory towers."

"Ah, but where would we be without you? I'm glad he's got his history locked down, but there's plenty more to help him with." The woman reached into her purse and quickly signed another check over to me.

Taking it was so hollow. In another life, I would've done this job for free, anything to help these kids make a better life and avoid my mistakes. Too bad I needed the money to survive, my only defense against Ed until Rabid came through for me.

If he came through, I had to remind myself. It hurt to doubt him, and if he'd abandoned me, I had no one but myself to blame.

We were all up, walking toward the door. Shirley and I lingered on the porch for a moment longer, leaning in close. I didn't like the uneasiness in her eyes.

"That man," she said. "Does he know you? He's been hanging around across the street since you sat down with Martin."

"Huh?" I turned around slowly.

Please don't let it be him. Please don't fucking let him be here.

Mercy wasn't in the cards for me today. I saw Ed sitting on his bike, leaning his gut into the handlebars, puffing away on half a cigarette.

I had to work very hard not to scream when I looked at her again. It was awful enough to hear his threats against dad, but if he started to go after Martin and Shirley too?

I'd go to the police, and get myself killed if it came to it. I had to. And that made my heart lodge in my throat like a fat, bitter stone.

"I'm not sure," I said, calm as I could manage. "Never

seen him before. Yeah, you're right to be concerned. I'm honestly surprised. This isn't a rough neighborhood."

Shirley cocked her head, staring at me. I didn't blame her one bit while I was babbling like a nervous idiot, trying to hide just how much my anxiety seethed underneath my skin.

"Shirley, listen." I took a deep breath. "If that man takes a step toward this house, call the cops. It's probably nothing, but you can't be too careful these days."

I had to go. Right now. Shirley reached out and caught my shoulder when I tried to get away.

"Wait! He's parked next to your car. Surely, you're not okay going down there alone? Let me walk you over."

"No! I'll be fine," I said, giving her a bitter smile. God. It was like trying to grin while being stabbed. "You can watch from the window to make sure I get out of here okay. Don't worry about me. I know how to talk to bikers if he tries anything. My dad was one."

Yeah, I knew how to talk to this one, I thought. *And it's never helped me one bit.*

I walked, feeling her eyes on me the entire time. By the time I got to my car, the nausea flipping my stomach upside down was total. I'd lied through my fucking teeth and it made me sick. For a second, I really considered revving my car and backing right over the asshole as hard as I could.

But that wouldn't get rid of him. Nothing short of a weapon wielded by an equally ruthless badass would at this point. I pulled out slow, steady, checking my rear view mirror and praying he'd follow me – but not too close. I wanted him away from this neighborhood ASAP.

Big Ed wasn't a total idiot. He waited a good minute until I'd turned the first corner before he started his bike. Didn't take him long to catch up. The asshole motioned in the rear view mirror when we were near the highway, gesturing toward a gas station where we'd met several times before.

Naturally, it was one without a camera outside, and minimal traffic buzzing around for this time of day. He had a real knack for picking places where we wouldn't be bothered while he whispered fresh death threats in my ear.

"Don't ever come near that house again!" I shouted it as soon as I was out of my car, slamming the door as he pulled up next to me. "This is between us. You've already fucked with my father. I won't let you look at that woman like that. Christ, she has an eight year old kid."

He chuckled. Nasty and menacing as always. "What? You think that's not the fucking reason I decided to hang around waiting for your ass? I figured the thought of me fucking the bitch and gutting the kid would do something to you. Do I look like a fucking retard to you?"

No. He looked like he'd just crawled up from the pits of hell, sent to torment me for all the missteps I'd made, a karmic debt collector to break me down for the rest of my miserable life.

"I know exactly what you look like," I snapped.

Clenching my purse tight to my chest, I wrapped the strap around my hand. I was ready to fight, hit him with the only thing I had if he came a step closer.

Ed seemed to sense the change. His eyes beamed dark interest. He stopped, tossed his cigarette on the ground, and stubbed it out with his boot. Then he cracked his knuckles, a sound that caused my belly to crawl toward my throat.

"Tough words coming from a woman who's put yourself in a world of shit. Only question is, you gonna put yourself deeper today, or what? Where's my fucking money, bitch? You're supposed to pay double after falling short last week. I ought to make it more after you bad mouthed me to that Rabid asshole."

Shit! How does he know?

There was no point in hiding it. "I didn't say anything he doesn't already know. Rabid's a better man than you and your idiots in Klamath, Ed. He's worthy of the Grizzlies patch."

I must've been absolutely out of my mind. Or maybe too many years being tormented by these pricks were finally boiling to the surface, ready to spill over in a reckless mess.

Ed squinted at me through the setting sunlight. "You wanna come up here and say that to my face, babe? You're bitch enough to say those words – don't think you're bitch enough to take the beating insulting these colors gets you. Come 'ere, I'll show you who's worthy of this motherfucking patch, you vicious cunt!"

He charged me like an overfed bull. Faster than I gave him credit for. I only had time to scream once before my back hit the car and I was lodged against his beefy chest, his hand clapped over my mouth. I halfheartedly swung the purse over my head, trying to hit him in the face. The angle was all wrong.

The monster had me, and now he whispered in my ear. "Don't even think about it, Chrissy. I *will* kill you, and fuck you in any order I damned well please if you take a swing at me. I don't give a shit what you've been telling your fuck buddy here in the Redding charter neither."

My bravery retreated in his brutal grip. Fear dominated. Even if I could've given the purse another swing at his ugly face, I wasn't sure I'd have the guts to pull it off.

"Guess you didn't know those boys are on good terms with us again? I dropped a little present for 'em off last night. So fucking good, they won't make a peep if I tell 'em I'm taking every dime you have – or even if I slit your scrawny throat. There's no getting out of this shithole you've buried yourself in, baby girl. And I'm gonna pile it all over your head until you fucking suffocate." Ed paused, crazy excitement in his evil voice. "Now, let's try this again. I've always been a three strikes kinda guy. Where's. My. Fucking. Money?"

His arms were locked tight around my neck, choking me little by little. The next ten seconds felt like an hour as I struggled to breathe, and realized with horror I couldn't. He had me beat. He could snap my neck back here and leave me paralyzed or dead, and no one would know.

If I could've prayed, I would've begged for mercy.

Mercy, or Rabid. God, what I would've given to have that man here right now.

My hands moved on pure instinct, offering up the purse. Ed ripped it out of my hands, pushed me to the ground. I barely had time to get my hands out before I collided with the pavement, getting a few scratches, gasping for air.

Things kept clattering onto the ground behind me. My phone, a roll of antacids, an old book with phone numbers of friends I'd lost years ago, a flimsy photo of dad next to his motorcycle outside Anchorage, grinning with a little redheaded girl at his side.

This wasn't the way I expected my life to flash before my eyes.

When I turned around, Ed had a knife in one hand, and he'd dropped the leather bag. He was going through my wallet, pulling out the flimsy bills I had stuffed in there. He found Shirley's check too.

Jesus, I never expected him to take the thirty bucks I had in there for food. Crawling toward him, I couldn't stop the tears, gushing like a broken fool.

"Please! I need that money to eat. How am I supposed to pay you anything if I starve?"

Amusement pulled at his lips. "You got a lot of fucking fat in all the right places, bitch. You'll live. Figure it the fuck out. I don't care if you've gotta rob a few places or suck a hundred dicks. Shit, maybe you live off some fucker's jizz and save a few extra nickels for me. Be a doll and sign this fucking thing over."

He pulled out a pen, shoving the check in my face. He was really demanding everything this time. If I didn't find some way to raise more money, I wouldn't be able to make my rent. I'd be homeless *and* starving.

"Sign it!" He bent down with his gut hanging, barking in my face so hard I felt his wretched spittle hit my cheek.

That was it. All I could take in his vile mist. I'd do anything to have this animal out of my face. I angrily scrawled my signature and his name, handing it over.

He headed toward his Harley and stopped next to my car. I watched as he took the knife in one fist, then slammed it into my front tire, tearing a gash across it. Air hissed out through the fissure in the rubber.

"What the fuck are you doing!?" I screamed. Anguish pressed so hard against my skull I thought I'd pass out.

No, no, no. This can't be happening. I've got to be asleep somewhere, suffering this nightmare.

I couldn't handle a car repair too. I fucking couldn't.

"I'm doing everything I can to give the Prez an excuse to let me bring you back to Klamath. I've got half a mind to throw you on my bike right now and take off. Shit, it'd be better for everybody. I'll get my dick wet in that red haired pussy of yours, and you'll get a couple hot meals a day in between having every hole fucked like no tomorrow. But I'm a nice guy. I'm a softie." His voice dripped sarcasm. "I'm gonna give your whore pussy a fighting chance. If you cough up next week's payment, I'll let you stay here until you finally fuck up. Won't shove poison down your old man's throat when the nurse's back is turned until you disappoint me again. Get your shit together, Chrissy. You've got seven days before I see if I need to visit again. You miss the next payment, your ass is mine, and daddy's a dead man."

I wilted right there. Listening to the sound of his engine growling was like the world ending. For all intents and purposes, it was.

My house of cards had finally collapsed and burned to ashes.

It was a little songbird landing on a branch overhead that finally stopped my shaking, stormy tears ripping at my eyes. I looked up, wondering how something so beautiful could exist in this hell.

I shifted, sat up, slowly tried to stuff my things back into my purse. My hands and knees hurt from where he'd shoved me to the ground. I didn't even want to think about how I was going to patch the tire with less than a hundred dollars in my bank account – everything in the world he hadn't ransacked from me. Also, all I had marked for my rent, and it wasn't nearly enough.

When I picked up my phone, I held it, shaking as my fingers went through my contacts. It stopped on Rabid's number. It took several tries calling him. I always hung up on the third ring, afraid he'd actually answer.

On the fourth try, I let it ring all the way. His voice mail switched on, and the mundane pre-recorded message was the best thing I'd heard all day. Why the hell had I been so blind until now?

I needed this man. Hell, I actually *wanted* his company

too. He'd offered a helping hand and so much else, and I'd been too fucking stupid to take it. No more.

"Rabid, it's Christa. I'm at the gas station off Cypress. If you're around this evening, I could really use some help." I couldn't stop the heartache and anguish from flowing into my voice. "Like, I could *really* fucking use it. I need you! You've got to come get me as quick as you can. My car's fucked. I've got no way to get home or fix it."

I just about left it at that. But my brain had no more filter, and I let the words come that would guarantee he showed up if he still gave a crap about me.

"Big Ed stole everything from me. Please. Come find me as soon as you get this."

I sounded like a little girl pleading for my father again. The sassy bitch ready to take on the world had been swept aside by Ed's assault. It should've horrified me, but somehow, it didn't.

I meant every word. I needed him to find me. I was ready to give him the truth and admit I couldn't face this on my own. And if he could help me wreck the bastard who'd given me a one week countdown to total slavery, then maybe he could help me straighten more out too.

Maybe he could prove letting someone else into my heart wasn't the disaster I'd always assumed, but something bright and unexpected as the little bird still singing in the trees.

It was about an hour before my phone rang. I was tucked into the driver's seat, trying to look normal to the gawky kid who came out of the gas station a half hour before to empty some trash. I hoped like hell he'd write me off as another poor girl in an old beater who'd pulled over to take a call.

If I had one more problem before Rabid showed up, I was going to break glass and scream.

My body was on overload. I'd fallen asleep. The phone woke me up.

The first thing I heard on the line was a motorcycle humming, and I smiled. Amazing how that sound had always offered either heaven or hell.

"Baby, are you okay?" His voice blasted into my ear. Intense. Questioning.

"I might be now that I've got you on the line."

"Hold on. I'm already on my way. When I get there, you're gonna tell me what the fuck's going on. Don't you dare cover anybody's ass."

I smiled. He was gruff, demanding, but it was all for me. "I think we're past that, Rabid. I'm not hiding anything from you for now on."

"Good. See you in a little bit."

The line went dead. Only took about five more minutes for him to roar up next to me. He killed his bike's engine and hopped off, running up to my window as I got out.

"Fucking shit! Where's the asshole who did this to you? He's a dead man." He reached out and touched my puffy face, probably at its worst since I'd escaped Fang. I certainly hadn't cried so hard.

"I'm glad to see you. Do you know that?" I threw my arms around him. No one had ever felt so *right* beneath my palms. "I'm sorry about last time. The kiss really freaked me out. I couldn't handle it. I ran away and –"

"Not now, babe." He pushed his finger across my lips. "We're not going there 'til I find the man who did this. Tell me the fucking truth. Tell me now. Was this really Ed and the Oregon crew?"

Our eyes locked. Slowly, I nodded my head. His eyes flickered, hellfire reflecting off diamonds, ready to kill and die for me if I had to. He looked like a lunatic, but the crazy bloodlust in his eyes was for me. All mine.

"He took everything. Stole my money and pushed me to the ground. I riled him up like an idiot." Rabid started shaking his head the instant I stopped talking, denying any attempt to find fault with myself.

Maybe he was right. Big Asshole was such a bully, he'd gotten all my wires crossed, tried to make me think I deserved this. Any sane logic said I didn't.

"Fuck!" Rabid bared his teeth. "Should've known not to let that piece of shit outta my sight. Where does he hang out? Has he hit the road home yet? How long ago did he leave?"

"I don't have a clue, Rabid. He comes and goes as he pleases. A lot more often lately. I think he's hanging around town for business with your club."

"Yeah," he said, as if he knew more. "Got a feeling his shit's done for now. I've gotta catch up with that motherfucker before he gets on the highway. You stay here, Christa."

He pulled me back toward my car. Wait, crap, he wasn't leaving me here, was he?

"Don't go!" I said, desperately tugging on his cut, pulling at the bear patch. He stopped. "He's stronger than he looks. Dangerous too. I don't need to tell you that. At least call in some help if you're really going after him. You can't do this alone!"

I was scared to death my plea was going to get him killed. If that happened, I wouldn't even fight the next time anyone from Oregon came after me. I'd give myself up and suffer everything I deserved for spilling Rabid's beautiful blood.

Jesus, in twenty-four years, nothing good had ever happened to me. It was a curse. Tragedy took everybody I cared about, and I'd lose him too if I let him slip out of sight. I just knew it.

"Baby, come on." His voice was soft, but determined. He leaned down, pulled me halfway off the driver's seat, into his arms. "You know I have to go. It's the only way outta this. Every minute he's walking around and breathing is one more minute you're in danger. That motherfucker's long overdue for a bullet in his evil brain. Let me do what I do best."

He threw his arms around me and squeezed. I threw myself at him, desperately pressing my lips to his. The kiss ignited an explosion in my brain. My vision blanked out into a black canvass, completely messed up while adrenaline overloaded my system.

Beautiful colors. Neon flashes matching the lightning in my blood. His mouth lit me up like a candle and I still wanted more, even when I was burning from head to toe.

This man knew how to kiss like nobody else. Probably because I wanted his lips on mine like nobody's business. His tongue swept over mine again and again, rough and possessive. He licked me sopping wet without even putting his face between my legs.

Jesus. I tumbled back to earth as it ended in a growl. Then his lips broke from mine and he stepped away.

"I'll be back for you as soon as I can. Here." He pulled out his wallet and rifled through the cash tucked inside, pushing a fistful of bills into my hands. "Get yourself a cab and something to eat. Wait for me. I'll call you as soon as the job's done. Got a funny feeling I won't have to go far. A shithead like him won't hit the road without visiting his favorite watering hole first. He's never leaving Redding alive."

My eyes bulged. Not just because he'd replaced everything the bastard had stolen in one stroke. Rabid talked about ruling life and death like it was the weather. I didn't have the strength to argue or beg.

I watched him mount his bike, fix his helmet, and then take off, speeding out the alleyway and into the dulling light. For a second, I thought I could sit there like a good girl, maybe dial up a cab, and find a bar to wait like he asked.

But that wasn't me. Ed tried to break my spirit, and Rabid restored it. Next thing I knew, my key was in the ignition, and I fastened my seat belt. I might break down trying to follow him with my tire slashed, but damn if I wasn't going to try.

I couldn't let him ride into battle without any backup. I'd keep my distance, but I had to know what was about to happen.

I had to make sure the man who was risking his life for me didn't die.

Rabid wasn't kidding about the watering hole. I'd only passed the dive just outside the city a couple times before, and the meager bar I'd owned put it to shame. The place was crawling with poorly concealed prostitutes and junkies.

When I first pulled up to park, I saw a man shooting up in the car next to me. He rocked back and forth, a rubber tourniquet around his arm, blasted out of his mind. Obviously such an addict, he couldn't wait to leave the parking lot before sampling the junk, presumably something he'd bought inside.

I didn't want to go in there. I told myself I'd give it five minutes. I recognized Ed's bike with the horse and bear skulls on it right away, and Rabid's was parked near it.

Night had fallen. Good thing the traffic going in and out of the bar was light, or else it would've been hard to trade the two big silhouettes that came out a minute later, angrily waving their arms.

They rounded the building and disappeared on the other side.

Shit. It had to be them.

I swallowed hard and slowly opened my door, tip toeing into the darkness.

Their voices were surprisingly quiet. At first, I thought I was following the wrong shadows.

Then Rabid's voice exploded. "I don't give a fuck what Blackjack says! I know you assholes are fucking with my club, same goddamned way you're trying to fuck with my girl. I'm gonna find out where you got that patch. No fucking way it came from a cartel boss. You're blowing smoke up our asses so you can set us on fire when our backs are turned."

Ed laughed. I'd recognize that awful, sandpaper sound anywhere. "Whatever you say, kid. I've been in this club a lot longer than you. You've gotta hold no punches and give no mercy in this world. The second you do, somebody else will eat you alive. If it's not the Prairie Pussies we're supposed to call our friends thanks to the deal your Prez cut, it's the fucking Mexicans."

"You really think you're a big man, don't you?" Rabid spat on the ground. "That's a fucking riot when you're really the most reckless, savage piece of shit I've ever met – and that includes the asswipes we used to call our brothers. They followed Fang off the fucking cliff like the lemmings they were. You're gonna do the same, and so are all your boys in Klamath."

"Yeah?" I knew that edge in Big Ed's voice. Rabid was getting to him, winding him up – probably trying to make him do something stupid.

"Last I checked, you fuckers are the ones who decided to go apeshit and kill the only bastard hard enough to give us a fighting chance. I'd give my left nut to have Fang back in charge. But I'm not gonna follow him to the grave either. I'll kiss Blackjack's ring as long as he doesn't let dumbfucks like you come into our territory and tell us how we ought to live."

Rabid laughed, low and booming, and then it abruptly stopped. "You're as funny as you are fat, asshole."

"Oh, yeah? Why the fuck's that? You wanna tell me before I hold you down with this gut and stick a knife in your pussy throat?"

"You won't do shit," Rabid growled. "Only pussy I see standing here's you. You're the one sneaking around in *our* goddamned town, telling chicks like mine what to do with club money. That fucking debt is ours to deal with because it's in our border. Or maybe we decide not to deal with it at all. You can eat shit if you think this brotherly truce changes a damned thing. You're not gonna come within spitting distance of my girl. Never again."

My heart was racing. Something insane was about to come to a head.

"Nah, brother, you got it all wrong." I cringed when I heard him say the b-word, and I could practically hear Rabid doing it too. "I'm taking what I'm owed. If Chrissy was really your old lady, you'd pay up like a good boy, and I know there's no fucking brand on that bitch. I've heard the talk around your clubhouse – you've got a bad case of puppy love for this scratched up cunt. You should've fucked her when you had your chance and thrown her away. She's not gonna be able to keep the cash flowing in, and you know what that means. I'll be the one doing the fucking soon in Klamath. She's a hot one – everything from the neck down, anyway. Fuck, maybe I can put a bag over that bitch's ugly head while I slam my cock up her –"

Hatred turned my veins to ice at about the same time Rabid snapped. His arms shot out, grabbed Ed by the throat, and threw him up against the wall with superhuman strength. Big Ed didn't have another second to react before Rabid's switchblade was out, buried in the demon's throat.

The monster's eyes went wide, searching, trying to understand the fatal pain that struck him like a bolt from the sky. Dark, filthy blood flowed out over Rabid's hands.

Ed croaked a couple times, shuddered, and began to die. His fat hands wrapped around Rabid's throat, but he was too weak, alive with shock and pain. But not for long.

I closed my eyes and counted to five. When I opened them, the big man was slumped over, his eyes shut, nothing moving except the blood pouring from his neck.

It was over just like that. The man who'd tormented me would never speak again, much less do anything else.

"Go tell your bullshit fantasies to whoever the fuck you meet in hell," Rabid growled and spat on him as he let go. Ed slumped to the ground.

He looked over in my direction and instantly cursed. "Fuck!"

I couldn't think about running. My lungs wouldn't

work, and neither would my feet. Rabid was on me like a wolf, tackling me to the ground. I screamed, and the hellish pressure on my spine lightened when he realized it was me.

"Christa, baby? Jesus fucking Christ." He stopped, lifted his knee off me, and ran his unbloodied hand through his hair. "Why the hell are you here? I told you to wait for me miles away from this shithole!"

Anger. Righteous and justified. I scuttled up on my hands and knees, looked at him, and lowered my face to the ground.

You know why. I thought it, but I didn't dare say it.

"Don't give me that fucking look. What the fuck ever, baby. Maybe it's better you saw me dispatch his evil ass after all." He paused. "Since you're here, make yourself useful. Go bring me the black bag on my bike. I'm gonna need it to clean this shit up."

He reached into his pocket and tossed me his keys. I moved mechanically, doing as he asked, trying to fully process the fact that I'd just watched him brutally kill the bastard who'd seemed too evil to die.

Big Ed was dead. He'd never torment me again – but of course his brothers up north might. I shook my head, refusing to think about it.

There was nothing to fear right now except getting caught by someone who wasn't another junkie or a creep. Tonight, Rabid gave me an ounce of reprieve and the first hope I'd had since forever.

The leather bag I'd retrieved from his bike was heavy.

When I brought it back to him, he tore it open, and brought out what looked like a thick plastic canister.

Rabid crouched on the ground, turned, and looked at me. "You don't need to watch this shit, baby. This next part's pretty fucking gruesome. Don't look – unless you really want to."

I turned my back. A minute later, there was a sizzling sound behind me, almost like bacon frying. My curiosity got the better of me. I looked back with my hand over my face and saw him spraying a solution over the corpse's hand.

The other one was already smoking at the fingertips. "What're you doing to him?" I whispered quietly, wondering if I really wanted an answer.

"Melting off his fingerprints and what's left of his fucked up face. Then this fat piece of shit's going in the dumpster." He said it so matter-of-factly. "The guy who owns this place hauls his own trash out to the country every weak and burns it. Too many junkies and too much contraband to risk turning it over to the city for waste disposal. He'll incinerate everything – including this fuck – but if anybody comes snooping around before he does, they'll never be able to identify this sack of shit."

I nodded glumly. All I needed to know. Jesus, this was his world, wasn't it?

I'd been around hard bikers and outlaws all my life, but I'd never seen how they handled life and death up close before. My stomach churned, but it wasn't full blown panic. There was only numbness, relief, and –

could it be? – gratitude. Admiration.

The last ones swelled my heart when I stopped and stared at the man who'd just done me the biggest favor in the world.

I took one more good look and nodded, thankful like I'd never been. Then I headed for the parking lot, hoping Rabid would join me as soon as he could.

I didn't regret a damned thing about tonight. Dad and I were safe, and I'd finally found someone worth opening my shell to. Someone who fought and killed for me.

I closed my eyes, standing next to my car, letting the warm breeze blow by while the stars twinkled in the sky. Those same stars watched us when I freaked out and ran. Now, they were going to watch me embrace the answers to my prayers.

When Rabid came stomping toward his bike, his boots and leather were dusty. He'd put his riding gloves on, but I could see a few reddish blood stains going up his arms.

"It's done," he said. "You're safe, Christa. I kept my promise, and I'll extend it anytime some asshole's stupid enough to fuck with you. You're *mine,* dammit. Nobody gives my woman a shred of shit unless they want to buy their souls a ticket straight to hell."

My ears pushed pleasant tingles through my body as his growl surrounded me. His hands hooked around me, tugged me to his chest, and we embraced for a long time, just listening to our heartbeats and soaking in the moonlight.

"Rabid…" His name was like a whirlwind on my

tongue. If only he wasn't still spotted with the dead man's blood. "You can't go back to the clubhouse like that. Follow me to my place. I'll help get you cleaned up."

He pulled back to look at me, quirking an eyebrow. "You sure you're ready for that? This shit's a lot to take in tonight, baby. We don't gotta rush anything – but you know I'm dying every fucking day I don't have you under me."

My lips trembled. "I'm ready for anything after tonight."

"Good," he rumbled, sliding his hands down lower. I gasped when they caught my ass and squeezed – hard. "Because there's no fucking way I could wait another night without going off like a nuclear warhead. I'll get the blood and dirt washed off, and then we're going to bed. We're fucking tonight, baby. I'll give you the ten minutes it takes on the road to think about that. Let it sink in. Let it curl that pretty red hair. If you can handle it by the time we get to your place, then you'll handle the same goddamned way my dick's gonna be slamming you tonight."

He squeezed me again, this time so hard my hips rolled forward. Big mistake. That V between my legs rocked into his hips, and I felt the massive ridge beneath his jeans I'd sensed a couple times before.

He was big, hard, and eager as all hell. All for me.

His lips crashed against mine. Hot, fiery, insatiable. His teeth sucked in my bottom lip and bit so hard he almost drew blood. I moaned into his mouth, craving his hurt, everything he wanted to give me.

He's right, I thought. *No more bullshit. This is what I've bought, and I'm ready to pay for it with every inch of my skin. It's not an obligation. I wouldn't want him so bad if it was.*

How long has it been since I've had a man? Years?

How long since it was a man like him? Never.

With a feral snarl, he released my ass, sliding one hand up my spine and fisting my red locks at their tips. "Give me another taste for the road, babe. I'm gonna be thinking about how wet and tight your pussy gets the whole way home."

We kissed. Explosively. Desperately.

The cauldron on my lips that was quintessentially Rabid melted me from the inside out. His tongue found mine and pushed hard, pouring his seething lust into me, igniting my own – I withered. Surrender never felt so fucking good.

"Get in and go, babe. I'll be right behind you if the fucked up tire gives out. We gotta leave *now*, before I take you right here. Trust me on this. I'm wrestling my own fucking dick with every heartbeat to make sure our first time's not happening in a shithole like this. I won't allow that fucking travesty, but I can't hold back shit for much longer."

Just then, a trashy looking couple stumbled through the parking lot, laughing. They slid by us, and I could smell the stink wafting off them. Worse than the dead man we'd left in the dumpster. They'd just helped him make his point.

I tore myself away from Rabid before anything else could happen. The car started up and moved without too much more destruction on the tire. Too bad I couldn't leave the POS here. Rabid was right behind me the whole way home.

It wasn't a stretch to feel his eyes melting through my car. Almost as bad as the non-stop ache between my legs. The heat, the wetness, the swelling made it hard to focus on the road. Lucky me it was a short trip.

I'd never been in heat before until now. He'd reduced me to an animal, nervous and tingling with anticipation.

It wasn't just the man he'd killed for me stirring my blood red hot. Every time we got close, my skin hummed like a magnet, drawn to him no matter how much my head resisted. The heart knew what it wanted. So did my wicked body.

I wanted to throw myself at him, tear off his clothes, and slide my tongue all over the glorious ink I knew he had on his chest. I couldn't stop thinking about what he'd feel like when his hard body shuddered between my legs, giving me the full inferno I'd only tasted in his fingers and his lips.

When we got to my place, I lingered in the car, trying to collect my wits and my breath. This was it. It had to be.

Rabid walked up and tapped on the window. "You coming, or what?"

I shut off the engine and got out. Something about the way he took my hand in his caused the fire to burn higher than when we'd kissed back in the parking lot. Raw sex took over everything like a rising wave, drowning whatever fears or doubts I had left.

We barely got through the door when he took off his cut and then the shirt underneath it. Jesus. If I thought he was a mountain, then he was actually a full *range* of rock hard peaks and wild, masculine edges. His muscles were packed together tight, whole slabs forming tight, delectable canyons in his abs. His chest was big and broad and hard enough to hold up the entire world.

The ink ran as wild as the rest of him. He had the roaring bear on his chest like all the other guys I'd seen in the club. The stripes rippling up his arms swung over his shoulders and formed dark flames around his neck. He was a walking canvass, painted like some bright jungle creature deadly to the touch.

There was no mistaking it – this man was dangerous as hell. I'd seen what he could do first hand. I refused to let myself be afraid. We were well past fear.

"You gonna gawk all night or help me wash this fucker's blood away?" he asked with a smile.

I smiled back, then tiptoed into the bathroom. "Just give me one minute."

Sweet Jesus. One minute. Sixty seconds until I lost my mind if I didn't run my hands all over that gorgeous body.

I swept the shower curtain aside and started running the water. He would've been content with a hot shower alone, but I was going to do him one better. I filled the tub with water and grabbed a washcloth.

When it was halfway full, I cracked the door and

looked at him. He was sitting on my bed like a tiger resting after a successful hunt.

"Come on in here. I'm ready." He stepped past me, into my small bathroom. "Sit down. I'll do the rest."

He didn't argue. I watched as he took a seat on the toilet, wringing the excess water out of my rag. He let out a low, satisfied throaty sound when I swept it over his neck, starting there and working down his arms, paying special attention to the rusty blood stains near his wrists. Little spots of the bastard's blood lined his entire arm, the last evidence of our crime to wipe away.

"Can I ask you something?" I whispered, hoping the question I had in mind wasn't too much for right now. He nodded. "How did it feel to kill him?"

"Almost as good as when I see you, babe. That's because he was your kill. Ours. I sent his ass to hell and I'll have to face the music with my brothers soon. I did it for you, and I don't regret shit. I'd do it all over again." He looked at me, eyes burning bright.

"Nobody rides your sweet ass but me from now on. Besides, Ed had it coming for the club. You just helped speed things along. They'll all see the light sooner or later. 'Til they do, it's you and me. That's all I ever needed besides this patch." He thumped his chest with one fist. "Killing for you's the same as killing for my brothers. Not something I think about after the job's done, unless I wanna add another mark to my skin."

He pointed to his right bicep. There were rows of jagged lines tattooed there, sets of five. Four lines cut with a diagonal slash, like something a kid would do to keep tally. I started to count, but after about eight, I decided I didn't really want to.

"I get it. Dad did his share of dirty stuff for the club too." Rabid looked up and gave me an understanding nod. "I just never understood how it could come so easy. How much I'd want it to happen. Not until you showed me."

Rabid snorted, leaning into the warm rag as I swept it over his shoulders. Oh, God. Those shoulders looked like something to grab and hold onto while we fucked with my feet off the ground. They were going to be the death of me, if every other inch of him wasn't first.

"Come on. Give yourself some credit. We oughta celebrate having that piece of shit dead. Don't tell me it was all me who opened your eyes."

I shook my head. "No. He was threatening to kill my dad. That's the real reason I put up with his threats for so long."

Rabid's hands formed fists on his thighs. His muscles rippled, swelled, amazing as watching a cobra coiling itself up for a strike.

"Motherfucker! I hope the devil's got a lotta bears, hungry and ripping his ass to pieces 'til the end of time. Killing him once in this lifetime's not enough." Rage hissed out his nostrils. "Figured there was something else eating you. You're not the kind to take shit from anybody, Christa. I like that."

I swallowed. Never knew it would be so hard to take compliments from a shirtless man chiseled like a god.

My eyes caught my own reflection in the mirror. Seeing the scars on my face threatened to kill the buzz running through my blood.

Seriously, now that I had him next to me, bare chested and beautiful, what did this man see in me?

Okay, I had the goods in the right places. But he was perfection, muscles and looks meant to draw a pretty face and a rocking body. And after what Fang did, I'd never have a pretty face again.

"You're a good man, Rabid. Killer or not," I said sadly. "There's not much here I can see worth liking. I treated you like a total bitch and I tried to run away like a coward until things got too hot. Then I ran to you, pulled you into my problems. You have no idea how grateful I am for everything, but doing charity must get pretty fucking –"

Tiresome. He never let me finish my thought.

He shot up like a bullet, ripped the rag from my hand, and threw it against the wall. It hit the water in the tub with a splash. I twisted in his arms. I knew he'd never hurt me, but it was scary as hell to see him looking at me with the same killer look he'd given Ed before he rammed the knife into his throat.

"Babe, you better close your little mouth before I shut it for you. I'm not gonna listen to a second more of this shit." He grabbed my head, jerking me around with more precision than a chiropractor. "Is this what you're worried about? *This?*"

He pointed to the long jagged scar arcing up my cheek, toward my right ear. I was too stunned to answer. He shook me again, vigorous but gentle. Commanding.

"Answer me! Is it?" Slowly, I nodded, turning against his hands in shame. There was no escape here. Rabid leaned down, pouring breath like fire into my ear. "I never thought a girl who's smart enough to tutor kids for a living could be so fucking blind. I see I'm gonna have to start from ground zero with you."

I blinked, steadying myself as he loosened his grip. "What's that supposed to mean?"

The iron grip was back, holding me in a death lock with one hand, then running the opposite over my face in a gentle caress. I squirmed, hating when he touched my glaring imperfections. Why couldn't he focus on the parts of me that weren't so fucking damaged?

"Means you don't know shit about me, and I'm gonna have to ram it home to make you understand." He rocked against my hips, harder than before, making me feel the full swollen outline of his hard-on against my ass.

God! Just give it to me or kill me now. My brain was on fire. No, make that *everything,* alive and burning with need.

"If I didn't think you were beautiful – every fucking inch of you – my dick wouldn't be like this. I wouldn't be thirty seconds away from shredding your clothes and smashing my face between your thighs 'til I suffocate." He shook me again, one fierce jerk, making me flail for a second before he caught me. "Baby, you'd better believe I'm gonna fuck those rocks right outta your head. And I'm not gonna stop 'til you're breathless, too damned tired to think about anything except how good my cock feels when it's balls deep inside you."

"Rabid!" He clapped one hand over my mouth and grabbed my hair with the other one.

He walked me out of the bathroom half-stooped over, stopping when we got into the bedroom. I tried to struggle, bite him, anything to make him understand this was crazy. Not how I ever imagined this going.

Rabid had other plans.

He swept me up into his arms, threw me over his shoulder, and carried me the last few steps to the bed before flinging me down. His weight held me down while he did what he promised, ripping my shirt off over my head, then working on my pants while he reached to pop my bra behind him.

I struggled for a second, but when his rock hard chest flattened my breasts, I couldn't think about anything at all. Nothing except how good he felt pressed against me.

His face rubbed on mine, scratching me with his stubble. He twisted his face, focusing on my scar with his kisses, burying it in lips and tongue.

I started laughing at how wild it was and tried to slap his chest. He didn't appreciate that. He reached up, pinned my wrists above my head, and maneuvered between my legs. He stared me down like the world was about to end as he rocked his hips against mine.

My jeans were halfway down, one less layer between us. God, even with his denim still in the way, he was so fucking hard against my panties. The friction in his long, rough strokes lit me up. I tried to fight him, tried to tell him to go more gently, but every thrust took my breath away.

Every thrust forced me to realize he was really into this, really into *me*. Scars and all.

When he was done making his point, running his tongue over my face, he moved to my mouth. Each kiss came harder than the one before. It was all hot breath, teeth, and tongue. He grabbed my bottom lip with his teeth and held it, growling into my mouth, making my whole body vibrate with rough, masculine energy.

I'd lost my shoes at some point, and my legs were folded around him now, begging him to fuck me closer, harder, deeper.

Rabid's stubble prickled along my neck as he lowered his head. He found one nipple and sucked it into his mouth. Pleasure ripped through me, and I almost came just from having this one tender part between his teeth.

His hands shifted. Now, he was holding me down by the hair with one fist. The other hand was on my left breast, warming it up for whenever his mouth got tired of my right nipple.

"Rabid...please!" I couldn't stop bucking against his dick. Clueless about what I was even begging for.

My hips rose and fell with a mind of their own. The muscles in my belly were wound so tight I thought I'd snap in two. This was a full body tease, showing me what the need to be fucked was really like.

Not want. Not desire. *Need.*

I reached up, hugged my arms around his neck, and rode the fiery thrusts coming between my legs. He was dry humping me into oblivion, if you could call the sopping wet mess against his jeans 'dry.'

"Fuck," Rabid whispered, taking his face off my nipple. "I could lick this nub all day, but I know all about how greedy the rest of a woman gets. I'd be a sick sonofabitch if I let everything else suffer."

I opened my mouth to answer, but he choked me off, drawing my other nipple into his mouth. He held me down, sucking hard and fast, swirling his tongue around and around in hypnotic, harsh loops.

I humped his dick like a mad woman. His name was Rabid, yeah, but I was the one foaming at the mouth, completely overtaken with this need to get him in me.

"Fuck. Me!" I managed to get it out when he stopped sucking my tit. "*Please.*"

"Not yet. You're gonna fuck my tongue first, baby. Forget everything that happened with your tits. You're gonna see what I can really do when I've got that little clit in my mouth, slapping it with my tongue 'til you blow."

I begged. I pleaded. I kicked my legs against him as he sank down, but he was determined.

He easily held my thighs to the bed like they were nothing, spreading them apart, opening me for him. His teeth caught my panties at the waistband and ripped. Everything came off, baring the hot wet slit to him, total proof of how sex crazed I'd become underneath him.

"Nice and pink," he growled. "Show me how tight you

get when you come. I wanna taste what's gonna be wrapped around my dick."

I tried to brace myself for his face going between my legs. But nothing in the world could've prepared me for the thunderbolt that struck me when his mouth hit my pussy.

He sucked. He licked. He fucked me with that tongue, deeper and faster and harder than any man's tongue should. I tossed my head back, thrashing above him, losing my mind as he raced me to the edge of the cliff and gave me one last push.

Climax.

Oh, fuck. Oh, Rabid. Oh, no!

Orgasm ripped through me with wild abandon. Merciless and rough as his tongue's endless strokes through my core, slinging pure fire, wicked and hot. I pinched my thighs so hard around his head it should've cracked his skull.

But he held me open, and I only realized later he was holding perfectly still, making me fuck his mouth with wild thrusts.

When I was coming down from it, he pushed one hand in front of his face, stretching me open. Two fingers sank into my pussy, and he pivoted his mouth above it all to continue licking my clit.

"No, no. I can't handle this again. It's too soon. Rabid, I need a little –"

"Rest?" he growled, in between licks. "You'll get it when I fucking say so. I told you I'm gonna show you all the ways I want you, baby girl. And that includes showing you what your body can do when I'm in charge. The shit you'll do for me doesn't understand the meaning of 'can't.'"

He wasn't kidding. He'd overpowered me, overtaken me, enslaved my flesh with his hands and mouth. I couldn't bear to think about what he still had waiting for me throbbing in his pants.

Maybe it wouldn't be so bad to come another time or two on his crazy tongue. He'd soften me up. After what I'd felt against my pussy, I knew I'd need to be loosened up before he pushed inside me. Only easy way I'd be able to take something so big – especially if he fucked the way he licked.

And that was a given, wasn't it?

I never got a chance to think about it. His fingers fucked me in rhythm with his tongue, pulling at my flesh and putting me back together, making me conform to his touch. He worked me harder when I jerked and gasped, reading my mind in every twitch and tingle.

Rabid read *everything*. I couldn't hide a damned thing anymore. I didn't want to.

His fingers fucked me at the same frantic, breakneck pace as his tongue when I started to feel the fireball building in my core. My *can't* died in the spiraling fire.

My pussy pulsed, slowly at first. Then a new shockwave tore through me – sudden, shocking, merciless.

I reached for the sheets and held on as I exploded from the bottom up. "God. God! *God!*"

I screamed to heaven over and over, but nothing was going to save me from him. My pussy pinched his fingers so tight, and still he kept fucking me, stroking my walls through the convulsions. The rock hard maniac between my legs had no pause, no on and off.

Colors blossomed before my eyes, beautiful and bright, some so wild I couldn't name them. Ecstasy squeezed me like a wet cloth, draining everything from my body. That moment, I was nothing but a breathless, shaking, rainbow watching mass, locked in pure pleasure. I could only buckle in and ride the wave, tearing at the sheets for dear life, desperate to stay grounded on this earth. The colors coalesced into one mega-fire and lost their luminescence, going hot white and then black.

Pleasure waned. Collapsing, I hit the bed and rolled, feeling new coolness on my pussy.

I reached down, realized he was gone, and looked to the edge of the bed. He was standing there, loosening his belt, watching me. Guess it was easy to admire the view with my legs lolled to their sides, wide open and ready.

"Helluva warm up, Christa," he said. "I'd lick that sweet pussy all day, but if we don't get down to business right now, I'm gonna start putting my fist through your fucking walls. And I don't think your landlord would like that shit. I'm already gonna fuck you so hard he hears it two floors up."

I laughed. A joke, I thought, but there was nothing funny about the way he looked at me when the bed sank with his weight. He crawled between my legs and rubbed his cock over my slit. One stroke told me he was bare.

Sweet Jesus.

I reached down and wrapped one hand around his shaft. It was even harder and thicker than I'd imagined, pulsing strong and alive in my palm. I rolled down toward his balls and then back up, perfect for a teasing stroke, marveling at every inch.

"I want this," I whispered. "Bad. Don't make me wait, Rabid. Fuck me."

He cocked his head, sliding forward to fuck my fist, a little preview of what was about to happen inside me. "Doesn't sound very convincing. You've got some idea now how much I like to tease."

Anger pulsed through me. Was he fucking serious?

I squeezed his dick, harder than I intended. He just pushed through my hand harder, asserting control.

"Who's teasing now, baby? You trying to make me shoot off all over your belly, or what?" He laughed when I shook my head in horror. "Yeah, I didn't think so. Put your fucking hands over your head if you're ready. Show me your whole body's begging for a fuck. Lucky for you, I like teasing like nobody's business, but I like fucking even more."

I let go of him and flopped back. Stretched out before him, pulsing my feet down his strong legs, imagining how hard they'd make him thrust. I was about to find out, assuming my skin didn't ignite before he got inside me.

Rabid grabbed his dick and aimed it for my entrance.

"All right, no more fucking around," he growled,

readying his hips. "It's now or never, baby, and I'm not stopping 'til I see the smoke curling off you from the way I'm gonna make you burn."

We locked eyes as he pushed in, one savage stroke that went all the way, not stopping until he was pressed up against my womb. *Balls deep* was an understatement. He filled me so completely, inch by impossible inch, that I nearly bowed up and came just from this fullness.

"Fuck!" he hissed, holding his warmth in mine. "Don't tell me you're a virgin, girl? This is the tightest pussy I've ever had around my dick in years. Shit, maybe since I was born."

I shook my head. No, not a virgin.

Damn if I didn't wish I was just then. The other men I'd given myself to were worthless compared to him. If he was an alpha, then they were omegas, Joe Averages who'd never know a dick this hard and strong unless it slapped them in the face.

And somehow, I had a feeling men like Rabid didn't go around clubbing weaker men with their dicks. I smiled at the stupid thought.

"What's so fucking funny?" he growled, pulled back and slammed into me, stretching me open, reminding me that the ten inches of rock hard muscle were all I ought to be thinking about just then. "You remembering how shitty everybody else is compared to this?"

Bastard read my mind this time. Literally. I threw my head back as he slammed into me again, sucking at my bottom lip.

God! How could two people fit together so perfectly?

"Yes!" I whispered, letting too much excitement slip out for my own good.

Rabid reached up and fisted my hair, giving me another thrust while he did. I moaned. He pulled hard, tucking his arm underneath my head, making me look at him.

"Good! By the time we're done tonight, you're gonna forget you ever fucked anybody before me. Try to keep up, baby. Try your fucking best. I wanna wind up half as sore as you're gonna be for the next week. Don't bullshit me, now. I know you can take it."

And take it, I did.

He rammed his dick harder as the tempo picked up. Our hearts thudded as one, and mine slammed my ribs as hard as he pushed me to the mattress. I seriously wondered if my old bed could take it. Its springs shrieked like mad every time Rabid pounded my ass down with his weight.

"Baby, baby, baby," he whispered, rough and steady as sandpaper. "Where the fuck you been hiding all my life? Your pussy's made for my dick. You feel it?"

Fuck yes, I did.

It didn't take long to realize I had nothing to worry about with his size. Our fusion was perfect, like my body was made for his, waiting twenty-four years to find the right man. Rabid fucked harder, gliding deeper into me, pulsing and stroking against my walls until I felt the fire like never before.

"I feel – oh, Jesus! Don't fucking stop!" Whatever he

made me feel, I wanted more. I wanted him to hurl me right over the edge and fill me with his fiery seed.

Snarling, he grabbed my hips, dragging his teeth over my throat in a love bite on the way to my ear. "Grab my neck and hold onto my ass with your legs. Hold on fucking tight. You wanna come hard, don't you?"

Holy shit. Is it even a question? I gave him a pleading look, sucking on my bottom lip. I'd never wanted *anything* so bad before, and he'd just found one more evil way to tease me, make me beg for my release.

His thrusts slowed, forcing me to fuck back if I wanted it. My blood fumed. My legs whipped up and curled around his rear. Digging my ankles into his flanks as hard as I could, I leaned up, pulling at his strong neck with my hands.

"Fuck me. Don't hold anything back. Show me how fast and hard you go on maximum." I could practically feel the sweat steaming out his pores as I whispered the challenge into his ear. "Fuck me like you want to break me – and don't you dare fucking stop for *anything!*"

Rabid gave me a look like I was out of my mind. Then I saw the last lights of sanity in his eyes fade too. His hips lurched forward, impacting me so hard his balls bounced on my ass, plunging his thickness rough and deep, just the way I liked it. His pubic bone scratched the itch raging in my clit.

So much for holding out. I saw white and started stabbing my nails into his neck, raking them down to his shoulders in a long, slow drag. We were way past being gentle.

He fucked me harder. Impossibly, achingly harder, impaling me on his pistoning length. I threw my head back and screamed bloody murder as everything beneath my waist seized up.

Next thing I knew, my pussy locked around his cock, begging to be filled. I saw white. My walls clenched, spasming so hard it hit my brain instantly, like someone had whiskey hooked straight to my veins.

I came in a jerking, scratching, spitting mess, coming completely undone on every beautiful inch of him. You haven't lived until sex controls everything except your brain stem.

And I was the one who'd summoned this earthquake, begged for it.

I'd challenged him to fuck me for sport, and he'd delivered. Oh, how he delivered.

Rabid growled, grabbed my ass off the bed, and pulled me up, holding it up in mid-air. I barely had the dexterity to brace my hands over my head. Thank God I lived an active enough life for this.

His cock hit me in places I couldn't even describe, shaking me apart, hammering me open for his relentless thrusts. G-spot? No way, this boy hit the *entire alphabet*, and I shook and gasped with every new sensation flooding me.

I hallucinated smoke coming off my body when it was finally waning. Not that it meant much, because he wasn't even close to finished.

He pulled out of me, hard as rock, his huge chest pumping air into his lungs to replenish everything we'd lost while fucking. I looked up through half-closed eyes, wondering how the hell he was ever going to top that.

Not that I doubted him. I hadn't felt him come yet, so I couldn't dismiss anything.

"Roll the fuck over, babe. Get on all fours." He gave my ass a little smack when I lingered a second too long.

I yelped, finding the energy to jump and do just as he said.

Crap. My clit was already swollen and aching again, a willing slave for his touch.

Maybe it was the ferocious ink crisscrossing his torso like tiger's stripes, or maybe it was just the raw power in his muscles that he sent through me with every thrust.

Whatever caused this crazy hunger, he'd turned me into a junkie for it.

Shaking, I listened to him growl, feeling the slow thunder front rolling through his throat, down his flesh, into me. Grabbing my hair, he mounted me from behind, planting his cock deep. I wiggled my ass against him.

We fucked harder and faster than before, free from the initial uncertainty. He hungered to learn my body as bad as I wanted to please him. Everything with this man was a slow burn, a wick blazing to ignite a full blown wildfire. My eyes rolled back and I punched the sheet in my hands, hoping I could stand another climax without waking all my neighbors.

My screams were the least of it too. The bed was

jerking beneath us now, bouncing and clattering, ready to go to pieces as he power fucked my pussy deep. The noise didn't make him pause once. Rabid fucked like he wanted the floor to fall out beneath us.

"Fuck, baby girl. You come for me again. You got at least two more to go before I bust this nut." I recognized an order when I heard one.

Whether I did or not, he wasn't leaving anything to chance. I felt his rough hand reach around my thigh, dive between my legs, and spread me open around his cock. He pinched my clit, making furious circles, swift and beckoning and perfectly matched to the rhythm of his cock pounding inside me.

My God, my God. Words weren't enough to handle this, and neither were prayers.

I'd officially lost track of how many times I'd come that night, but I did it again, feeling my pussy cream on his cock as everything below my waist exploded. Grabbing me by the shoulders, Rabid pinned my little ass to the bed with his weight, alternating between grinding and thrusting so deep he touched my cervix.

Can't stop. Can't. Fucking. Stop. Coming!

This sex was like a seizure. Or maybe a storm, so powerful it ripped apart everything in its path without a second thought. My body was going full primal now, sucking and coming and pulling at his cock, starving to wring the come from his balls. I wanted him to bust inside me, just like he promised.

I needed his heat, his fire, his everything.

"Please. Come with me," I pleaded, in between the hoarse spasms reaching up to my throat. "*Please. Rabid, please.*"

He laughed, fucked me deeper, lengthening his strokes. "You gotta do better than that, baby. Beg me to fill you up. Fucking beg, Christa."

I started to, but my throat was too tight, too overwhelmed with the pleasure popping in every nerve. When my vision went white, bursting with rainbow stars, I couldn't even think about anything at all. I just screamed.

Rabid clapped his hand over my mouth and pulled my hair tighter with the other hand. I swore he was going to rip my ponytail off in the mad race to fully claim me. Somewhere in the ecstasy, I realized he didn't want me to beg with words.

My pussy, my body, was doing all the hard work for me. His thrusts were totally frenzied now, fucking me right through the convulsions, turning me inside-out. He rammed my face into the nearest pillow, the better to brace my bones for the savage hammering that came next.

His whole body tilted into mine and he snarled into my ear. "Don't move a goddamned inch. Keep your legs open and take every fucking drop. I'm gonna shoot you full 'til I collapse, baby, and your little pussy's gonna join me in the storm, leave us both breathless."

Storm? No, this was an honest-to-God hurricane.

The bed rocked like a freight train coming uncoupled.

I whimpered. I folded. I screamed my throat raw when

he ripped my head up and growled, biting into my throat like some wild beast.

Pleasure, pain, and a thousand sensations I couldn't identify took full possession. I lost control, gave it up to the madman balls deep in my twitching cunt, starting to jerk and pulse and melt.

"Fuck!" he growled it through his teeth, still locked onto my shoulder, needling me with the full fury of the tension winding up in his body for the grand finale.

Rabid came. Lava jets flowed into me, fierce as everything else he'd done tonight, filling the emptiness so good it finally cured the wanton craving I'd had all night. He doused me in fire, seed overflowing, filling me and spilling out of the spaces where our tender flesh joined and writhed.

The last orgasm that rocketed me out of my body made me wonder if the bed had really fallen through the floor after all. My muscles clenched so hard everything went white and numb. I fucked straight through the colors and blinding white light to a new dimension of pleasure that was truly pure, stripped of everything except this pulsing fire exploding inside me.

Feeling his teeth leaving my skin was the first thing that brought me home. There'd be one hell of a hickey there tomorrow, if he didn't leave his teeth marked in my skin like putty. I hoped I had a shirt to cover it.

He leaned in and smothered my lips with his, staying rooted in me, even though he was going soft. It was like he didn't want his seed to come out, wanted to keep it buried in me until I soaked it up, bathing myself in his essence.

My tongue was limp at first. But a few delicious swirls of his against mine had me licking right back, savoring the softer calm returning to our flesh.

I had a feeling it wouldn't last long. His hand reached underneath me, found my nipple, and gave it a warming pinch. I moaned into his mouth, breaking the kiss for sorely needed breath.

"What the hell?" I whispered. "Don't you ever rest?"

"Not when you're underneath me, babe. You're mine. You're new and shiny, everything I wanna fuck 'til my hips won't work. But fuck, you'd better believe I wouldn't give a shit if I'd fucked you a thousand times. I'm never gonna get sick of this. I thought your pussy was like a fine shot of Jack, and I was a fucking fool."

I looked at him, loving the warmth lighting up his dark eyes. "What, then?"

"Your pussy's fucking heroin. I never did the shit, but I saw enough guys who did to know. This is the kinda shit that turns a man into something depraved, makes him a totally desperate junkie for this and only fucking this." His breathing grew sharper, shallower. The hand on my breast glided down my soft belly, reached lower, and cupped my pussy.

"Fuck," he growled, low and ruthless. He squeezed, and we both rasped when I felt his seed trickle out around his fingers.

It wasn't just an act, something tender and sweet to say after sex in his own crazy biker way. He really meant to claim me, own me, and never, ever let go.

"You think I'm satisfied feeling my seed inside you? Think again."

He squeezed tighter, pushed two fingers into my wetness. I sucked in a sharp breath. God, how could I want him again so soon after more than an hour of nonstop fucking?

"What does it take?" I whispered, amused and genuinely curious. What the hell did it take to ever satisfy him?

"You wearing my brand. Right here's a good spot for it." He touched the soft skin in the center of my lower back. "You're total sex now. You'd be a fucking knockout with my name inked in your skin, right where I can see it. Better get used to fucking on all fours, baby, 'cause we're gonna be doing it a lot – right in between all the other ways I'm gonna take you."

Holy, holy shit. Was he really asking me to be his old lady? My head was spinning – spinning right off after the flurry of sweat and sex.

"Rabid..." I turned over, pushing his hand away, unsure what the hell to say. He stopped me, clapping his hand over my mouth.

"I don't need an answer tonight. Just think about it. Think hard whenever you wake up tomorrow. This isn't a night for that kinda shit. Thinking doesn't go good with everything else I've got planned for your sweet little cunt. All you gotta know is I want you, babe. I'd kill and dismember a man for this hot fucking pussy – no bullshit."

I knew he wasn't joking. The edge in his voice was the same just before he murdered Ed. It should've made me jump up and run, but I loved it. This was an animal passion I'd never fathomed outside my own dark fantasies, a passion that was real because it was so damned psychotic.

He forced his hand between my thighs, found my clit, and rubbed. The tension in my muscles instantly withered.

Not fair.

He knew how to work my body too well, and I still didn't have a clue how to handle him, let alone work him over. His lips replaced the hand over my mouth. When he started running his free hand through my red hair, pushing me up to meet his mouth, I automatically opened my legs.

His hips rocked against my belly, his dick growing hard and hungry.

Yes, there'd be *a lot* to think about very soon. But tonight, there was nothing to worry about except how bright he lit me up and made me burn.

VI: Deceived (Rabid)

She moaned when I kissed her the next morning, shifting lazily in the bed. I loved the way those cherry-chestnut locks falling off her head looked when they were flopping in my hand while I fucked her, but this was beautiful too.

I could've laid next to her all damned day if it wasn't for the all the shit threatening to tarnish this piece of heaven I'd ripped from the sky. Just as well, because she'd need time to think long and hard about what I'd offered her last night.

It wasn't just the heat of the moment. I wanted her to be my old lady. Fuck, I wanted it since I decided I wanted my dick inside her, since I first washed her bleeding cuts and laid a kiss on those lips underneath the stars.

She'd think and get me an answer, yeah.

Obviously, I had 'no' wasn't a serious option. No wasn't in my fucking vocabulary when it came to this chick.

She was *mine*, dammit. Mine when she was curled up next to me, making me hard just having her skin on mine. Mine when she was going nuclear on my dick. Mine when she woke up later and felt the soreness I'd no doubt left in her pussy.

I wasn't sorry for that shit at all. Same way my heart swelled with pride when I looked at the bruises I'd left on her neck with my teeth. I *wanted* her to think about me every time she moved. It'd be the perfect reminder of everything we'd had tonight, everything I'd done for her, every way I'd ravaged her sweet body and left it to smolder.

Fuck, it was hard to leave. Did I already say that?

I slid my clothes on, unable to resist planting one more kiss on her forehead before I went. "Sleep tight, baby. I'll be back by evening."

I left her some money on the way out with a little note attached to get the tire fixed on her car.

Soon, I was on my Harley, riding into the early morning sun. The shit I had in my bag felt like it was burning a fucking hole in the compartment behind me. I'd taken it off Big Dead Ed before I stripped his face and fingerprints with the acid.

Two patches soaked in somebody's blood. Both had the Spanish crap I couldn't pronounce at the bottom, right beneath the cartel's symbolic bird and cactus.

Yeah, the asshole was just as sloppy screwing over my club as he was getting drink and hobbling onto his bike. Killing one cartel boss was a fucking miracle, but three?

Nobody would call it anything other than pure bullshit. My bros wouldn't be happy to see it when I laid it out for 'em, but they'd swallow the sudden fondness they had for the Oregon fucks. And I'd be lying if I said part of me didn't enjoy imagining Asphalt and a couple other dudes eating their crow raw and rotten.

I stopped by a local joint for a breakfast sandwich and coffee. I'd need to keep my eyes pried open today after all the life she'd sucked outta me. And shit, I still wanted more. I'd let Christa's pussy put me right into my grave if I wasn't careful.

My phone rang while I was about to dig into my food. I saw Brass' number and cursed.

"Yeah? What's going on, bro?"

"You'd better get your ass over to the clubhouse this second. Shit's going down." That was the VP talking, and not my friend.

"What the fuck? I'm on my way over right now."

"Hurry the hell up. Get ready to talk to the Prez. I hope to fucking God you haven't done something as stupid as I think."

"Yeah? What's that?" I growled, but the line was dead.

I wolfed down my food angrily, pissed that my one night of peace was already gone with the morning light. Everything about the Veep's tone said I was due for a beating, or maybe something worse.

God damn it. Good thing I'd fucked her at least five times last night. It might be a week or two before I'd be able to again, if my brothers were going to be massive dicks and start swinging before I could show them what I'd found.

There were a lot of bikes parked outside when I got

through the gate. Too fucking many. None of them ours.

Shit. I shouldn't have assumed Ed was the only asshole from Klamath in our territory. They couldn't have known we'd take the bait with his bullshit about the cartel before he sprung his trap, so he'd brought his boys for backup.

I checked the holster holding my handgun before I went inside. Roman was waiting by the door like a bulldog. He took one severe look at me and stood, smashing his knuckles together.

"Calm the fuck down! I know you've all been waiting for me. Brass told me."

"Prez is waiting for you in his office," he said, barely giving me enough space to squeeze past him on my way down the hall.

There were several strangers wearing our patch over by the bar. Greasy looking, dead eyed bastards, the kind who were the norm in this club before our little revolution. They all looked at me like vultures waiting for a big meal.

Shit!

No fear. I walked into Blackjack's office and found the old man perched behind his desk. He kicked his leg underneath the table, pushing the chair out for me, and pointed. Soon as I tried to sit, he popped up, uppercutting me in the jaw so hard I swore I lost a fucking tooth.

"Motherfuck!" I growled, tasting copper in the blood. A quick check with my tongue told me everything was all there. Surprising. "Christ, Prez. I thought you'd at least try talking with your mouth first before you brought out your fists."

He didn't say anything. I saw why a second later, when the door popped open, and Brass walked in. My bro looked at me like he'd caught me stealing his bike, a look of outrage and sadness.

"Cut the shit, son," Blackjack growled. "We both know you killed the bastard. So do the boys from Klamath. They showed up here this morning, demanding to know why the fuck their VP didn't return last night. They would've put lead in a few people if I hadn't managed to talk their asses out of it, backed by Roman's fists."

"Look, I fucked up on one thing, I'll admit that." Shit, make that two. I'd forgotten my fucking bag in my bike while I was stewing, too pissed to remember the smoking gun I had outside.

"One thing?" Brass gave me an evil smile. "Brother, you're in the deepest shit anyone's been in since we took down Fang and his friends. If you killed a brother in this organization – an officer, no less – you know what happens next."

We locked eyes. Yeah, I damned well did. The fucks in southern Oregon would be taking a vote soon once Blackjack told them what I'd done. They'd vote for my head on a platter, but not before they stripped my patch and everything remotely Grizzlies MC related on my skin. And if this charter didn't want an all-out blood war between brothers, Redding would vote to stand down and let them have their justice.

All kosher according to club charter. I was looking at a

violent, bloody death.

"I'm only going to ask you once, Rabid. We know the truth, and this is just a fucking formality, but it needs to be done." Blackjack took a breath and leaned forward. "Did you murder Big Ed last night?"

What the fuck was the point in hiding it? Truth or lie, I was dead as soon as I admitted it. And I was ready to face that, as long as I could get their assurance my girl would be safe.

"Answer him, asshole," Brass growled, slamming a not-so-brotherly hand on my shoulder.

"I took him out with a stab to the throat," I said, never breaking eye contact with my evil looking Prez. "It was at that shithole on the edge of town, the Pig's Tail or whatever the fuck it's called, where all the junkies and whores hang out. Caught up to him right before he was about to blow town. I found him drunk and tipsy inside the bar, got him to come out back, and we had words. Our talk ended with my blade in his fucking jugular, just like I planned the minute I got there."

I stood, ripping Brass' hand off my shoulder. Spreading my hands on the Prez's desk, I stooped down to his level, glaring at him.

"Before you kill me, Prez, there's something you ought to know. Just two things."

"Yeah? Spill it. Better do it fast." The merciless expression on his face looked like it was about to set his long gray hair on fire.

"My girl's been in debt to the Klamath crew for a few

years. Christa took a loan from their fucked up club running some kinda bar up there. They've been harassing her ever since, sending brothers down here to fuck with her whenever she's the least bit late. Yesterday, our buddy Ed slashed her tire and roughed her up. I wasn't gonna take that shit. I also knew he was lying through his fucking teeth when he dropped that cartel boss patch for Brass – and this time I got proof. You gotta let me show you before I get the blow to the face I probably deserve. I found two more bloody cartel patches stuffed in Ed's pocked before I dumped his body, just like the one he gave Brass. They're in my bike. Just say the word and walk me out, I'll let you see it with your own damned eyes."

Blackjack snorted. Leaning back in his high leather chair, his hands twitched on the table. It was like watching a transistor waiting to blow. I braced for the impact, ready for both the Prez and the VP to go to work, breaking everything on my face to smithereens. And that was if the Prez didn't pull his gun and put me outta my misery with a clean shot before the Klamath boys did.

"I don't need to see shit, Rabid," he finally said. "Everybody in this room's on the same page. I knew Rip and his Veep were blowing smoke up our asses the second Brass laid that fucking thing out on the table."

Jaw, meet floor. After I finished picking my mouth up off the sticky ground, I swiveled, staring at Brass. He nodded.

"What the fuck? Then what the hell was the point of that bullshit brawl in church last time?"

"The point was to keep it on the down low before any dumb fuckers got impulsive, brother." Brass stepped forward, giving me the evil eye. "You just made our job a helluva a lot harder. Honestly, if the jackass you killed wasn't fucking with Christa, I'd punch you right through the goddamned wall."

I bared my teeth, the only instinct after a threat like that. But the rest of my brain, apart from the lizard section, realized he was right. Not that I was ready to admit I'd fucked up or apologize.

Shit, if only they'd told me, instead of this cloak and dagger shit! We wouldn't be cooped up here with some very angry assholes from Klamath outside this office right now.

"I ought to give them your ass anyway for this." Blackjack's voice was stone cold. "But then I'd be no better than Fang. You're taxing this club right to hell, son. I'm not going to let you die, but the heap of shit reserved for you just landed on the whole club."

"Why pull any punches if everybody knows where we stand?" I asked, guilt tugging at my heart. "Shit, when the rest of the charters find out Klamath tried to screw national, they'll stand down without threatening you, Prez."

"No, they'll help us do the job when they find out the Klamath fucks have been working with the cartel," Blackjack said.

Fuck, I almost had to hold my jaw to keep it from hitting the ground again. So, they were bigger bastards than even I'd thought. I balled fists, fully ready to march out and fight the assholes in the bar all alone if I had to. Exactly the kinda deadly hot head shit the two men in the room with me were trying to avoid.

"Christ." I shook my head, all I could do to ignore the impulse. "How long's this been going on?"

"Nobody knows," Brass said. "Might've started under Fang. Maybe they only went nuts in the last few weeks, purely because they don't approve of the new leadership. We wanted to get the jump on 'em. Now, thanks to you offing their VP, we never will."

Shit. That cut deep. I was perfectly willing and ready to spill my own blood to keep Christa safe. But having any brothers stuffer for it was almost as bad as her taking the pain herself.

"Say the word," I said. "I'll buy you guys time. Whatever it takes. I'll go with 'em right now if you think it'll help. That's what they're expecting. I can handle whatever the fuck they wanna deal out. They can't kill me 'til our charters both vote on it, and you deliver the results, Prez."

"No." Blackjack shook his head, his eyes wide and maybe slightly impressed. Guess he never expected me to offer up my own hide. "They'll know we're onto them whether they've got you or not. Rip and his crew are dumb, but the cartel sure as fuck isn't. The Mexicans will see us pulling reserves away from the fight when we go to confront the boys up north."

"Then, what? We tell them to fuck off and expect

they'll just walk outta here?"

"They damned well better," Blackjack growled. "That's their only choice if they don't want half their crew winding up dead today. Roman's assured me all our brothers are quicker shots than they are. We'll kill them in this clubhouse if they try to start shit here."

Damn. There was nothing worse than a club's HQ turning into a fucking war zone.

The three of us looked at each other, letting the realization set in that this was the only way out. I was ready. The ink all over my body burned like a shield. My blood seethed, taking the tattoos' heat, ready to give the ultimate sacrifice for this brotherhood, and for her too.

"I'm ready when you are, brothers."

Blackjack stood up. Brass clapped me on the shoulder, this time giving me the brotherly grip I'd felt a hundred times before.

"I've always got your back, and you know it. Even when you're making shit ten times harder than it needs to be. You were there for me and Missy when things got bad. I'm doing the same for you and Christa." He paused, heading toward the door with me while Blackjack got his bearings on his half-healed leg. "Oh, but you'd better hurry the fuck up and claim this girl if you really want her. If I find out she's just another fucking slut to you, I swear I'm gonna –"

He raised his fist, and I pushed it down hard. "Already working on it, bro. Settle your ass down."

"All right," Blackjack said, growling through the pain

in his hip. "Let's go."

Roman joined us as soon as we stepped out. So did several other guys who'd been lingering on the opposite side of the bar, Asphalt and several prospects, keeping watch on our shitty guests.

"You, Marrow." Blackjack called the name of a skinny, dirty looking man with an eye patch when we were just a couple feet away. "Let's talk."

The five Klamath boys walked up and took their places next to us. Goddamn, they were ugly. It shouldn't have been so easy to see who the evil fuckers were just looking at them, but it was.

"Well? Is this piece of shit coming with us, or what?" Marrow pointed at me, a killer glint in his eye.

"You guys can pack up your shit and leave Redding, that's what. I'll give you three minutes before we start shooting. Rabid's not going anywhere." Blackjack would've stared them down just the same, even if he didn't have Roman's wall of muscle behind him. Tough motherfucker.

"You gotta be shitting me!" Marrow twisted his head and spat tobacco on the floor. "I'm gonna ask you again, *brother,* because I think you must've fucked up your head in there talking to him. Are you sure you wanna make this mistake? You know what it fucking means."

"Yeah, I do. Soon as Rip hears, he'll hit every other Prez in the five state area and try to brand this mother charter a rogue group with a kill order. Go a-fucking-head. If you think I give a shit, you're wrong."

Marrow's good eye twitched. Snarling, he reached right for me, tried to get his hand around my throat. I was faster. Started pounding my fists into his chest while his boys surrounded me, slamming punches into my spine. I hit the floor hard, and some asshole's boot was on my back.

The world exploded with men screaming, roaring, fighting. I rolled, getting the upper hand on one of the greasy motherfuckers. My fists wouldn't stop 'til his hot blood stained my knuckles, pounding his nasty little face over and over and over.

Then there was a bang like the end of the world. Everybody stopped moving.

"The next fucking shot's going right through the skulls of anybody wearing an Oregon patch!" Roman thundered, his magnum in hand. The hole he'd put through the ceiling was still smoking. "Pick your asses up and leave, or I'll carry you outside in fucking body bags."

Brass and Asphalt helped me off the floor. The asshole I'd been pounding on scampered away like a wounded rat, covering his busted nose.

"Then go ahead and shoot me right through the fucking chest," Marrow snarled, walking right up to our big man and standing like a peacock. "I'm not leaving unless that cocksucker Rabid's handcuffed and stuffed on the back of somebody's bike. Shoot me, big man. *Shoot me!* Rip'll find out one way or another, and then he won't even need that vote to bring every free man in the rest of the Grizzlies MC down on this fucked up charter! Now, you gonna pop that fucking thing in my ribs or what?"

For a second, I seriously thought Roman was gonna unload hellfire into his chest. But he raised his gun, and smashed it across the asshole's face instead. Several teeth exploded from his mouth and hit the floor, bouncing like popcorn kernels.

Marrow reached for the holster near his hip. Roman struck him again, bashing his wrist so hard I swore it snapped. The asshole howled, toppling backward as pain tore through him. His brothers caught him, helped him stand straight.

"Get the fuck out," Blackjack growled. "Last warning before we take more than blood and teeth!"

One by one, we watched the fuckers slink away. I was sorely tempted to lunge and give them one more parting shot. But I'd lit enough shit on fire for one day, and now were in full damage control.

"Round up all the brothers," the Prez said. "Have them ready for church by evening. I've got a lot of fucking calls to make to the other charters. Gotta dial before Rip does it first."

Brass and I sat the bar with several other guys, waiting for everybody else. We nursed our shots, careful not to get totally fucking plastered. Old Southpaw was at the end of the bar, staring into his beer and shaking his head every so often. The bitter look on his face said he was way too old for this shit.

Roman sipped a big bottle of mud he slipped his

whiskey into, some kinda black stout with a kick. I swore it'd be easier to get a horse drunk than the dude next to me.

"You should've come to us sooner about the girl," the giant growled, giving me the evil eye. "The Prez could've put her up in a safe place."

Damned annoying. He'd been filled in on all the gritty details since the blowout this morning.

"Look, I know the line's thin between my shit and club biz. But if you think anybody here wouldn't protect his girl before bringing the whole club into it, then you must've downed more of that mud than I thought."

Roman looked at his bottle and scowled, adding another shot of Jack to the mix. "The line's fucking nonexistent, brother. You know it."

Brass laughed. I turned, wondering if my next words would get a fist to the face. What was one more blow after the Klamath assholes peppered my back with bruises?

"Yeah? What about that you and that Sally chick?" I narrowed my eyes, sucking more napalm down my throat. "Is that something you're gonna keep to yourself, or will the club wind up finding out she's a cartel mule or some shit in a couple months?"

Roman's bottle hit the counter just short of fracturing. "She's no threat to the club, motherfucker. She's nothing to me. We're finished. Don't even say her fucking name."

Bullshit. I almost fucking called him on it too. The fires roaring in his eyes didn't say anything close to finished. I knew that look too – I'd seen it staring back at me in the mirror a thousand times 'til I'd finally had a piece of Christa.

Waking up today and washing my face, there was a different blaze in these eyes. I'd finally fucking had her, and now I wanted more. More everything. More of her hot little lips, more of those curves, more of her beautifully imperfect face tensing up and going rosy before she lost her mind on my cock.

Fuck. Just remembering last night got me hard as steel, and I had to look away from the bitter hulk next to me. Last thing I needed was my brain connecting arousal with our wall of an Enforcer or some shit. I'd never been into dick – not that there's anything wrong with that – but just thinking it meant I was gonna have to fuck my girl half a dozen times to bleach my brain.

"Rabid's right," Brass said. "I know I've done my share of putting the club through the fucking wringer for my old lady and her little sis. Dammit, though, these complications are easily avoided if we can see 'em coming. If there's anything we need to know about the mystery chick, Roman, you'd better –"

"You saying I'm holding out on something, Veep?" Roman slid off the bench and stood, towering over us. Brass shook his head. "Cause if you are, you're full of shit. I'll tell you fucks one more time – Sally's nothing you need to worry about, and neither do I. She's history – over and done. You think I'll ever hold shit back from the club that's important, then you'd better find a new Sergeant-at-Arms. I don't play weasel. I aim direct."

He got up and stomped away, shooting me one last dark look. Next to me, Brass shrugged.

"Guess we'll never get the real story outta him. I tried."

I swung around and punched him in the arm. He hit me right back, and I laughed as the sting rolled up my shoulder.

"Leave the poor bastard alone. He's smarter than either of us – he knows there's easier ways to get pussy than pure hell." I slammed another shot down my throat.

Brass raised his eyebrows. "Come the fuck on, brother. You're a sucker just like me. You've gotta know damned well there's a difference between easy pussy and pussy that belongs to a woman worth wearing your brand."

"Yeah," I said, trying not to give the boy too much credit. "I'm learning that the hard way. Good fucking thing it's been worth it."

"And it only gets better when you make it official. Man the fuck up and go all in. If I hear the week's gone and that redhead's still not wearing your mark, I'm gonna laugh at your lazy ass."

I pinched my jaw tight. Great, like I really needed another challenge on top of all this other shit.

On second thought, maybe it was *exactly* what I needed.

I told my baby I'd give her time to think about what I'd offered last night. But I was one impatient SOB.

Soon as I saw her, I'd follow up on the most important question of my life, right after I finished pumping my balls dry inside her velvet cunt. I'd never get sick of fucking her, and the only thing better would be taking her long and hard when I could actually call her my old lady in between thrusts.

Church was about what I expected. Blackjack spelled everything out, and more than a few brothers growled their discontent, pissed to realize there was more going on behind the scenes. They all understood the Prez's reasoning, even if they didn't like it.

We were staring down the barrel of a fucking shotgun.

The club was barely holding its line against the cartel with some help from our new friends in the Prairie Devils MC. Going to war with Rip's crew was a certainty, and it had the potential to fuck us over with their Mexican support, besides causing more discord in the national organization.

We were all tired and ready for a drinks by the time it ended. The thirst for booze was just about the only thing that kept some guys from getting their fists bloody.

Suddenly, Blackjack jerked up from his chair and turned, ripping the huge Grizzlies MC banner off the wall.

Half the guys slouching in their chairs sat up. I blinked, watched the old Prez clamber onto the table, ignoring the hellfire in his bullet wound.

"You see these colors, brothers?" He pulled the flag open in his wide arms. "You'd fucking better. I want everybody in this room to peel their eyes open and take a good long look. This is what we're fighting for. I've served under this bear for thirty years. I was there when he was just a cub with half-inch fangs. I watched him grow into the big tough bastard we all know today. Like you, I helped tame him, get him back on track, when he started to go crazy. If anybody in this room thinks we've got a grizzly on our patch because we want to look like badasses, think the fuck again. The bear's the biggest and the baddest because he's *free*. King of the wilderness. Nobody fucks with a fifteen hundred pound giant with claws.

"He eats, sleeps, and fucks wherever and however he damned well pleases. Once upon a time, big grizzlies like this roamed California before they were hunted to extinction. Now, it's just us grizzlies on our bikes, keeping the dream alive. If any one of you is ready to give up and lay down because we've all been scorched, pick your ass up, and walk out the door right now. Roman will take your patch.

"This is our club. These are our colors. We live our lives like men, and we'll die like them too. You've got about forty eight hours to drink and fuck yourselves senseless before I decide how we're gonna hit the fucking traitors sitting over the border. Get your shit together, and never, ever forget what this patch means on your cuts. I want you to *feel it* when you're partying, loving, and even when you're drawing your last breath. This club's our home and this bear's our father. Make him proud."

Brass held out a hand to the Prez, but he jumped down on his own, gracefully pinning the Grizzlies MC standard back in place. When the bear's face emerged on the field of black, my heart sputtered pure adrenaline.

The old man accomplished his mission. He'd amped us up like a motherfucker.

Prez picked up the bear claw and slapped it down on the wood, adjourning the meeting. We all hugged him on the way out. Some guys had tears in their eyes.

Me, I was coming apart. I was ready to kill and die for these colors, the only thing in the world that brought comfort and sense to my life besides the chick I was about to make my old lady.

"I want you out of the clubhouse tonight, son," Blackjack growled into my ear when it was my turn to embrace him.

"Huh?"

"Go home. Get a hot meal in you. Then spend the rest of the evening with the woman who's helped you get into so much trouble."

I smiled. "Gotcha, Prez. Thanks for reminding us what really matters."

"I didn't do shit," he snapped. "You boys all know what's right and worthy in your hearts."

Christ, his eyes were bright. Blackjack had been the Enforcer under Fang, and he'd always led us through the toughest shit since I'd patched in. He always got crazy and motivated during a fight, but I never saw him look like this, not even when we wrecked Fang and put him in the President's seat.

They say that patch on his chest does strange things to a man. I believed it as I walked away, turning away from joining my brothers at the bar. A few steps later, I was outside, heading for the garage.

A couple prospects came running up. Lean, muscular guys in their early twenties, Beam and Stryker.

"Your woman's here," Stryker said.

"We fixed her car up good. Free of charge," Beam chimed in. "I know she's not officially tied to the club yet, but I figured you'd want it that way."

I gave them brotherly slaps on the shoulders and pushed through them. Shit, I was about to head right out to my girl. I never expected to find her here.

It felt like a million years since morning, when I'd left her sleeping like an angel. She was leaning on the junker she drove, shiny new rubber wrapped around the tire Big Ed fucked up as his last evil act in this world.

It took me a second to process what she was wearing. Fucking shit. Forget the rubber wrapped around the wheel. I wanted her wrapped around my cock right this second, the best way in the world to burn off all the crazy, righteous energy Blackjack's speech jolted into me. She didn't know showing up in *that* was testing me like a missile ready for launch.

Skinny, tight jeans pulled her nice, full ass up, ripe for attention. A low cut tank top held her girls, and fuck if I didn't want to bury my face right in them.

Christ, did she even have a bra on underneath?

Jealousy and want shot through me, both wrestling for the upper hand. Thinking about those pissant prospects getting such a sweet view of her goods pissed me right off, but I couldn't stay mad if she'd dressed like that for me.

"Baby," I greeted her, pulling her mouth to mine before she could say another word. "You look so fucking hot."

Dammit, her lips were good. Tasting her was like biting into fresh strawberries doused in creamy sex. No, I'd never put that sugary girly stuff in my mouth, but I wanted to lick and suck and bite these lips all fucking day. They could taste like bubblegum and cherries for all I knew.

She flattened her hands on my chest, trying to push me away, when the kiss got to be too much. I wasn't done by half. I rocked into her, flattening her against the hood, bending over and clenching her thighs while my tongue probed deeper, dancing hers silly.

This kiss wasn't just a how-do-you-do. I made damned well sure it got the message across, a little omen of all the ways I'd fuck her later.

Fuck, fuck. What was this girl doing to my taste buds? How was she zapping every nerve like lightning at once?

Didn't have a damned clue, but I knew how to stop her. I'd slam myself to the hilt and shake her 'til I couldn't anymore. But only after I held her down and lapped her sweet pussy. I'd lick and suck and finger-fuck what she had 'til I felt her squirt in my fucking mouth.

"Rabid!" She called my name when I finally took my lips off hers. "Jesus. A girl needs to breathe, you know."

No, I didn't. I was ready to move in for another kiss when she slid out underneath me, sneaky and fast like a cat.

"What's wrong, babe? Don't tell me you didn't just enjoy that as much as I did."

Okay, maybe it was hard for me to believe anyone else could feel the shit I had screaming in my veins. I wanted to tear her tank top off right here and fuck her on top of the car, anything to satisfy the bloodhound howling in my pants.

She blushed. Those little marks on her face were almost invisible when she went all cherry. And I knew she could turn about three times brighter when she came on my dick.

"I figured this was the safest place to get the car fixed. I'm still trying to get over yesterday. Do your guys know what happened?" she asked, giving me a serious look.

"They know enough. The rest is all club business you don't need to worry about. You're safe. Nobody's gonna fuck with you again." I reached for her, trying to get a hand around her waist.

Fuck if she didn't squirm away again. Damn it, one more time and I was gonna lunge, throw her to the ground, and have my way. Didn't give a shit if every other brother inside saw it. Wouldn't be the first time other guys watched me fuck. Plenty of brothers watched me when I left my door open, giving it to whores in the past.

Guess they wanted to learn a few new moves from a boss.

But shit, something about Christa turned me crazy fucking jealous. Maybe I wouldn't be able to fuck her at the clubhouse after all, not when I had the urge to beat any eyeballs out of their sockets for undressing her.

"Seriously? The other guys in Klamath won't come looking for their dead man? I met their President, Rip, more times than I ever wanted to. He's not the type to let go of a grudge."

Shit. Using the old club business schtick wasn't gonna work on this spitfire. It was easy to forget she'd been deep in this world for some time, 'til she opened her mouth.

"Christa, baby, the main fuck that matters is in his grave. We both know that. You watched me put him there. He can't come back."

"But the others…"

"Fuck 'em. They'll be dealt with. Me and my bros are part of the mother charter. That makes us the biggest dicks around. We'll wreck anyone and anything who tries to fuck with us, even if they're supposed to be our brothers. You understand that? I'd kill that fucker, Ed, in broad daylight a hundred times over if it'd make you feel better. You've got nothing to worry about. Read my fucking lips –*nothing*."

"I hope you're right." She swallowed, surrendering to my grasp.

"I always am. I promised you Ed would die. Now, refresh my memory, what the hell happened?" She turned away, unused to having the truth thrown at her like this. Too bad. "Come on, baby girl. Lay it on me. What happened after I said the fucker was done?"

"You killed him," she whispered.

"Damned straight. I'm gonna say it here and now, even

though it's getting deep into club biz – soon, you won't have to worry about any of those fuckers above the Norcal border. Give it a week. Just trust me."

"You've earned a little trust, I guess." She winked. "Can't totally let my guard down. I've got to be careful with a man like you."

"Yeah? Why the fuck's that?"

"Because if I open up and give you a little trust, you might take everything else."

Fucking funny. I laughed. "Babe, I'm already rocking your whole damned world, and I'm about to do it some more tonight. Whatever you give me, I'm gonna keep it safe, and send it back to you as pure gold."

She moved in for a kiss. About damned time. I pursed my lips, tongue hungry as hell. For some reason, she stopped less than an inch away, looking over my shoulder.

"Rabid? Who's that?"

I turned and my heart dove like a flying ace. There was Red beaming the evil eye, standing against the wall with a cig in her mouth, puffing on her own green jealousy. Fuck.

"Hold up. I'll be right back."

Christa tried to grab for me. I shot her a warning look and she dropped back, giving me the space to drive this little bitch away. I was in no mood for her shit.

"What're you doing here? You know I don't appreciate eavesdropping. I thought I drilled where we stand into your fucking skull the last time we –"

"Rabid, stop!" she snapped. "I'm sorry. I just wanted to

see who exactly it is you're so much happier with than me. I had to see *her.*"

"Happier?" I nearly shook my head right off. "Red, your first mistake's comparing yourself to the woman I'm about to claim as my old lady. Your second fuck up's thinking I was gushing love instead of lust every time we fucked."

Shit. I thought I could make it short, sweet, and get away without the waterworks. But they were lining her eyes. Tears trickled, smearing mascara down her face. If this crap kept up, she'd never get off me and move onto other things. No brother wanted to fuck a weepy whore.

"Drag your ass inside and have a drink. You've been around long enough to know when the brothers need a little privacy with each other or their women. You can take your smoke breaks somewhere else."

She leaned forward, her little hands balled into fists. "I didn't see your name on this wall. Guess it doesn't have enough ugly pits and lines in it for your liking. You only like that beat up little slut because she doesn't have a backbone. She can't protect herself and sort out her own problems. What is it with you men? You throw away the beautiful things you take for granted every time some ugly hag looks at you with puppy eyes!"

Oh, fuck. She didn't really say that, and right in my girl's earshot too!?

I lunged, ready to grab the bitch by the hair and slam her against the wall. I'd drum her right outta the fucking club here and now, make her know with absolute certainty that she wasn't welcome here anymore with a poison tongue like that.

"Shit!" I swore. I barely caught the lacy red collar thing she wore around her neck and it tore off in my hand.

Red didn't stop. She went running back inside. My boots pounded pavement, and I was halfway up the steps, ready to break down the door, when I turned back and saw Christa looking at the ground.

What the fuck was I doing? Wasting precious time I could be spending with her, chasing this cheap hole I'd never stick my dick in again?

Not fucking worth it, I thought. *Fuck her. She'll fuck up soon enough and some other brother will be the one to toss her out on her defiant little ass. Everything I've gotta worry about's standing right over there.*

"Baby, I'm sorry as hell you had to hear that."

Christa turned away from me. I put my hand on her shoulder, ready to spin her around. Fuck, she was tense.

"I heard what she said, Rabid. Old flame. I get it." The electric edge in her voice said she didn't. "Is it true?"

She spun around, shooting me a fiery glare. Red was so fucking wrong about this woman being a pushover, and that's why my cock turned to steel. I liked a fight, long as my dick went where it belonged in the end.

"Do you really just want me because you've got some kinda Messiah complex? You want to save me? Is that it?"

Jesus Christ! Where the fuck was this brimstone coming from?

"No, baby! That bitch is whacked outta her gourd. If

we didn't have better shit to do tonight, I'd march right in there and throw her over the gate. She's done with me and done with this club. *You're* the only one I'm ever gonna want. I told you – I want you to be my old lady. I'd never offer that to any chick who put a second thought in my skull!"

She blinked, her face hot and red, overwhelmed. I grabbed her, pinned her to my chest, stroking her soft hair. There was another big difference.

Red's hair was always fake, shaggy, smelled like it was soaked in perfume. Never cared while I was drunk and needed to get my dick wet. But Christa's was all natural, sweet and soft, with just a hint of some honey and her own intoxicating smell.

"Did you think about what I told you last night?" I growled it. Now, I was the bastard on edge, and about to go over it if she got scared.

"Yeah."

"Well?" I cocked my head, tightening my hold. Fuck, she looked beautiful with the setting sun catching her hair, turning it ruby. "Are you gonna give me a yes?"

Please fucking give it up, babe, I thought. *I'm gonna go rocketing right into the sun if you keep me waiting another second.*

She smiled, forming little dimples I wanted to lick on my way to biting her bottom lip. "Being an old lady sounds kinda nice. If you're sure you'll never get tired of kissing this messed up face, I'm willing to give it a shot."

Blood shot through my heart like a grenade going off.

I picked her up, lifted her right off the goddamned ground. She started screaming, laughing, pounding playfully on my back. Fuck the car. We could pick that up later.

"Rabid! Put me down!"

"Not 'til you cut that shit out and give me a kiss. I'm gonna get my brand on you real soon," I said, carrying her over to my bike and putting her down the backseat. "But not 'til I've fucked all that horseshit uncertainty outta your bones. How much more do I need to kiss and lick and fuck for you to realize I want this? I want you so bad it's hard to breathe, like I'm fucking drowning. You're gonna give it a shot, yeah, but you don't need to worry about shit. You already hit the only bullzeye that matters, and I'm gonna make you see it."

I reached for her face, cupped her chin, and turned her toward me. I shoved my lips on hers and gave her a kiss so rough I made her squirm. Lightening up when she kissed back, our lips moved like dancers, high on love and anticipation.

I tore myself away after a minute. Had to, or else we'd never get outta this place. It was hell resisting the urge to take those lips again.

Soon. Real fucking soon.

There was just one more part I needed to taste to make her see.

"This, baby." I planted my lips on the jagged scar going up her temple. "This is what I want. Every beautiful inch of you."

Something about feeling her skin on mine turned me into a total madman. Once I started, I couldn't fucking stop. Not 'til her head was tipped back and I was moving down her face, making a direct line for her mouth, plunging my desperate lips into hers one more time to finish.

"This, this, *this*." I growled through the kiss, loud as I could before tying my tongue up in hers made words impossible.

One hand went to her thigh while I brushed her sweet little lips with my tongue. Couldn't resist the urge to head for the center, where her skinny jeans hid her pussy. Fucking couldn't.

My fingers cupped her there and squeezed. She moaned, flooding my hand with heat.

Fuck, fuck, fuck...

It was like a tiny hot spring in her pants. I started to lose my mind, one rough pull away from unbuttoning her and taking that pussy with my tongue on this bike.

Too bad what I said earlier stood, with the same mad energy I'd felt when Blackjack renewed our oaths to the club. No other brother was gonna see her bare curves and pink perfection but me.

Nobody!

I squeezed her harder, finding her clit through all the denim and fabric. She gurgled into my lips, and I smiled through the kiss, knowing I'd found the right spot.

No, fuck no. This was all mine. Nobody else's.

Mine. I wanted to brand it on her ass and scratch it

into her bones. I wanted to tattoo the fucking word on her naked skin with my teeth, right above where her cleavage started and sucked me into heaven. Fuck, I wanted to walk her around town with a leash around her neck and one hand on her ass, ready to kick the shit outta anybody who even looked at her with a little drool on his lips.

I was fucked, destined to be a maniac 'til I fucked her so many times my brain was as numb as my dick, all I could do to shut the voice up in my head screaming that fatal fucking M-word, and two more just as dangerous.

Mine. Soon. Forever.

I just had to be patient for once in my life. If I could wait a little longer without going ape, it'd be all official with my ink on her skin and a jacket on her shoulders. PROPERTY OF RABID sounded pretty damned good right about now, a perfect way to wrap this up. But hell, make that unwrapped, because having her naked underneath me twenty-four-seven sounded even better.

"Let's go." I ripped myself away, all I could do to break the insane addiction to her flesh. I reached behind her and pushed the spare helmet into her hands.

"Where are we going?"

"Somewhere we can unwind for the night. Not your apartment. It was good for a first time, yeah, but I can think of far better places to fuck your brains out besides an old bed and paper thin walls. Hold on tight, baby. Might as well get your fingers used to running over my body now because they're gonna be holding onto me all night."

The engine roared to life. Helmets on, I tore outta the

garage and headed for the gate, waiting five agonizing seconds for the thing to open. My dick was ready to jump ahead of us and go flying down the street.

It would've been perfect if I hadn't looked behind me. I caught a flash of Red in my mirror, standing there by the door. The little slut must've snuck and poked her head out the second she heard my motorcycle growling.

Well, fuck her anyway. She'd be gone soon enough, and I'd never have to worry about her jealous shit ever upsetting my girl again.

Nothing was gonna come between my old lady and me, especially not something as stupid as that.

For the first time, I could see my future laid out in front of me, something I'd never seen before in almost three decades of passing through life. No, scratch that. My future was behind me with its pretty little hands hugging my abs, and I promised right then I'd never let it slip outta my sight again.

"Jesus. Are you sure you can afford this place?" I laughed when I saw her mouth hanging open.

It was the best resort Redding had to offer, and from now on, my old lady was getting nothing but the very best. I shook my head, packed up our helmets, and headed inside. She seriously had no idea how I was gonna turn her life on its head.

The smart dressed shit at the counter turned his head, trying to hide the derision and fear in his face at the big biker asshole coming toward him. When I was right in front of him, he couldn't ignore it anymore.

"Yes? Can I help you?"

"Need a room for tonight. Cash." I reached into my wallet, pulled out three one hundreds, and slammed them on the table. "Will this get us something with a jacuzzi, or am I gonna need to pay more for that?"

The idiot looked like his eyes were gonna pop outta his head. "No, sir. That'll do just fine."

I thumped my fingers on the counter while he typed our shit in. Turning around, I caught a glimpse of Christa ogling the huge chandelier hanging over the leather seats in the lobby. A man in a tux was playing a piano in the corner – classical shit. I didn't know fuck about Beethoven, but I knew what made my woman smile, and seeing her happy put a grin on my face.

"Here you are, sir. Valet service is available around the clock, breakfast at five thirty, and twenty-four hour room service with complete a drink menu at this number." He stabbed a chubby finger into the piece of paper. "If you need our wifi password, you'll find it –"

"Fuck, just give me the damned keycards." I ripped the leathery folder outta his hands and walked towards Christa.

She didn't see me coming when I came up behind her and wrapped a possessive arm around her waist, giving her a hard tug toward me. She squealed. Just the kinda sound that made my cock beat like a jackhammer in my jeans. It was far too similar to the way she'd be yowling when I pounded her into the fancy ass bed soon.

"Come on, babe. Room's all ready. Let's go."

The place was nothing short of classy. I'd considered splurging and taking a few sluts here in the past, but none of them were worth it. They were quick, trashy fucks meant for rutting out the tension pooling in my balls. The redheaded beauty at my side was the first woman worth a damned thing, the first one worth fucking surrounded by ritz and glamor.

Shit, what was I thinking? She'd be worth my dick any place. Something about the classy stuff put my cock on edge, though. Right now, it was raging to do all the things to her that'd defile this rich, cultured shit. Yeah, I was a twisted barbarian at heart, but my dirty impulses obviously pleased her too.

We rode an elevator up to our suite on the twelfth floor. Soft jazz played inside, and the stars were starting to come out through the glass. Christa shook her head every time she looked at me.

"I can't believe you did this. Nobody's ever treated me to anything this wonderful. Ugh, just wish I'd had some notice. I feel totally underdressed." She looked at what she was wearing and snorted.

Underdressed? Was she fucking serious? There'd be plenty of time to freshen up later. Maybe after I locked her in our room and fucked her 'til it didn't matter. And last I checked, there was no dress code for sliding my dick into her pussy except buck naked.

Naked. Fuck.

My fist popped out and slammed the elevator to stop.

We halted near the seventh floor. She looked at me, eyes wide with surprise.

"I need a taste, baby. Right now while we're here in mid-air. I'm not gonna make it to our room if I don't feel your lips on mine right fucking now."

She slid right into my arms and I tugged her pretty red hair in my fist. My mouth crashed against hers, raging like a motherfucker, rabid as my name. My free hand reached around, hugging one hip. I squeezed her ass so hard she moaned into my mouth.

For a second, I thought I'd pass the fuck out with all the blood surging into my dick. Those sweet pink nipples of hers were plush against my chest, begging to be sucked and bitten.

Christ.

I took my hand off her ass and brought it around, slamming her gently against the glass while I shoved my fingers down her jeans and panties. Sopping fucking wet. Just what I thought.

"Rabid, this is —"

Crazy, she was about to say. I choked her off by pressing my thumb to her swollen clit and circling it like the doorbell to nirvana. Crazy? Sure, but it wasn't like I knew how to do any of this sane. Hell, I could barely control myself for five goddamned seconds when she wanted me.

The urge to throw her down and fuck her right on the elevator floor was overwhelming me. Two stiff fingers plunged inside her, feeling that wet, warm, quivering velvet I'd have around my dick soon. These soft walls were gonna shake tonight, quake and burn with every inch of her.

My dick never felt like this in my entire fucking life. It was like I'd downed a handful of the blue shit, and the bastard in my pants was so strong he'd beaten my brain into a coma, taking full control of everything. Bad analogy, though, because I knew I'd need my pulse checked if it ever took a fucking pill to get hard for this woman.

"Fuck, baby. You wanna get fucked right here, don't you? No bullshitting, girl." I scraped my stubble across her neck and sucked the spot beneath the ear.

If the noises she made were supposed to make me stop, they didn't do shit. A second later, I had her wrapped up in my hands, one hand down her pants, pulling her tank top down with my teeth to get my mouth on those tits.

All of a sudden the elevator jerked. I swore, spinning around just in time to see the door pop open. A well dressed old couple stared at us like we were Martians.

Christa froze, completely mortified. Still had two fingers deep in her pussy, and the lunatic bulge in my pants would've been noticeable to anybody who wasn't blind.

Shit. Fuck. I made my decision in about two seconds.

I nodded at the old man and his wife, drew my hand outta her pants, and picked her up. Christa flushed beet red and hugged my neck numbly as I passed between the old folks. I charged down the hall like a bull, not stopping for anything.

It wasn't like I had a choice. Another minute or two, and my dick was gonna go off like a stick of dynamite, blow this whole place to kingdom come if I didn't have her naked and wriggling underneath me.

I kicked open the door to the stairs. "Hold on tight," I growled, making sure she did before I started up the stairs.

We took the last few floors quickly. I must've set a record for climbing five or six flights of stairs, and the burn in my legs still didn't come close to matching the fire in my balls. What did it matter? A little workout would give us hurricane force sex instead of just stormy loving.

I never fucked harder than right after I was running for my life or spilling some fucker's blood. Preferably both. But these shitty stairs would do, anything to get my blood thudding harder. Adrenaline bored into my brain, channeling my killer instincts into pure primal need.

"Rabid, Jesus Christ! I *cannot* believe what you did back there." She shook her head, ashamed and infuriated when we finally reached the door to our room.

"It worked, didn't it?" I grinned, slamming the keycard into its slot and pushing it open. She didn't follow, just stood outside with her arms crossed.

"Come the fuck on. That old boy in the hall looked like he'd been around the block a time or two. It's nothing he hasn't seen before in his wilder days. Trust me."

"They were old enough to be my grandparents!" She sighed, giving her head another shake. If only she knew how it made her tits bounce. "I'm starting to wonder what

I've gotten myself into…"

Oh, no. Fuck no. I wasn't about to listen to any second thoughts.

I stepped out into the hall, grabbed her again, and shoved her against the opposite wall. "Baby, give me a chance, and I'll show you how deep this heart goes. I'm not asking. I'm saying you're gonna do it, and you're gonna love it, even when I make an ass outta myself."

I leaned my lips in close, just enough to tease, and sensed the heat on her skin. She wasn't fooling anybody with that feisty shit. My cock jerked on instinct when I saw the lights in her eyes.

"It's your choice how we fuck, but I'm having you in the next five minutes. Now, you can follow me inside and take my dick in a nice warm bed with some privacy, or I'll throw you down here and we'll fuck in the middle of this hall. Don't think I won't do it. You saw what happened in the elevator."

She squirmed, amused fury flashing in her eyes. The girl's face said her front lobes didn't know what she wanted, but the heat in her skin told another story. I laughed, grasping her wrists and pinning them to the wall.

I rubbed close, making sure she felt my stubble and the molten bulge about to blaze right through my pants. Fuck, I swore I could practically feel her wet pussy begging for me between two layers of denim.

"You're a pig!" she spat, trying to stay angry, doing her damnedest not to laugh. "Just tell me, is there any part of being an old lady that still lets me be a lady?"

I shrugged. "We're about to wine and dine and bathe in fancy salts when my dick's not inside you. That's gotta count for something, right?"

She snorted. "You're arrogant. You're so sure a fancy dinner and a nice room makes up for embarrassing me. How do you know I won't just slap you across the face and walk out of here right this instant?"

"Your nipples are still like bullets for one thing," I growled, bowing my chest out, feeling those little pinpricks on my torso. "And I'm willing to bet your pussy's still melting all over itself for my dick. How the fuck you gonna get home in one piece dripping cream all over the place? You'll slip and break your neck."

She smiled. "Oh, so you're protecting me again?"

I didn't answer. I just nipped at her neck, gliding my tongue along her pale skin. Fucking shit, she was hot. I tasted lava lust rolling in her veins with every lick, every inch of my skin pressed to hers.

Once my hands started, they couldn't fucking stop. They were total puppets for my dick, and he was working overtime to make sure he got inside her before blowing up like a fucking kid on prom night.

"You know damned well what I'm doing," I snarled, trying to make out the words like a human being instead of a demon. "Are you gonna melt like a good girl and open those hot legs up for me, or am I gonna have to hammer 'em apart?"

I rocked against her, pressing my hard cock to her pussy. I'd rub holes in our jeans right here and make us both come in our fucking pants if she didn't give it up soon.

Yeah, I really was that maniacal. This girl blurred the ying and yang and a thousand other things I couldn't describe in my screwed up system. She turned me to lightning the same way a rod draws current. I had to strike her deep, strike her hard, strike her 'til I blended right into her.

Her breath hitched. I was still dry humping her when I covered her mouth, one second ahead of the mushy scream pouring out her throat.

"Gahd! Rahbit! Fuckh!"

I grinned, sucking her right nip through her shirt. The nice girl drowned in the dirty little succubus lusting after what I had grinding on her clit, surrendering a little more each time I humped her. My thrusts were coming harder, faster, meaner.

Something about knowing anybody could walk right in on us made it all the more electrifying. Her legs started to tremble around mine. Perfect signal to go full throttle.

I thrust against her so hard her little ass bounced back over and over, dangerously close to putting a hole through the wall. Snarling, I reached down, popped her shirt and bra, and stuffed that bud I'd been teasing in my mouth.

Christa instantly tensed up, scrunched her face, and exploded. Her hips did all the work this time. She wrapped her legs around me, panting and grinding like a madwoman, bucking me so hard I really thought I'd lose it in my pants.

Fuck, fuck. I rubbed back so hard it hurt – and the pain did me a favor, prevented me from losing my load. The hand clamped over her lips was like covering a furnace vent. She poured pure smoke into my palm, gurgling her pleasure, biting into my finger when her orgasm peaked.

She came hard. Pride roared in my heart, knowing it was just a warm up for everything else I had planned tonight.

I helped steady her when she came down from her high. Her legs were shaky and her throat must've been dry as fuck. She licked her licks and looked at me, green eyes blazing, cheeks a whole new shade of red I'd never seen in my life.

"Hurry up and catch your breath, baby girl. You know it's time."

She didn't even think about fighting me anymore as I took her by the hand and led her inside our room. I gave her a minute to admire the awesome view. The place overlooked the entire city, opening up on the mountains in the distance.

I smiled. Maybe we hadn't missed much having that elevator fuck interrupted after all.

"Clothes off. Or you want me to do that for you too?" I grabbed her by the shoulder, pulled her to my mouth again.

Heaven. Hellfire. Fucking mercy.

Her tongue plunged eagerly into my mouth. Didn't have a single complaint about it, but I wasn't the kind to let a woman lead either. I cupped my arm around her waist and threw her on the bed, covering her with my body, fucking her lips with my tongue.

"I'm not a helpless kitten," she purred, dodging my next kiss. "I have claws. If you want to play rough, Rabid, I can give it right back to you."

"I'd like to feel that shit, babe. Better show me soon." I wouldn't stop rocking my hips into hers for anything, addicted to that hot wet heat where her legs met. "Come on, before I make you come in your pants again."

She shook her head furiously, trying to protest through her moans. Then she managed to get her hands between us. One brushed the granite in my pants on their way to her belt, working it off like mad.

I gave her some space and stared, feeling my eyes start to melt as she tore her jeans down. I brushed them away with one fist, dipping into her panties, plunging my fingers deep. High time we picked up where we'd left off in the elevator.

She squirmed into my hand. I found her clit and pinched it, alternating my strokes. Her jeans were around her ankles, and after a minute I decided all this shit had to come off.

"Lift that ass," I growled, helping her with a push.

Her panties were like a wet rag. I tore them off and hurled them across the room. Didn't have a fucking clue where they landed. Not like it mattered – she wouldn't be needing them again for hours.

I worked my fingers good and deep on her bare cunt, feeling that wetness, imagining how hot and slick she'd be on my cock soon.

"Rabid...oh! Oh! There."

There. I memorized the place that made her jump and flush with pure pleasure. I did it with all the girls I'd ever fucked more than once, but I took extra care with her. In a few more months, I'd know exactly how to make my old lady come within seconds.

Fuck, *my* old lady. *Mine.*

My dick thumped like I'd grown a second heart below the belt at the thought. I worked my fingers faster, measuring every moan, every gasp, every ripple flowing through her curves. My free hand worked at her bra, tearing it off and sending it to join her long lost panties.

Her thighs collapsed on my hand. The scars lining her face disappeared in steaming red. I smiled, realizing it was an easy way to start the countdown before she came.

One. Two.

Three, four, five.

I pulled my hand away. Two more seconds and she would've blown. She looked at me like I'd just robbed her blind. Guess I had making her wait like this.

"What the fuck?"

"Thought you'd say that. I'm not the only fucker here with a dirty mouth." I yanked her to the edge of the bed, sliding to my knees. "You're gonna come on my filthy lips, baby, one lick for every nasty thing that comes streaming outta your mouth. Start talking."

Her eyebrows went up. I didn't give her a second longer to adjust before I buried my face between her thighs. Licked my way up both her inner thighs, dangerously close to the hot wet center. Stopped just short of hitting the target 'til I heard her speak.

"Bastard!" Her fists hit the bed. "Asshole. Fuck me, Rabid. *Please.*"

Sugar and spice. Everything fucking nice was there, everything I liked to hear while she convulsed on my tongue. Lucky for her, I always kept my word, and it was time to reward her.

Her legs hooked around my shoulders and started trying to close right away. Growling, I held her open, sliding my tongue up her cunt. Licking, sucking, fucking her with every lap, I held her down 'til she came undone.

"Oh, oh, fuck. Fuck. *Fuck!*"

She was singing my favorite word like a mantra. I flipped my face up just in time to smother her clit, circling it like a madman as she blew on my face. Sweet cream gushed into my mouth, urging me on, feeding my hunger.

I fucking buried her, smothered myself between her thighs. I licked her so hard and fast and relentlessly she couldn't even breathe.

Only her pussy got relief. Her thighs pinched tight around my head like a vice. Her senseless jabber was like a siren blasting in my ears, and that was the muffled version. It must've been like a jet screaming through the room with my ears uncovered.

Instinct took over. She rocked her hips against my face, strong and full, hips I'd use one day to make our kids.

Holy fucking shit. Just thinking about knocking her up

caused my dick to drool napalm in my pants. It was too soon for that, but it wasn't as far off as I thought.

I buried my face in her decadent cunt and went wild, licking 'til her throat seized up and she couldn't even scream, just gasp and pant and grind on my face.

Breathless was a big bullshit understatement by the time I finished.

I lay there and turned my back to undress while she was catching up on oxygen. When I dropped my pants, my dick sprang out, so hard it hurt. I gave it a quick pump with one hand to make sure it hadn't gone numb from the blue balls I'd been suffering.

Imagine my surprise when I felt her little hand reach around my thigh, right on top of mine. I spun around. The mischievous smile on her face said she had more energy than I'd given her credit for.

"Baby, don't you need a breather?"

Shut up, man. Why the fuck did I want her to hold off on my cock a second longer? Maybe because I was afraid I'd self-combust and blow the windows out of the room when I started filling her holes.

"Not while you're standing there naked," she said, replacing my grip on my dick with her own. "An old lady needs to learn how to give good head, right? You tell me if I'm on my way to doing it right. I want you in my mouth, Rabid."

Fuck! No man with a pulse would say no to that. I turned, maybe a little too eagerly, giving my swollen cock completely over to her fist. Tried to brace myself for her mouth and fucking failed.

Nothing – and I mean *nothing* – could've prepared me for those soft pink lips drawing down my length.

Motherfucking mercy. I needed it in spades.

I couldn't tell if she knew how to suck good or if I was just so damned turned on because it was *her*. The first thought got my jealousy going. If she sucked a mean dick, it meant she'd learned it from somebody else.

I laced my fingers with her hair and jerked her head forward, making her take it harder, thrusting back and forth into her little mouth.

Whatever, maybe she'd had a few dicks before, but I was damned well going to be the last. These lips, these tits, this pussy…every beautiful inch of her belonged to me now. And I was crazy fucking determined to ravage every inch of her so hard it'd wipe away every last trace of any stupid bastard who'd come before me. I'd teach her a thousand times more than any little pissant who snuck into that pussy before I claimed it for the rest of eternity.

"Shit!" I jerked when her tongue hit the ridge underneath my cock, rolling up toward the small slit in the middle. "How'd you get to be so fucking good?"

She rolled her shoulders and sped up her licks, giving me a little shrug. Smart girl. This was no time for talking, and any answer she gave me was gonna take away from the total perfection gliding toward my balls.

Christa sucked me so good and deep I thought she'd choke. I tried to throttle back to avoid gagging her a couple times, but fuck if she didn't push her head deeper anyway, anything to swallow every inch and then some.

She got little more than halfway down my dick before it was too much. Impressive. Most chicks balked at less than that, including the whores I'd had before.

Fuck, fuck, fuck.

Her tongue swept deeper, seemingly everywhere at once like a goddamned ninja. My balls tightened up, burning, begging for release. I thought about letting loose right down her throat.

But every time I caught those tits bobbing and that pussy underneath, I knew I needed something more. There'd be plenty of time later for popping off in her mouth after she was overflowing with my come.

"Stop, baby." I fisted her dark red locks and pulled her head away. "That was fucking amazing. But your mouth can't come on my dick the way your pussy can. Spread your legs. We both know where I belong right now."

Smiling, she flopped back on the bed, opening wide for me. Pink, wet, and perfect. Wasting one more second would've been a travesty.

I fell onto my arms and mounted her, sinking deep, relishing her heat. I told myself I wouldn't unload 'til she came on my cock a time or two, but it wasn't gonna be easy. Her velvet clung tight, clenched around me like a second mouth, only warmer and wetter.

Shit! This was the kinda pussy that could make a man's brains come out his ears.

I fucked it anyway. Oh, Christ, how I fucked it.

Her tits flopped wild when my thrusts picked up. I

couldn't decide whether to keep my hands on them or grab her ass, pull her deeper onto my cock. I wanted to grab everything on this woman at once, loving the way she rippled and groaned every time I dug in to the hilt.

Couldn't stop the growls rumbling through my throat neither. She activated something primal, that crazy killer instinct to love her as much as I wanted to keep her safe. I couldn't figure out what she'd done to me.

I'd kill for her in a heartbeat, but I also wanted to fuck her so hard she ripped apart. I wanted to screw her so hard it hurt and leave marks all over her, but I'd fucking mutilate anyone who truly tried to put another scratch on her holy skin. The big fancy bed held up well under my assault, creaking and throttling her hips back to mine each time I pounded down.

Her pussy drove me absolutely loco each time I plunged deeper. A couple minutes in, she started tensing up, thrashing her head from side to side. Sweet, sexy satisfaction hissed in my veins. I knew she was on the verge and trying to fight it.

Too bad. I wasn't letting up one second. I was gonna push her into free fall.

"Hook your legs around me, baby." I slowed, grabbing her by the ankles, bending them up 'til her feet rested snug on my shoulders. "I'm gonna tap you deeper than ever. You feel it coming on, just let it go. I want you to squirt all over my dick."

"Oh, God!" The dirty talk caused her pussy to clench tighter around me. "Make me, make me."

Request granted.

I went full throttle, unable to hold back, slamming her pussy so hard the whole bed rippled. How could this girl be so responsive?

She gasped and blossomed fire red right before her orgasm took hold. I started chugging my hips like a fucking train when she flexed her toes around my neck and screamed. She was a sight to behold laid out underneath my thrusts, hands over her head, tits flopping, screaming and clenching at the mess of pillows and bunched up sheets above for leverage.

Oh, fuck. So much for holding back.

Her pussy was jerking my dick off like two soft, endless hands gliding over it when the lava in my nuts erupted. I howled, thrust so deep I rubbed my dick against the entrance to her womb, growling all the way.

"Fuck, baby, I'm coming! Drain me good."

She went from red to purple. Her screams became totally breathless. I joined her a second later, paralyzed as all my muscles tensed and lightning shot through my cock. Seed pumped out in hot jets, a primal geyser dead set on hurling deep inside her.

A surge of pure pleasure like nothing I'd felt in my life slapped my skull. I rocked into her hips, still trying to fuck her as my cock was in full meltdown. Her pussy sucked me off so hard I had to flatten my hands on the bed to keep from collapsing right on her, overwhelmed by the fire spitting outta my balls.

We came together, snarling and breathless like two

mating beasts. You better believe I pumped every damned drop of come I could squeeze outta my balls into her. And I still wanted to flood her with more, make her drip my stuff for days.

Christ, she fucking drained me. I could feel our cream spilling out around where I was fused to her, leaving a big wet stain on the bed. Cool air brushed my back from the vents, beckoning me back to life, cooling the red hot engine of my body with my own sweat.

"Fuck, girl. You're gonna kill me before I get my brand on you, aren't you?"

She'd gone from red to purple at some point while orgasm wracked her body. For a second, I thought I'd have to do CPR just to make sure she was breathing. But then she opened those emerald green eyes and looked at me.

"No, no. You're going to do me in first." Her hips rocked, keeping my dick lodged in her.

I couldn't even go soft. I was hard and numb, loving just being in her warmth, deep in the pool of sex we'd created.

"Bullshit. You respond to me like heaven because you know you're mine." I leaned down, hovering just a couple inches above those addicting lips. "I treat everything I own well. You know that?"

Her legs slid over my shoulders, gliding down my back, and stopped just above my ass. She pinched them together and jerked me forward, deeper into her, teasing me to fuck her again.

Careful, babe, I thought. *You might just get what you want.*

"Yeah," she cooed. "I'm starting to figure that out. When do I get one of those cool leather jackets with your patch, anyway?"

I grinned. "Soon as we're done giving this bed the best fucking workout it's ever gonna have."

She smiled, fresh mischief overtaking the exhaustion in her eyes. "Guess we'd better get to work, then. I have a feeling a place like this sees some kinky, rich creeps sometimes."

Oh, that pissed me right off. A challenge, huh? My dick rose to the task, hardening back to steel and regaining its sensitivity.

"Babe, if you think I can't fuck you harder and sicker than every other wrinkly asshole who's ever been in this place with an escort, then you'd better get used to carrying a pillow with you tomorrow." She quirked an eyebrow as my hips began to rock. "You'll need it just to sit down after all the fucking we're doing tonight. Screw the restaurant. We'll order in and I'll feed you bites of lobster while you're riding my dick."

She laughed. I was only half-joking. Shit, I was gonna take her in every position, every corner of this room before the night was over, including the jacuzzi.

I drove deep and hard, watching while pleasure sealed her eyes shut. Soon, the laughter was gone. The entire room lit up with her moans and the steady thump of the bed as I fucked myself stupid.

So began the best two days of my life. I fucked that girl seventeen ways from Sunday. Yeah, I said *seventeen,* because just seven didn't begin to describe the carnal rodeo going on in that room.

We finally left the resort for a bite in town the second night. Christa had finally taken the stick outta her ass and she was alive like I'd never seen her, putting me to shame with the way she downed beer and whiskey. She glugged hers straight while I tried to keep up, mixing my shit with ginger ale like I usually did.

Course, I would've beaten her in a heartbeat if I didn't have to drive. But fuck, this girl could drink like an old lady, and that made me grin like a fool.

"Careful, babe. You're gonna fall off my cock later tonight if you keep it up," I said at the bar, watching her knock down another shot.

"*Again,* Rabid? You weren't kidding about being sore." She smiled, shaking her head. Her small hand landed on my thigh and then reached over when nobody was looking, giving my cock a quick squeeze.

"You're lucky I like it as much as you do."

"Like it?" I took a long pull from my beer. "Baby girl, I *need* it like oxygen when it's you and me. Don't think I'll ever go more than a day without tangling that hair in my fist and getting between your legs. 'Til we got together, I never thought I'd find anything that could match riding with the wind in my face and the road growling beneath me. Getting in bed with you proved me wrong."

I reached over, swept her hair aside, and tasted her lips. This kiss was sweeter and headier than any buzz this fucking watering hole could offer, even if it was a fancier hole than I was used to.

Whatever. Anything for her. She was getting nothing but the best from now on, everything she deserved for choosing me and accepting all the insane shit that came with this patch and the brand going on her skin real soon.

I brushed the red tipped claw patch on the front of my cut. I thought about the club, furrowing my brow at all the crap we still had do to do make sure those assholes in southern Oregon never bothered us again. There'd be a battle this week or next for sure.

Blackjack wasn't a patient man, and neither was Brass. They'd want to hit the fuckers hard, stomp the rotten apples like Rip, and maybe keep a few good guys left to help form a new charter tightly under our control up there. *Maybe,* assuming they weren't all evil assholes, and that was a real possibility from everything I'd seen.

I didn't trust a single one of the shits who'd paid us a visit at the clubhouse, demanding my head. If this was a biker bar, I would've been looking over my shoulder, anything to make sure some sneaky bastard wasn't prowling around, about to get the jump on me.

"What's that one mean, anyway?" Christa tapped the claw patch I'd just brushed. "Guess I'd better start learning this stuff if I'm becoming a club woman."

Yeah, the girl was right about that. "You really wanna know?"

I set my beer down and leaned close, making sure none of the civvies could hear.

"This one's called first blood. It's the first patch I got after earning my bottom rocker. The club was already starting to have trouble with the Mexicans creeping north. I went down to LA with some guys, Blackjack leading us. They had an old warehouse holding all the shit they brought up from Mexico. Blackjack and me planted the bomb that started the place on fire. Burned up all their drugs for cash and turned a few of the fuckers locked inside into crispy critters. That was the first time I killed for the club, and the red claw marks the occasion."

Her eyes were huge. She blinked, smoothing her face. "Jesus."

"Yeah." I sipped my beer. "Don't tell me that shit scares you?"

"No," she said after a pause. "I know what this life is all about. My dad was no stranger to doing whatever needed to be done to protect his club."

"Anything else you wanna know?" I looked at her. Now was a better time than any to lay my cards out, as long as she didn't want me to spill shit that was for the club's eyes and ears only.

"Are you ever going to tell me your real name?" She flashed a wicked smile. "I'm perfectly happy calling you Rabid forever, buuut…"

"It's Charlie. Charlie Tellard." Fuck, giving up that secret was tough. "My ma wanted to go with something classic. All her choice. The deadbeat asshole who walked out on her while she was pregnant didn't have much say in the matter. This name's all on her."

She cocked her head. "I like it, Charlie. Tells me there's a man with a good heart underneath the badass."

Her fingers rolled up my cut and grabbed the collar of my shirt. Maybe giving her my real name wasn't so bad after all if it got her wet. I smashed my lips on hers.

Yeah, no way was I ever getting sick of kissing this. My dick started throbbing in my jeans again, hotter than ever with some booze in my system. No matter how many times we kissed and fucked, I was ready for more. This girl taught me the meaning of *insatiable*.

"Why Rabid?" she asked, pulling away. "There's got to be a story behind that."

"Blackjack came up with that one. We were at a big rally in Spokane, lots of other clubs representing, one-percenters and casual riders alike. This club from New England cut us off at the bar, trying to wave their dicks in our territory, thinking we were some little pussy group from the west coast. Blackjack tried to hold us back, keep shit calm. Their Prez was being a fucking ass. Words were said and I was ready to fight. When the fucker pushed me, it was the last straw."

She shook her head, knowing what was coming.

"I went nuclear. I broke the asshole's nose while all his guys were beating on me. I was new to my patch and very motivated. I couldn't even feel them while I was wailing on that fucker. Blackjack and the crew had to break through the circle just to pull me out and break it up before I killed him. Said I was like a rabid dog or something. The name stuck."

"You like tough odds. I can respect that." She smiled.

"Just respect it? Baby, you'd better love it. I had a couple broken ribs when that fight was over and it didn't faze me one bit. I've been this way all my life and I'm not stopping now. I'm a reasonable man. I always do right by my brothers and my woman, and I'll give anybody a couple chances before I let my fists do the talking. But when it's time for that, you'd better watch the fuck out. I *will* break anybody who deserves it, even if they're busting me piece by piece. That includes anybody who disrespects you. You're mine now. Nobody gives you shit except me."

"Yeah? You going to give me something tonight?" She batted her eyes.

Tease. Good thing I loved every morsel she stirred up in me.

I reached for her thigh, growling with satisfaction when I felt how warm she was beneath her jeans. Her tongue darted over her bottom lip, obviously turned on and a little drunk. Fucking perfect by my standards.

My girl knew the answer. Some crotchety old tourist watched us from the corner. I kissed her deep, filling her mouth with everything I was gonna do to her, more than words could ever say.

"Come on. Let's get the fuck outta here. I'd rather have you than waste more time on another beer and have to wait."

We paid our tab and she followed me out to my bike.

It was a quick drive back, just as the stars were coming out. Nice reminder of how she'd been resistant as fuck the first time we rode under a sky like this. Now, she was all mine, and I was only beginning to mark her.

I'd turned her around, brought her into my arms and into my bed. Hell yes. She was mine, dammit, I was never letting go. Not for fucking anything.

Somebody would have to reach down from the sky and take me away from her before I quit. And that wasn't gonna happen, not with my heart beating strong, sending blood and lightning through my veins. Tonight, it beat like a war drum, strong and tingly in a way that almost freaked me out.

This love shit was kinda scary. Luckily, I was ready, and I knew I'd be ready for anything by the time I laid her down with my brand tattooed on her skin.

VII: Complicated (Christa)

The bike ride went by in a blink, and that was a good thing. My muscles ached with the aftershocks of all the sex we'd had the longer I was on the motorcycle, and my pussy ached more at the thought of what was to come.

We were in the parking lot, taking off our helmets, when his phone rang.

"Yeah? What's up?" Rabid growled, annoyed at the interruption.

"You'd better get your ass to the clubhouse by six tomorrow, brother. Roman's got the prospects out on patrols, taking shifts. Word on the street says the Oregon boys are back in town." Brass' voice boomed through the receiver.

"Fuck. Are you sure?"

"Not yet, but there's a damned good chance it's true. Don't think our local supporters and hangarounds would be bullshitting about seeing dudes with our patches who aren't in our club otherwise. They're back here for blood, and we've gotta be ready. I'm making the rounds and keeping watch on Missy and her sis so nothing fucking crazy happens. Get your girl to the clubhouse tomorrow and make sure she stays there 'til this shit blows over…"

Brass was still talking, but he'd lowered his voice. I couldn't make out the rest.

Rabid looked like he'd bitten into a lemon. "All right. Hit me back when you've got more. We'll be there."

The phone snapped shut and he stuffed it into his pocket. We packed up our helmets and he turned to me. "Bad news, babe –"

"I heard. Sounds like we'd better make the most of this night." I sighed, wondering if this is how those military girls feel before their men ship out overseas.

"Damned straight. We've got a few good hours before we'd better try to get some shut eye. We'll be checking out at five sharp tomorrow morning." He grabbed my hand, and I followed him toward the hotel.

The parking lot was packed, so we had to take a space further back. We were crossing the last row of cars when a man on the ground yelled out, kneeling next to his tire. His car was jacked up. Looked like quite the clunker for a place like this, worse than the old beast I drove.

"Hey! Think you can give a guy a hand, mister?"

Rabid's jaw clenched, and so did his grip on my hand. He gave me a warning look and stepped toward the man.

"Yeah? What do you need?" Ground man looked up, an older man, and he stared at us for several seconds before Rabid bowed up. "What the fuck? You're the guy from the bar!"

Heavy boots pounded the pavement right behind me. I

spun, just in time to get knocked flat on the ground by a thick silhouette. More footsteps clattered past, heading for my man. I tried to call out to warn him, but a cold hand slammed over my mouth.

Another hand tore at my hair, holding it, pinning me to the ground. I squealed into the mystery palm, but it was no use. Everything came out muffled.

More hands were on me, lifting me up, carrying me away at lightning speed.

All I could hear were the scuffles in the distance, Rabid roaring, men cursing. Someone howled in pain. Then there was a massive blast from a gun.

I was about to bite the hand around my mouth when they all let go at once. I hit some narrow, confined space and rolled. Something crashed above me, and the world went dark. I didn't realize they'd thrown me into the trunk of a car until we started moving.

"Rabid! Oh my God. Help me! Help!" I started pounding on the metal overhead as hard as I could. It was surprisingly difficult in such a narrow space, hard to get the right leverage to throw my arms into it.

And I didn't know if it would even do any good. But I had to try something, had to try to get away. These had to be the men from Klamath, and things were sure to get worse every minute I was in their hands.

I sucked in a deep breath and screamed so hard I nearly burst my lungs. "Rabid!"

"Cut it out, you fucking cunt." Something blunt smashed me in the head. There was a flash of red, and everything started spinning.

I barely had time to roll over before I blacked out. One of the seats behind me was pulled down, and a man had a knife to my throat, reaching through the space connecting to the trunk.

"You scream or hit that trunk again, I *will* bleed you out right here. Same fucking way your lovebird killed our Veep."

Why was this so familiar? Flashbacks came, rapid fire.

I saw Fang holding the knife to my throat again, recording his little threats on video to send to Blackjack and his crew during their rebellion. The dead man had set to work on me then, trying to pump me for information I didn't have. He beat me across the face with the blunt handle, just like the man in the trunk, a warm up before he started carving the ugly scars I'd have forever going up each cheek.

I'd been a hostage before. I could do it again, just as long as Rabid was okay.

God, please let him be okay. Don't let him be dead.

The man with the knife was a nasty looking bastard with an eye patch. Bruises peppered the skin over his jaw and around his lone good eye. "Remember me, bitch? It's Marrow. I helped trash your fucking dive when you didn't pay up and tried to blow town. Did you really think you'd get away from us? Hmmm?"

I shook my head. No.

Just give him what he wants. Buy time. Stay alive.

Stay breathing for Rabid. He's okay – he fucking has to

be!

My thoughts raced as fast as my heart, a pulse so manic it shook my entire body.

"Big Eddy told me about your daddy too. We'll be back for him when we're done having our fun with you and your fuck buddy. We'll give those old farts at the nursing home a fucking show they'll never forget."

"No!" Adrenaline rattled my throat. I couldn't help it. The knife twitched, pressing closer, one ounce of pressure away from digging into me and drawing blood.

Dad. Fuck! I'm so sorry.

Tears came, hot and explosive, as if the fire in my brain was spilling out my eyes.

"Cry all you want, baby, it isn't gonna help. But don't fucking worry." He snorted. "Some good will come of this. Settling score with both of you assholes just might keep our brothers from killing each other all the way between Redding and Klamath Falls. Blackjack's a reasonable man. He'll understand."

Wrong, wrong, so fucking wrong. I wanted to scream it in his face. But I didn't dare as long as he could kill me with a quick swipe of his wrist.

The car drove on. There was nothing more to say.

The bastard with his knife to my throat relaxed after a while, satisfied that he'd scared me into submission. He had to know I wouldn't try to pop the trunk either while we were speeding down the highway, probably heading north.

We'd be across the Oregon border soon. Nothing else

mattered just then except knowing Rabid was safe. If he was still free, still in one piece, he'd come for me. If he wasn't...

The other possibility hurt so much it formed a lump in my throat. I'd gone from hating his guts to loving him. Jesus, I hadn't even said it either. The universe was fair, wasn't it?

I couldn't die before I saw him again. I swore I wouldn't miss another chance to tell him everything, say the dreaded L-word. If only we escaped this alive.

The car rumbled and jerked, turning tight corners as it headed through the mountains, onward toward destiny. Death or defiance waited up ahead. Only time would tell which.

"Come on! Get the fuck up!" Marrow didn't bother opening the trunk

He yanked me into the back of the car through the narrow space where he'd held his weapon, pushing down the other seat to make room. I went flying out carelessly and banged my knees on the trunk when I tried to twist.

"Okay, okay!" It was all I could manage with him ripping my hair out of my head, jerking me through the passenger door.

I'd never been inside the Klamath Falls clubhouse before. I recognized it, though, a large concrete building that looked like it had been a police station or a post office once. Several other guys walked ahead of us. They flung the entry door open and held it for Marrow, who pushed me through it.

The stink that hit me in the face instantly said this wasn't like the one in Redding. It was like somebody died in there – maybe many somebodies. I swallowed hard, hoping I wouldn't be the latest to add to their sick body count.

"The fuck? Do I have to do everything to get your ass to move? Go!" The bastard slapped me on the ass.

It was more like a fist than an open hand. One more bruise I'd have there tomorrow – if I lived to see another day. He pushed me against the wall when we were next to a door. The greasy biker ripped it open and pushed me inside.

I held my hands out and hit the wall hard, thankful I didn't fall.

"Sit and keep still 'til the Prez comes to see you, bitch. You're our property now." The door slammed shut behind him.

No, I'd never be theirs. Not in body, mind, or soul. I'd already given everything to Rabid, wherever he was.

The room was completely dark. Thinking about my old man was all I had to keep me sane. I wanted to freak every time my foot brushed something on the floor, thinking it was a rat.

Probably just debris. It didn't move much. My fingers slid over the wall, searching for a light switch. Five or ten minutes must have passed before I gave up, leaning against the wall in the darkness. I stayed perfectly still.

Hoping. Praying. Trying not to scream.

If Rabid got away, he'd come for me soon with his men. He'd free me. I'd be back in his arms in no time, and we'd both live happily ever –

The door swung open, shattering my optimism. Marrow stepped inside and marched to the room's center, giving the string attached to a light bulb overhead a hard jerk. I felt like an idiot for not finding it before.

A tall, heavily bearded man I recognized was right behind him, looking like an angry Norse god. Rip. I'd only met the bastard a couple times when he came to my bar, and he always had some skank at his side.

When the bitch behind him stepped in on her bright red heels, at first I thought she was another slut. Then I thought I was seeing things.

I blinked, and the woman didn't disappear. My heart caught in my throat. Jesus, there was no mistaking her, she was really there.

Red. The club slut who'd upset Rabid and given me the evil eye. Now, I was starting to understand how these assholes had gotten the upper hand and surprised us. They had a rat in Redding all along.

"Hiii," Red cooed, stepping close. "Surprised to see me?"

I shook my head and spat at the ground. My spit landed on the toe of her over-polished hooker shoe. She looked down, then raised her head, locking eyes with me. Then the bitch's teeth came out.

She slapped me across the face so hard the impact twisted my head to the side.

"Stupid skank! Can't you see who's got you by the throat, or are you just retarded? You've disrespected me enough. You stole my man. I'll kill you before I let you take anything else away from me."

Go ahead, I thought with a smirk. *Something tells me you've never so much as sliced a steak in your miserable life.*

"Red, Red. Down, girl." Rip laughed, pulling her away with a rough hand to the shoulder. "It's been a long time, Little Miss Kimmel."

"Not long enough." Yeah, my sarcastic tongue was probably going to get me killed, but if I did I was going out with a few parting shots.

"Fuck." Rip stopped when he was just a couple inches from my face, close enough to feel the overgrown bristles sprouting on his chin. "My boys weren't bullshitting. I remember you being a lot prettier when you were serving drinks to the crew. Fang did a fucking number on you, didn't he?"

His fat fingers touched my cheek, tracing the longest scar. I twisted my head, throwing him off.

The big man stood up, grunted, and shook his head. "Looks aside, you're still the same cunt I remember. Defiant. Fucking ungrateful. Only now your debt to this club's in blood – not just money."

Hate lit up his dark eyes. I watched his arm tense and tried to brace myself. There wasn't enough time. His hand crashed against my face, ten times harder than Red's, temporarily blinding me.

"You think this is a fucking joke, bitch!? You killed an

officer in this club, my right hand man!" He stepped back, trembling with rage. "You were dead the second Marrow threw you in the damned trunk. Only question is how much fun we're gonna have before your heart stops."

Red smiled at me from her perch in the corner. She walked up behind the Prez, who looked like he was about to keel over from the rage shooting through his veins.

If only I were that lucky.

"Easy, Prez," Red whispered, soft and almost seductive. "You're too close to this little rat to work her over without cutting her throat. Let me start in on her. I'll save the final blow for you. Promise."

Rip spun, arm raised. Red's eyes widened with fear, stretching her dark mascara rings like a craven raccoon.

"I'm calling the shots here. This is my fucking club. You're lucky I didn't kill that other fucking rat on the spot. Both these fucks owe a debt to *me,* not you. You're just a pretty looking tip line." Growling, he looked her up and down, eyes openly sticking to her ass.

Yep, that was the Rip I knew. A nasty, violent, demanding pig. Except now the pig was a wild boar, and he was going to eat me alive.

Why was it like they were talking about two people anyway? Wasn't it enough that I was here for their torture? Who else did they have?

"Whatever you say, boss." The whore smiled sweetly. "I just like to have my fun. You can beat me any old day with the torture. But I bet I can do a few things to their hearts."

"Whatever," Rip snorted, pacing the room. He stopped next to the half-cracked door and roared through it. "Hey! Where is that other piece of shit? Bring him in here."

It can't be.

Oh, but it was. A second later, Marrow and another bulldog faced creep marched Rabid through the door. His face had dried blood on it and a couple patchy bruises.

My heart sank. For the first time since I'd gotten here, the nightmare seemed real and permanent. Him being here meant the Redding crew wouldn't know what happened. By the time they figured it out, it could easily be too late.

The men swung their arms and threw him into the opposite corner of the room. My man hit the wall hard with an *oomph.* He landed, coming out of his fugue state to sit up straight.

Rabid finally looked at me, and his eyes swelled with everything bad.

Horror. Anguish. Apologies. Shame.

The fissures in my heart burned and scratched like broken glass. He turned his head away, shaking it slightly.

Rip shuffled. He snorted, then headed for the door, pointing a finger at Red on his way out. "You got thirty minutes. Make it good. My fists aren't gonna wait any longer. Come on, boys."

The men left the room, slamming the door shut behind them. It was just us and Red. Ignoring me, she clicked by on her heels, heading for Rabid. She crouched down next to him, cupped his face in her hands.

"Oh, baby. I wish you didn't have to learn your lesson this way. I begged them to take it easy on you." She swept a quick, cautious hand over his cheek.

My half-dead heartbeat suddenly picked up, thumping with jealousy. God damn it. Common sense told me I should've been more worried about the bikers – not this stupid slut trying to get underneath my skin.

But my heart didn't know any better, and I wanted to make her bleed as bad as I wanted out of here. I wanted to rip her apart with my bare hands, even if it was the last thing I ever did.

Rabid kicked his legs, pushing himself back against the wall, grunting with pain. They'd definitely beaten him. I wondered how many bones they'd broken – maybe that was why he didn't try to stand.

Red put her hand against the wall and helped herself down, resting on her knees, trying to stroke his brow. "All your ouchies will be gone in no time. I'll help. I'll talk him out of making them worse, I promise. We'll figure something out. We can get past this, baby. You're meant to be my old man. We just got ourselves a little off track…"

Rabid's head rolled, half-conscious, trying to get away from her despite slipping the concussion probably rattling his brain. And the stupid bitch kept trying to touch him – my man!

I stumbled up, ignoring the ache in my knees, and flew toward her. She screamed when I kicked her in the spine, grabbing at her hair. She thrashed, pulling me onto the floor. We rolled, hissing and tearing at each other's hair, scratching and screaming. The door burst open and boots thundered around us.

Marrow ripped me off the floor and slammed me against the wall. "Fucking shit! Are you bitches stupid?" He aimed his one good eye at Red. "Prez's gonna cut your time down to zero if you can't control this cunt. Here, take this."

Holding me against the wall with one hand, he reached into his pocket and handed her a switchblade. Red fumbled it in her hands so pathetically I almost rolled my eyes. Then the blade popped out, shiny and cold. She smiled, her little button eyes filling with her new power.

"We'll be okay now. Promise. I'll call if I need anything."

With a snarl, Marrow released me, waving to his buddy. Deja vu. The door slammed shut and we were alone, but this time the bitch facing me brandished her blade. He'd given her the upper hand.

"There's still room on that ugly face for a few more lines," she said, stepping close to me. "Think I can make some pretty patterns? There's a limit to what even Rabid can love – unless he's a lot sicker than I think."

She paused, turned, and looked at him. "Baby, will you love me as much as her if I put those scars on my face? I can make myself look just like her if you want, only I'll be hotter."

Rabid and I looked at each other, sharing a mad gaze. I didn't even care about her insults and threats. This bitch was certifiably crazy, and that made her more dangerous than I thought.

I folded my arms. The movement caught her peripheral vision. She darted toward me, slapped me across the face. The second knife of the night pressed against my throat.

"Don't you fucking move unless I tell you, bitch!" she screamed. "I'll cut a hole in your fucking neck and drag your tongue right through it. I ought to do it anyway for kissing what's mine. You don't deserve to even speak to him!"

Rabid twisted in the corner, trying to stand, growling the whole time. He staggered and fell over when he was halfway up, clawing at the wall for support. Tears clouded my eyes. His injuries were worse than I thought.

Red watched him collapse too, and the raging murder in her deflated. "Oh, baby. You're struggling too hard. Sit still. Try not to hurt yourself. This'll all be over soon."

She leaned next to him. I considered trying to jump her again, but she had the blade in her fist. The knife was so sharp she'd easily kill me if she got a lucky hit. And luck was definitely plentiful with a weapon like that.

"There, there." She ran her fingers through his bloody hair. "I'll tell you what, baby. I won't cut her. I'll leave that up to Rip. She has to die one way or another, that's the agreement I made. But she doesn't have to suffer first."

His face snapped up. The look he gave her chilled my blood to sub-zero. Even if every bone in his body was shattered, he looked like he could ignite the entire room, vaporizing this cruel bitch purring her sickly fake concern into his ear.

And she wouldn't fucking stop.

"This is how it's going to go down. We've got twenty minutes before Rip does his thing. That's just enough time for me to fuck you silly right here on the floor while the bitch in the corner watches. We'll let her see how a real woman pleases you." Red licked her lips and put her hand on his crotch.

Fire shot through my veins. *Hold back. Just a little bit longer.*

Resisting the urge to throw myself at her was pure hell. But if I embraced the instinct to fly forward and gouge out her eyes, I'd get myself killed, and probably Rabid too.

My old man squirmed on the ground. He fought. His hand flew up, knocked her bright red fingernails away from his dick. I knew a bulge in those jeans when I saw it, and right now he wasn't hard. Small relief.

Disgusted, Red put her hands on her hips, thumbing the switchblade. "God. How can such a beautiful man be so fucking stupid?"

"I dunno. How can such an ugly whore be so fucking delusional?" I said it to get her away from him.

She pivoted toward me, new anger shining in her eyes. A smirk pulled at her lips.

"I'll get to you soon enough, bitch. Here, I'll tell you exactly what's going to happen." She licked her lips. "You're a dead girl, Christa. If Rabid knows what's good for him, he'll leave you buried in some pit and run away with me. It's not too late for him. I can talk Rip into sparing him – I know I can!"

"Red, you'll never talk anybody into jack shit. Even if you could, I'd rather die than go anywhere with you," Rabid growled, reaching for her leg. "I swear I'll fucking kill you myself, you fucked up little –"

Red screamed, slashing the blade across his arm. Her shoe flailed, kicked him in the face. He lost his grip in the commotion. I watched, horrified, as Rabid rolled, grabbing at the long, jagged red stripe seeping from his forearm.

"Oh my God. Baby, I'm so fucking sorry." Red stumbled backward, her mouth hanging open in horror. She looked at me again, blade pointed like an accusing finger. "This is your fault! You made me hurt him, you bitch!"

She flew forward, punching, kicking, and swinging her blade. I tried to cover myself, kneeling on the ground. She slapped and punched but she didn't stab. A feral growl echoed through the room as the whore went crazy. Then she stepped back, panting for breath when she'd gotten it out of her system.

"You're dead, thieving cunt. But not before you make a choice, the last one you'll ever be offered." She smiled. "You can watch me have sex with him right here, right now – or I'll bring all the guys in and have them fill your holes as much as they can until Rip's ready to slice out your throat. Rabid and I'll watch. What's it going to be?"

Fire invaded my heart. The bitch was stupid, but she

was downright evil too. I refused to look at her. There was no good option in this monstrous choice she'd offered.

"Well?"

"Leave her the fuck alone. You're a cowardly little shit, Red. You've fucking betrayed everyone around you and signed your death warrant." Rabid looked up, his fists curled, still losing blood from the cut on his arm.

"It sounds like you're too angry to fuck me right now, baby. That's okay. I know we'll get through this – we're meant to." She cleared her throat, turning back to me. "Last chance, Christa. Are you going to pick an option, or should I just start in on you right now?"

I stared right through her. If looks could've burned, then she would've melted on the spot. Shame the universe wasn't that kind. Uncertainty filled her eyes, and she tightened her grip on the blade, alternating her gaze between Rabid and me.

"Okay. Fine. We'll do it my way." Red drew a deep breath. "Christa, you're going to get the shit fucked out of you before you die. Rabid, baby, I want you to see everything. You'll want her a lot less after she's had a few dicks down her throat."

The fuse was lit. Tense silence reigned as I tried to keep my heart from beating out of my chest, letting the vile fate she'd picked sink in. Rabid exploded, hurled himself at her, and caught the asshole off guard.

She went flying, hit the wall hard. I swung for her face. Caught her hair in one hand and pulled it until she screamed, praying we could finish her before the men burst in. Then the stupid heels she had on caused her to topple over.

She took me with her. We hit the ground hard, and I lost all the air in my lungs. Next thing I knew, Rabid wasn't fighting her anymore. Something icy-hot slid down my neck.

Sharp pain filled my nerves. I reached up and touched just below her knife, feeling the trickle of blood running around my collar.

Jesus! No! My other hand reached for her wrist and I pulled as hard as I could.

"Don't. Neither one of you move. This thing's happening. Let it, or I'll cut this bitch's throat out now."

I caught Rabid's eyes. I was her hostage now, and he knew it. The raging seas in his eyes looked on helplessly, searching for another opportunity to turn this around.

Fuck. Why couldn't we get one lucky break?

"You really hate me, don't you? Both of you!" Her eyes were completely crazy. She pushed her face against mine, snarling, knife twitching at my throat. "Let's see how you like this, bitch. Maybe I can kiss away everything you've stolen before you're full of Grizzlies dick. Here, I'll warm you up for the last cock you're ever going to enjoy in this life…"

Something hot and tight pressed against my mouth.

What. The. Fuck?

The whore was actually kissing me. Her filthy tongue pushed past my lips and my stomach heaved. I struggled, hating how there was no way to move my head that wouldn't end in her cutting my jugular. She had me trapped in her madness, her cruelty, her –

Wait.

Maybe I wasn't as trapped as I thought. A brain running on pure survival comes up with some crazy ideas. And I had one that just might work.

I cleared my mind. My eyes shot to Rabid, and held his gaze the entire time, focusing entirely on my man as I started to feel my lips again. I kissed her back.

My hands gently wrapped around the whore's shoulders, and I stiffened, moaning into her mouth.

She spluttered, her eyes flashing like I was the crazy one. Good. Exactly what I needed her to think.

Baby, no. Don't fucking do this, Rabid mouthed, shaking his head.

I had to ignore him. Had to play along. Had to survive.

Just like I thought, she rose to the challenge. Red pulled away for a second and looked at me in disgust, but then her mouth was on me, hard and aggressive. She tried to suffocate me with her gross tongue.

I sucked it deep, twining it with mine. Frustration steamed through her every time she moved her mouth on mine, kissing me so hard it hurt, angry that her sick torture wasn't paying off. I waited until her hand slid between my legs and started to rub before I moved my tongue away from hers.

My teeth snapped down, hard enough to break. The bitch managed to get her tongue out of my mouth before it was too late, but I caught her bottom lip. I bit her hard, tasting blood, and held on, rolling on the floor in desperate strokes to avoid the knife.

The shock of feeling my teeth go through her lip weakened her grip. Red screamed, blubbering like a baby when she finally pulled away with her torn up mouth, bleeding bright crimson.

Rabid's war cry filled the whole room. He lunged, jerked her off me, rolling on the floor with her. Everything around me became a tangle of arms and legs and twisting bodies.

I hit the wall and scrambled to my feet, watching as he tore the blade out of her hand. Red sobbed and spit blood. His arm hooked tight around her neck and squeezed, hard enough to choke off her breath.

Footsteps thudded outside. "Rabid! Look out, they're coming."

He nodded. The door flew open. Rip, Marrow, and a couple other goons piled in. They took one look at me against the wall and then saw Red.

"Fucking shit." It was all their President managed before Rabid lunged, jabbing the switchblade into his thigh.

Guns came out. They were fast, but Rabid was even faster.

He managed to pull the weapon out of Rip's holster before he could, and he aimed it at the President's spine, slowly pulling himself up, dragging the gun up to the man's head.

"Nobody fucking moves, or I'll blow this bastard's

brains out. Get the fuck out of this room if you want to see him alive again." I flinched at his cold, killer tone.

"We're not leaving 'til we know he's alive, asshole. Let him fucking go!" Marrow barked.

"Idiot, do what this jackass says." Rip's eyes were wide with fear. His beard trembled like a tumbleweed glued to his chin. "You heard him! Go!"

Slowly, the men backed away into the hall, never taking their eyes off them. Rabid looked at me. Red lay on the ground, crying and writhing in pain, fingers pressed tight to her injured mouth.

Let's see who's got scars now, bitch, I thought, grim satisfaction humming in my blood.

It wasn't time to celebrate yet. I didn't have a clue how we were going to actually get out of here. One little slip with Rip as hostage, and we'd both be dead. And it was a long way between Klamath and Redding, even if we could secure a ride and head out. They'd come roaring after us and shoot out our tires the second his gun wasn't against the bastard's head.

I swallowed. Rabid looked at me, the same long odds in his eyes.

"Let's go," he whispered. "Everybody outta my fucking way!"

The men in the halls stared at us like wild animals when they saw he had their leader with a gun to his head. Rip was a heavy man, and it looked like Rabid was trying to drag him. I kept my switchblade ready for stabbing at a moment's notice, edging past the dangerous looking men, and hoping they wouldn't lunge for me.

None of them were brave enough to try. Rabid's headlock was tight, and Rip blubbered the whole way down the hall, toward their garages.

When we got outside, motorcycles were rumbling. Lots of motorcycles. There must've been more than a dozen.

Rabid spun, pointed his finger at one-eyed Marrow. "What the fuck is this? You trying to get the jump on us? I'll blow this bastard's brains out right here – I swear to Christ!"

His hand trembled. My heart caught in my throat and I tried to stand behind him, the only protection I had from the men slowly following us. Marrow came to a stop just a couple feet away and smiled.

"Let him go, asshole. You both know there's no way out. You try to stuff him in one of our cars, we'll fucking shoot the tires out and drag you up against the wall where you belong. You kill him, you lose your leverage. Fucking idiots!" he spat. "You're goddamned right we're jumping your asses! Nobody fucks us over!"

"Rabid!" I called out, eyes locked on the ugly bastard's hand, knowing he was about to draw.

Rabid hesitated. He couldn't pull his gun away from Rip's temple and risk the Prez getting out. My turn.

I threw myself at Marrow and plunged the switchblade right into his guts. He stopped, dead in his tracks, his lone eye wide with disbelief. He sputtered in my face one time and then hit the ground. His weight nearly pulled me over with him. I had to pull on the blade with both hands to keep it from sticking in him.

Growling, the others circled us. I matched Rabid's steps, keeping my bloody dagger aimed at them, ready to lash out like a cornered beast.

Marrow was still alive, groaning on the ground, holding the bleeding hole I'd torn in his stomach.

"Anybody else? Just try me! There's *two* of us you've got to deal with." A big man with a wiry mustache looked like he was about to try it. I jabbed the blade toward his face a couple times and bared my teeth. "Don't. Next time, I'm going for an eye. Go on. Get back. Bring your man inside if you want him to live."

"Baby, we've got to go," Rabid said, stabbing his handgun tighter to the man's head. "You're gonna tell 'em to give us the keys to that old LTD over there, and you're gonna tell us what the fuck's out there. You got more men surrounding this place? Trying to block us from getting out?"

"What're you talking –"

Rabid smashed him in the head with his free hand. "Shut up, motherfucker! You know damned well what I'm saying. Whose fucking bikes are out there? Sounds like the end of the world."

It really did. The growl was getting louder, and men were yelling somewhere behind the big brick wall built around the clubhouse. Rip sniffed, choking back the blood Rabid struck from his nose. I never thought I'd live to see the big evil bastard so defeated. It caused me to smile, even through all this.

"Okay, asshole. Let's do it the hard way. We're going for a walk to see what we're dealing with, and you're coming with."

"No, no!" Rip started to struggle, kick and scream when we'd crossed half the long strip of pavement leading to the gate. "It's got to be the Mexicans. They know I fucked up. Turn back – turn the fuck back! I'd rather die with your bullet in my brain than what they do to kill a man. Stop, stop, *fucking stop!*"

My heart was pounding so hard I thought I'd pass out. The Klamath President was terrified, and that scared me. I almost put my hand on Rabid's shoulder and begged him to turn around. But he was so confident, so determined to keep going, to see what was waiting behind the wall.

Nothing ever tested my faith in him like this. But I realized just then the love and trust I had for this man was unconditional. If the men with the mystery bikes were going to kill us, we'd die together.

I held my tongue, forced myself forward step by concrete step, and prayed it would be enough.

VIII: The Longest Night (Rabid)

My heart chugged like a jet engine in my chest. I stopped being scared for myself the minute those motherfuckers took me and started beating on me. My thoughts began and ended with her, sweet Christa, my old lady now and forever.

Flash forward. I had to make sure our forever didn't end here. The jackass in my headlock couldn't stop shaking like a fucking leaf every time I jabbed the gun into his brain stem.

For once, he had good reason to puss out. If the cartel was really waiting outside the clubhouse, they'd give us all the most agonizing deaths we could imagine, worse than the sick, fucked up shit I wanted to do to Rip and Red for putting my girl here.

"Rabid, Rabid, please don't do this shit. We can talk. We can figure this shit out. We're both on the same side now – I never wanted to work with those bastards anyway –"

Jesus Christ. It didn't matter how much I fed my fists – every word this piece of shit said just made them hungrier. I wanted to throw him to the ground and pistol whip him 'til his fucking skull broke.

Instead, I settled for constricting his throat, choking off his pathetic whimpers.

"I'm only gonna say it one more time – shut your fucking mouth. We're going out there. You should've thought about becoming a goddamned baby before you turned rat and started working with the cartel, asshole."

Christa and I shared a look. Her eyes were huge, ready to pop out. It tugged at my heart, making the stone cold mask I was wearing that much harder to keep on. I felt like hell for putting her here, letting us get captured and dragged into this shit.

Something out there was seriously fucked. There were too many motorcycles, and the Mexicans never used them in those numbers. Not unless they'd decided to trade their humvees and pickups for Harleys.

I motioned to Christa with my head, told her to stay behind the wall. We were parallel with the gate now, and I took several steps toward it, stopping just short of putting myself in front of the bars.

"Who the fuck's out there!" I growled. "Show yourselves! I've got this fucking pussy Prez and I'll put a bullet right through his brain if you don't –"

"You'll do no such thing. Not yet." A familiar voice. Blackjack stepped in front of the gate with Asphalt and Roman at his side.

Holy fucking shit.

My hand shook so hard I nearly put that bullet in Rip's

head anyway. Blackjack kept coming 'til we were face to face. He looked me up and down. The boys next to him had their rifles trained at the fuckheads behind us, an extra sight for sore eyes.

"Glad to see you're still in one piece, son. Tell them to open the fucking gate, or we'll do it ourselves." His eyes fell to the asshole bleeding and crying in my arms. "Jesus. Have some respect for yourself, Rip. I'll make it quicker and cleaner than the cartel."

I shoved the gun into his temple 'til he squealed. Shit, if this kept up, I'd work my way through his skull long before a bullet reached there. "You heard the man," I snarled. "Tell your fucks to open sesame."

"Open the – ow! – open the goddamned gate!" Rip barked.

The men behind us hesitated. A large guy with a mustache nodded, and then walked back into the garage. About five seconds later, there was a whirring noise, and the gate started to slide open.

Fuck, my brothers were a sight for sore eyes. Brass flashed me a salute on his way in. I didn't dare let up the death grip I had on the Klamath Prez, but I looked at Christa, watching the relief flood her eyes.

We'd survived. We were gonna be all right. If any of these jackasses were gonna try anything, they'd do it right –

A gunshot rang out. I spun, my finger one little tap from pulling the trigger and putting the fuck in my grip outta his misery.

"Rabid!" Christa called my name.

I held up a palm. "Stay the fuck back, babe. Stay with the club while we sort this shit."

Beam and Stryker nodded and motioned to her, letting me know she was in good hands. Wise decision. Those boys were gonna earn their patches sooner than they thought.

I dragged his fat ass back to where my brothers were grouped.

The nasty looking one-eyed wonder lay dead in the garage, a new and fatal hole in his chest next to the one my girl had given him. Amazing that Marrow tried to do something stupid with his guts torn up. Growling, Roman pointed the rifle at the small gaggle of Klamath boys, his lips peeled back.

"Anybody else wanna try to rush our Prez? You'll get some of this."

There was a soft, feminine murmur. Red staggered through the doorway, her hand still over her busted mouth, looking at the dead man on the floor.

Fuck. She was next on the list as soon as Blackjack gave the word about Rip's fate. No fucking way would that bitch walk outta here alive for what she'd done.

I never liked killing women – much less one I'd fucked – but I'd do it to protect my club and my old lady. The cunt's jealousy put us here, and soon it would put her into a shallow grave.

"Prez?" I looked at Blackjack.

Everybody was quiet. He stepped forward, marching

right up to the big Klamath boy with the mustache. He flinched when the Prez was close, one hand poised over the weapon he had in his pocket.

"Keep that thing in your pants, and you're in charge now, boy." Blackjack's cold eyes watched as the man's mustache twitched. Slowly, he lowered his hand away from his pocket. "What's your name?"

"Blow."

Several guys snorted. Blackjack just shook his head.

"You fucks sure do know how to pick 'em. All right, Blow, let's play truth or dare. Tell me the truth, and I'll give your Prez a nice, clean shot to the head. You guys get to walk away alive if there's no evidence you followed your leader off the cliff, working with the Mexicans. You'll keep your patches long as you behave yourselves, and some help from the Portland crew will make sure you do."

Blackjack reached by his belt and pulled out his switchblade, brandishing it in one hand. "You dare me by doing anything stupid – any of you – and I'll have Roman gun you all down when I give the signal for my boy Rabid to finish this shit."

Blow shrugged. "You're the boss."

"You fucking rat!" Rip spat. My signal to squeeze his throat for the hundredth time.

Christ. How many times was I gonna choke and pistol whip this fucker before the Prez let me shoot him? Red took the opportunity to scamper back inside, away from the pow-wow going on out here. Didn't fucking matter. I'd be coming for her skank ass soon enough.

"We heard it all behind the gate. Is it true? Your asshole Prez been working with the cartel? I already know, but I need to hear it from the horse's mouth." Blackjack was judge, jury, and executioner right then.

"Yeah. None of us liked it." Blow looked at his dead brother, Marrow, on the ground. "Uh, none of us who are still breathing, anyway. It was Rip's idea. He couldn't handle the way you started doing shit after Fang died. And when Ed didn't come home, it set him off. He told the Mexicans they could operate, kill, and deal in our territory as long as they left us alone."

"Shit. You sure we can't waste all these fucking pricks, Prez?" Roman growled, pumping the gun in his hands.

"Not as long as these boys are cooperating. I'll be the judge of that." Blackjack nodded, walked toward Blow, close enough to make him step back. Our Prez looked over all the whacked out looking Klamath men. "You've all got a chance to start over clean. This man here told me the truth without blowing smoke up my ass. I expect everybody standing here to do the same. We'll hang around long enough to do some background checks, some interviews, just to make sure everybody's story checks out. But as far as I'm concerned, I've heard all I need to today."

My hand tightened on the gun. Blackjack looked at me. "Rabid. It's time."

"No, no, fuck, no!" I kneed Rip in the ass and pushed him to the floor, my gun to the back of his head. "This is fucking crazy, Blackjack, a big mistake. Just let me –"

I pulled the trigger. No use in letting that fuck take up

any more precious air breathing. Blow and several Klamath guys winced as the Prez fell, dead by his own gun.

Well, mine now. I'd be keeping it as a trophy, one more kill for the club, one more payment for laying down justice over chaos.

Blow looked relieved. Nobody wearing our patch would dare turn our backs on any of these fuckers, but maybe in time they could be trusted after all.

"Back against the wall. Everybody!" Roman barked, herding them into the corner.

Blackjack nodded at me, satisfied. "Make sure the body gets burned. Take his patches before you do. We'll pull off what's ours for the club. Hope to hell this is one of the last guys we'll be killing with the bear on his back."

Nodding, I tucked the gun into my empty holster. I was ready to take off and hug my girl for the first time since they'd taken us. There was just one thing left.

"Prez, wait. What about the bitch inside?"

Blackjack turned. I let him see all the fury and death swirling in my eyes, everything I wanted to unleash on that cunt for what she'd done to Christa and the club.

"She's all yours." He looked behind me. "Brass, help your brother make sure she gets out of the clubhouse, wrapped up tight. Last thing we need today are more crazy bitches running around. Don't let her out of your sights alive."

I nodded, looking past him to Christa. She was hanging with the prospects and sipping a bottle of water.

Fuck, it was good to see her safe. Prez made the right call. He always did, and so did I.

"How the fuck did you find us?" I asked Brass, heading into their clubhouse.

He grinned. "Had a couple prospects add your hotel to their patrol. I know it's easy to overlook shit when you're drunk on love. I did the same when I was claiming Missy. You're damned lucky they caught those fuckers leaving the lot, right after we got off the phone. Not so lucky they were too outnumbered to stop 'em."

"Yeah, well, luck's shaping up on our side after all. Maybe this shit's for the best. Close fucking call, though. I thought we were fucked before you guys pulled up."

"Later than I liked, yeah." He ripped open a cabinet behind the bar. Empty. "Fuck, where is that bitch? Never expected one of our own sluts would turn rat."

"Me neither." I tore through someone's room, ripping open the closet and coughing when a bunch of a stale weed came tumbling out.

Shit. I was getting pissed, desperate to drag that bitch outta her nest.

Brass hung back, going through shit in the main living area while I hit the back. I walked past the room where they'd been holding us. Little drops of our blood stained the floor beneath the dull light.

If it wasn't for the half-open door, I would've missed her. When I caught the small flash of red, too high off the ground to be blood, I wheeled around and kicked the door open.

She was on the ground like a dog. Red looked at me with wide eyes and a torn lip. Jesus. Putting her outta her misery was doing her a favor. She'd never kiss a man in any way he'd enjoy with the way my girl shredded her lips.

"Rabid, please –"

I ripped her up by the hair, jerking her on her feet and shoving her out the door. "Don't you ever fucking 'Rabid' me again. You know what's coming."

She started to cry, harder when I marched her down the hall and she ran into Brass. The VP gave her the same death stare I did, only his was all business. Mine was seriously personal.

The girl was too fucked up to sob. Goddamn, it was hard to hear that shit, but what she'd done was burned into my brain. I'd destroy her not-so-pretty face with my bare hands before I let her pathetic sobs get under my skin.

"How do you wanna do this?" Brass asked, walking next to me as I nudged her toward the door.

"Let's take the bitch to some abandoned ranch. There's plenty just past the Oregon border."

"No, brother, I mean –"

I looked at him, and his eyes widened when he saw the rage in my face. "Slow. Clean across the throat. I've already wasted enough time dealing with this fucking cunt. I can't believe I ever saw anything except pure evil."

I stopped, shook my head, listening to her whimper. "We'll throw her in a ditch and toss dirt over it before she quits breathing. Better than what she really deserves. Come on, I just want to get this shit over with."

He nodded. We were outside now, heading past Roman, Asphalt, and the rest. Blackjack hung back, a smoke hanging out of his mouth. He looked at the weeping whore, then saw us, and gave a cold nod.

Death sentence. Quick and easy – too fucking easy after what she'd done.

Whatever – at least the cunt would feel a shred of my old lady's fear and pain before we finished her off.

We headed for the van parked next to the bikes, just inside the clubhouse gates. I motioned to the prospects to get the door open. I was about to hurl the bitch inside when Christa came running up.

Fuck, what bad timing. Not that I could blame her for wanting to look into the eyes of the woman who'd tried to kill us one last time.

"Hold up!" she yelled, running toward. "Rabid, wait. You don't have to do it this way."

God damn. Maybe she wasn't here to look at the defeated slut one last time before she headed off to slaughter. I gritted my teeth, ready to let her down as gently as I could.

I had to remember she wasn't totally in my world. Not yet. And even when she was, the old ladies weren't killers who took care of business like us. They had good hearts, and sometimes they went soft.

I held up my free hand, feeling the bitch wriggling in my other one.

"Yeah, baby, actually we do. You can't talk me outta this. Don't tell me you want this treacherous bitch to walk. You know damned well what she did!"

Christa looked at me, her eyes big and pleading. "Yeah, I do."

Brass stood behind her. He shot me an understanding look. My brother understood how it was with these women, and he was ready to help me separate her if he had to so we could finish this dirty business.

"Come on, baby girl. It'll be all right." I tried to soothe her over one last time. "Just let us do our thing. We'll take a little trip and be back here to go home real –"

I stopped talking when I saw her become a blur. She hurled herself forward with a guttural, earsplitting scream like nothing I'd ever heard. She shocked the shit outta me so much the whore went tumbling out of my hands. By the time my fucking ears stopped ringing, they were both on the ground, and my girl was stabbing her in the chest, over and over.

"Piece of shit! You'll never touch my man again in this lifetime!"

My eyes went to Brass. His mouth was hanging open, same as mine.

Red squawked a couple times, making that gurgling sound I'd heard plenty of fuckers make before the reaper drags them down to hell. I put a hand on my girl's shoulder, instinctively ready to pull her away.

Then again, why the fuck should I?

I let her work the switchblade 'til the whore went

silent. Her blood streamed out around us, a murderous river, one last stain to bleach away in this miserable place.

When Red wasn't moving anymore, I put both hands on my girl's shoulders. Pulling her up, I reached into her hands, grabbed the bloody knife, and threw it on the ground.

She was shaking in my arms, covered in the dead whore's blood. I gave her a squeeze so tight she felt it in her bones.

"I'm sorry, Rabid, I'm so sorry. I couldn't let you kill her. I had to do her myself. I *had* to feel her blood and watch her go white after what she did..."

"You did good, baby. There's nothing left to explain. Shit, you even saved us some time." I paused, planting a slow, full kiss on her forehead. "We're done here. Let's go home."

We all cleaned up. Once with the Klamath boys, best as we could, and later that evening at our clubhouse. Soon as we got to Redding, we hit the shower. I undressed her and washed the blood off, taking my time in the shower.

She was tired. I expected her to clean up and crash in my old bed before we went back to her place later. I didn't expect to feel her hand wrapped around my cock.

"Baby, what the fuck you doing?"

"Shhh." She hissed it long and low, drawing her lips up to mine. This kiss went right to my guts and exploded, hot like a shot of warm whiskey after riding in the cold. "Just fuck me, Rabid. I need you inside me."

Her hold on my cock tightened. Strange and totally unexpected. Killing does strange things to a man's head, and apparently to a woman's too. Fuck if I was gonna deny her.

Hot blood throbbed in my veins, circling down to the hard, ready flesh pumping in her hand. I rolled my hips one time, fucking her fist, groaning against her neck.

The animal inside me ripped right through his cage. I was either amped up from watching our tormentors die, or maybe I was desperate to fuck her 'til I forgot all about that shit. She squealed with surprise and delight as I grabbed her, pushed her against the wall, and forced her hands above her head.

Christ, I'd never get tired of that ass. I watched it bob as the water rolled down it, rubbing my dick in the snug crevice where her cheeks met. One hand fisted her wet red hair, and the other I reached around her thigh, plunging two fingers into the hotter wetness between her legs.

She jerked against me and moaned.

So fucking wet. So fucking ready. So fucking wild.

"I love you, babe. You know that?" I hooked my head around, raking my stubble against her soft cheek, locking my tongue with hers.

Oh, fuck. My fingers slipped out, ordered away by my cock.

I had to have her right now, or I was gonna go off like a bomb right there in the shower. My body pushed against hers, flattening her to the wall, and I pushed into that hot, sweet heat. She gasped pure pleasure when I slid deep, tapping her womb, holding myself in the fiery silk I was about to own.

"I love you too," she whispered when I finally let up on her mouth.

"I know you do, baby. Now, fuck me like a lover." I drew back and thrust in, loving the way her soft curves rocked against my hard muscles. "Fuck me like this is the first fuck of the rest of your life. Fuck me like you're dying to get my come inside you. Fuck me like you know we just came back from the brink of death – because we did."

She pursed her lips, showing her teeth, and hissed as I drove inside her harder. I kept it good and slow, making her do the work, growling when her hips began to move against mine. This was a slow build like a pot starting to boil.

We'd both come our brains out – exactly what we needed to forget the shit that happened in Klamath. I growled, thrust harder, every time I thought about those fuckers we'd killed tarnishing her brain. I wanted every part of this girl to belong to me. *Me* – nothing and nobody else – even the thoughts in her own rosy red head.

Her hips were bucking back against mine more feverishly, feeding the tempo in my blood. I let out a growl, reached for her nipple, and squeezed.

I could never do the slow and sensual shit very long. The only love I'd ever know was raw, real, and deep as fuck. Didn't take a damned thing away from the pounding in my heart, that thick fiery feel of lust mixed with nothing else I'd ever felt for a girl 'til Christa.

Love. Sticky, wet, and burning.

My hips sped up. I rocked her right into the wall, gliding through her wetness, filling her completely. We fucked so hard my balls swung up and smacked her clit. She groaned, edging closer, begging me to bring her to that blazing white place where there was nothing to worry about but twitching muscles and brains licked in flames.

"Oh...oh...oh my God." I grinned, watching her fingers curl on the hand she had planted against the wall. She'd come soon, and I wanted it to be hard as fuck. "Rabid!"

Hearing my name, I thrust like a fucking maniac, pounding her into the tile, trying to hold in my load for just a few seconds longer. Wasn't easy – not with the way my woman's ass rippled each time I drove balls deep.

Her pussy constricted around me a second later. Rhythmic waves of pure, tempting velvet surrounded my dick. Calling me home, calling me to let go, hounding me to shoot my seed where it belonged.

"Fuck! Hold on, baby, I'm coming with you."

She arched her back and screamed as my load tore loose. I plowed through her convulsing pussy and held my dick deep, spitting hot fire into her, branding her from the inside-out. I swear to fuck my toes tried to curl like hers I came so hard, twitching head to toe.

Every muscle flexed, bathed in heat, pooling their energy to hurl my come into her body.

This was the alpha and the omega of fucking right here. Only thing better would be breeding her. We'd get there one day. I'd flush her pills down the toilet and fuck every drop of white I could into her womb the day she said she was ready for a kid.

For now, we fucked to heal instead, riding a wave of white lightning. My nuts were down to dry spasms when it was over, and they still didn't want to stop. I wanted to empty everything I had in this woman 'til she didn't have a single molecule that wasn't owned by me.

I drew outta her and watched my come slide down her thigh. My jealous brain forced me to cup her pussy. I thumbed her clit, pushing what was left back inside her, burying a piece of me in that perfect cunt.

"You feel better, baby?" I asked, nipping at her earlobe.

She squirmed and moaned, turning to face me. "You know I do. I was worried about you. I thought they really hurt you back there…"

I shook my head. "Fuck no. I got off light. A few sick bruises tomorrow and maybe a hairline fracture or two somewhere. I've had worse like those busted ribs I told you about in the past. I played dumb and weak so they wouldn't kill either one of us before we killed them."

She laid her head on my chest. Wasn't hard to tell the girl wasn't real interested in the fine logistics of war, and I didn't blame her one bit.

Soon, we'd step outta the shower and lay down 'til we could hold our eyes open without that exhausted burn surrounding them. Sleep sounded good.

Then I'd make sure her shit was sorted out forever, starting with a proper brand going on her.

We crashed at her place for the next three days. We slept and fucked and ordered all kinds of takeout.

I only left for a few hours, headed for the clubhouse to debrief with my brothers. The Prez was confident the boys he'd left living in Klamath would be able to give the club a clean start. Underneath the very careful eye of our own charter and Portland, of course. We'd keep those sorry fucks in line so they never defied us again.

We all sat around the table, Blackjack at the head, one hand on the bear paw serving as his gavel. "It's been a long, tough road, brothers. And we're only halfway home. We can't say we've got a clean slate 'til the cartel's been pushed back over the border where they belong, and we've got good, solid charters all the way from Redding to San Diego. This state's Grizzlies territory, dammit. Never forget it. Don't let it outta your sight 'til it's a reality again."

Everybody nodded solemnly, myself included. There were more battles to be fought. We were finally beating the Mexicans, but they had a lot of tricks up their sleeves, a lot of blood to spill before they went home quietly.

"All right. Now's the time to lay down less important business if you've got it," Blackjack growled, looking us over one-by-one.

My turn to raise my hand. Brass nodded. He knew what was coming because I'd talked to him about it before church. Blackjack looked at me and motioned with his hand.

"Let's hear it."

"Prez, you talk a lot about clean slates, and we're all behind you. You know the only long-term path for this club is building more legit shit and letting the black market shit slide. I know we can do it too. The Devils did – and friends or not, we're ten times the men those fucks are."

Brothers laughed. The MC a few states over might be our allies now, but we still got our friendly jabs in. Talking shit outlasted slinging bullets.

"That place we bought off Bear Mountain road's been in limbo for more than a month. I think it's time we put it to good use – how 'bout a full service bar with girls? We can make it our kinda bar, something everybody riding a hog up Highway Five will wanna hit to wet their whistles."

"You had me at the chicks," Asphalt growled. "I'm always up for another place to get my dick wet. Fucking in the clubhouse all the time gets old."

"Shut the fuck up, brother," Brass chimed in. "We keep our whores and tramps here. The city will yank our shit in a second if we think about letting our strippers fuck around for money. Rabid's right – it's all about making money legit. We gotta keep our noses clean to do that. They'll flash their tits and serve drinks, but nothing else."

Roman looked at me. "I like it. We'll have the manpower to keep shit in line as soon as the cartel's broken."

Blackjack shook his head. "It's a good idea, son. We'll revisit it in a few months. Right now, we need every man we can spare making sure our neighbor charters stay in line. We've got everybody else pulling double duty to keep the cartel fuckers off our backs. Managing a place like that's a full time job. Shit, we don't even have time for interviews with outsiders right now."

"What if I've already got the perfect gal in mind?"

"Gal?" Asphalt's eyes shot up and he snorted. "Oh, fuck. I see where this shit's going. You wanna put your new old lady in charge after she almost got you killed."

I gave him the evil eye, but I didn't deny it. "That's the plan. Christa's come a long way. She's done this gig once with the nasty fucks up in Klamath, and it only failed because they drove the other customers away with their shit. Think about it. If we can build some good cred with other clubs passing through for a drink, maybe we won't have to keep eyes in the back of our fucking heads all the time. We'll be able to fight anything south one hundred percent."

"It'll give us a chance to scope out anybody who wants to fuck with us before they get the drop too," Roman said.

Blackjack looked torn. Holding the bear claw, he turned it over in his hand, as if he could feel how many lives and fates had been decided by that thing.

"Fuck it. I'm going to allow this. A club gets nowhere without taking some risks. As long as everybody here around this table's in one piece, we can afford a few." The gavel came down hard. "We'll get the renovations started next week and see about the licensing shit. If all goes well, we can have it up and running by fall. Don't tell me anybody's gonna insist on a vote, because the yays clearly have it."

I looked around the room, trying to hide my shitty grin. Brass and Roman were pleased. Asphalt and old Southpaw looked ambivalent. Stryker and Beam were neutral – the smart choice for prospects still trying to earn their patch.

"Congratulations, son." The gavel hit the table again. "Tell your girl she's the proud new manager of our latest, greatest titty bar. I'll talk to her more about it in person at the party next week."

"You got it, Prez." I sat back down and Brass slapped my back, grinning ear to ear.

He was trying to reel me into the life of a settled man with an old lady like him, stable and sticky sweet. Fuck if I didn't find myself liking it. Couldn't tell if I was getting old or just too deep in this lovestruck shit.

I never thought going out for rides and drinks with our girls on the weekends would sound better than soaking myself in whiskey while railing two whores. It did.

Later that evening, we were at the tattoo parlor. The place was friendly to the club, just a few short blocks from the empty building I was dying to show her.

The needle gun hummed in the corner. I sat a few feet away, listening to that sound, trying to think about nasty and ugly shit so my dick wouldn't bust right through my pants. I knew there was no holding back the wood when I saw the final product.

It took the skinny freak inked from head to toe another half hour to finish. When it was done, he stepped aside, and Christa sat up. Her face was bright red, scared and proud all at once to show me the thing I'd been waiting for.

The dark ink hugged the spot on her low back, just above her ass, right where I'd always imagined it.

PROPERTY OF RABID, GRIZZLES MC CALIFORNIA.

A wreath of dark, tangled thorns surrounded it like an evil looking halo. They were locked together, twisted tight, same fucking thing we were gonna be tonight when this was done.

"Here it is," she whispered, sliding off the bench and walking toward me. "Hope you like –"

Didn't give her a chance to finish. I ripped her off the floor and held her high in my arms before the words were even outta her mouth. "Baby, it's fucking beautiful. It's gonna look even better when your jacket comes in next week. I want you wearing that shit all the time and nothing else."

The freak in the corner laughed. I shot him a dirty look, but I was too damned happy to think about throat punching anybody for eavesdropping. Much less the man who'd branded her for me.

My lips crashed on hers like an avalanche. I pulled her close, kissed her so fucking hard she moaned into my mouth. I considered grinding her clit through her pants right there – but not with the dude still watching us, pretending he wasn't while he cleaned up.

Fuck. Even my kinda kink had limits. Some of these tattoo artists were real *Freaks* with a capital F.

"Come on, baby. Let's take a walk while the ink dries. I got something I need to show you."

I took her by the hand and we headed out. The sun shined high and hot like a motherfucker, but it was the prettiest motherfucker I'd ever seen hanging in the sky. We covered the two blocks fast.

Didn't realize how fast I was going 'til she begged me to slow down. The hell with that. I grabbed her and threw her over my shoulder, carrying her the rest of the way while she beat on my back and laughed.

The girl's confusion only added to the sweet mischief seething in my blood when we got to the empty place. I plucked the key outta my pocket and undid the lock on the door, then walked her inside.

"Rabid? Why are we standing in an abandoned building?"

"It's gonna be your kingdom in a few months," I said, taking a wide walk around the place. "Prez gave the go ahead for renovations today. Congratulations, babe. You're about to be the manager of the club's brand new bar – the one you should've had up in Oregon."

Her jaw dropped. She clenched her hands instead of running toward me like I expected.

What the fuck?

I stepped closer, sliding a rough hand up her shoulder. "What's up? Don't you like it?"

"I do, Rabid. I really do. It's just that…I hadn't ever thought much about giving it a second shot. It's like a blow to the face. Management's a full time job too. I know that from the first time around, and this place looks a lot bigger than my little hole in the wall."

"Damned right," I growled, eyeing the high ceilings. "You're gonna make it work like a stripper doing overtime. You'll have a good budget to start too. Obviously, this place needs to be profitable someday, but the club's got plenty of money to get you off the ground. No debts and no liabilities neither without an ownership stake. Not right away, anyway."

She sniffed, fighting tears. Finally, her soft hands went around me, hugged me tight.

There went my cock again. That unruly fucker just wouldn't lay down when she was wrapped around me, even when it was supposed to be all tender and sweet. I'd fuck my dick stupid later for its shit.

"I want to do this," she said, beaming her bright green eyes into mine. "But I also want to keep tutoring."

Shit. I hadn't thought about that.

"Oh. Fuck. I thought you were just doing that shit to make quick coin with Ed breathing down your neck."

Christa shook her pretty head. "No. I really like the kids I'm working with. I'm giving something back, helping them make sure they avoid the mistakes I made when I was young."

I slapped her ass. "You still are. Young enough to do whatever the fuck you want. Listen, we can work something out. I'll make sure the Prez gets somebody in as backup too for the times you want to take off and teach."

Her face softened. Then she laughed, and I was in high heaven.

"Really? It's that easy?"

"Yeah, it is. Whatever I say goes. You ought to know by now I always get my way. Doesn't matter how deep I gotta dive to get there. Long as you're my old lady, you're getting your way too. Whatever the fuck you want." The last sentence was pure thunder, shaking my bones because I damned well meant it.

"God, I love you!" she jumped right into my arms for the second time that day.

We kissed and kissed for the next ten minutes, long as I could take without throwing her down on the gutted floor and fucking her right there. I didn't even give a shit about the pedestrians gawking at us through the windows as they walked by.

They understood the Grizzlies MC owned this town. The club didn't keep a secret, and neither did I. When my lips were on hers, the whole world realized who owned this woman 'til he drew his last breath.

IX: Learning To Accept (Christa)

Blood was the price I paid for the most perfect week of my life. I couldn't wait to start getting set up for the bar in the autumn. No, scratch that.

I could barely wait for anything these days. Living my life safe and free, being his old lady, tutoring the kids. The world was so bright and new it was almost overwhelming. I could've managed it easier, if only I could get a good night's sleep.

But Rabid wasn't interested in that. And every time he put his hands and lips on me, neither was I.

We woke up in bed together one morning, about a week after I'd gotten branded and he showed me the new bar site.

I wrapped my hand around his cock as he pressed his lips to mine, a good morning kiss I'd never forget. Only way I wanted to wake up for the rest of my life.

One, two, three kisses, and his fingers were grabbing at my hair. He took hold and worked my face to his just like he wanted. His tongue darted in and out, deep and possessive, rhythmic as the pulse tap dancing in my blood.

Jesus Christ. How was it possible to want a man so much when you'd had him practically every night?

My body didn't have any answers. The flesh was insatiable, and it hummed when his skin was on mine. Wet heat flooded my core; hungry, slick emptiness begging to be filled.

"That's how you wake me up, babe?" he growled with a smile. "Careful. You're gonna get a couple loads in this pussy before you've even had your morning coffee."

"Fuck the coffee." He laughed. I was dead serious, giving his dick a squeeze. "You know what I want."

His tattoos and hard muscles were sexy as ever. But there was something extra adorable about him when we first woke up. I ran my hand through his messy crop of dark brown hair, inhaling his scent. Pure masculine need surrounded me, and I wasn't just talking about the hands on my ass.

Rabid was everywhere. His scent soaked into the sheets, wafted off his skin, invaded me with the same wondrous curiosity as everything else about him.

He pushed one hand between my thighs, spread them apart, guiding them toward his waiting cock. He was hard in seconds, hot steel throbbing in my hand.

The twitch in his dark eyes ordered me to ride his cock.

Not so fast. I resisted. I wanted to have some fun first.

I slipped out of his groggy grasp and led my mouth to my fist. Hearing the surprised groan rumbling in his throat when I drew his swollen tip past my lips sent more tense heat purring through my core.

Sucking him off was a total joy. I went deep, went hard, pressing my tongue tight to the crown lining his head. In just weeks, I'd learned his soft spots, and one day I'd make him come wrapped around my tongue.

His abs stiffened underneath my resting hand. I reached down and played with his balls, marveling as they drew tighter and harder, ready to burst at the seams.

Fuck. For this man, I'd be filthy.

I'd fuck him, suck him, take his come anywhere. I was his old lady now, damn it. And I knew enough to realize a good old lady had all the skills of a whore and the love of an angel to keep her man satisfied. I wanted to work his body until he couldn't think, rupturing inside me, fused to any opening he chose.

My cheeks were on fire as I bobbed my head. Ground zero for the fire racing down my body, a full body lick charged with lust, eradicating everything except the wanton need to have him inside me, to feel his dick turn to granite before it exploded.

I was so focused on pleasing his cock with my mouth that I didn't realize how lazily I'd left my legs laying near his head. Growling, he jerked my head up by the hair, then picked my legs up and threw them over his shoulders.

"Rabid, this is supposed to be all for you right –"

"Fuck that shit. I know it is, baby. You wanna work it like I want? Then you'll come 'til your eyes roll white with my dick in your mouth. Keep sucking while I hold your thighs open."

There was no asking. No compromise. Rabid gave the

commands that made me wet, and I never said no, even when part of me wanted to.

I realized how stupid 'no' sounded the instant his tongue curled inside me.

Oh, God. Oh, fuck. Oh, no.

I tried to match his pace. I sucked his dick harder, pumping the base with my hand, nudging his balls in my other palm. He growled into my pussy like a starving lover, hungry to possess me, crazy to make me come.

And the feral need in my own body embraced his licks. After a minute, it was twice as hard to focus on his dick. He was miles ahead of me in multi-tasking.

I went numb every time he growled his pleasure, sucking my clit into his mouth. He held it there in rapture, a flicking, nibbling, wavering pleasure that made me see red.

Fuck. *No!*

I wanted to make him come so bad. I wanted to fight through the pleasure, show him I had full control even with what he was doing to my body. But the pleasure was too intense. My thighs began shaking in his rough hands, and my pussy tensed up, giving the sharp tingle that let me know climax was imminent.

Rabid knew it too. He squeezed my thighs harder, so rough it almost hurt, furiously swiping his tongue across my clit. His teeth pinched harder, and I was over the edge before I knew what hit me.

I screamed with my mouth half filled with his cock. My lips tightened into a tight ring, and his hips thrust, fucking my lips while I lost my mind.

The convulsions made me see stars. For a second, I saw what a total slut I'd become in this bed with him, and I didn't regret it for a single second. Even in sex, he challenged me, and I looked forward to a lifetime together learning to please him better than he did me.

He sucked and lapped at my pussy until my ass went soft. I had to take his cock out for precious air, panting and beaten, feeling the need for more between my legs.

"Flip over, baby." Rabid smacked my ass, helping me reposition with his hands. "Fucking shit. You almost had me. Nearly lost this nut in your mouth while you were coming."

"Yeah?" My heart swelled with pride. Maybe I was getting better at this than I thought. "There's always next time. You'd better get in and hold on tight. My pussy's going to milk every drop out of your balls."

He bared his teeth. My signal to grab his dick and help guide it into me. I straddled him, trying not to give away how bad I still needed it as his length filled me. Jesus, I always forgot how big he was until he was up in me, curling and stretching my soft wet walls apart.

Rabid grabbed my ass. The sucking counted as our foreplay. He showed me what he was after in every fierce thud of his hips against mine. The bed rocked madly beneath us, pitching and whining with his thrusts.

I tried to keep up with the frantic pace. Thankfully, his hands were there to move me along, faster and smoother than anything I could've done myself. I glided over him, riding fast and hard, clenching my teeth every time my clit dragged against his pubic bone.

His hands dug into my ass cheeks. It should've hurt, but the pleasure overwhelmed everything, tuning my senses to love in every sensation he shot through me.

"Ah, fuck. Come the fuck on, baby girl. I wanna see you sweat."

He fucked harder. Faster. Sweat steamed on my skin, and so did a bright red blush. It was like feeling my whole body gradually submerge into a hot, steamy pool of pleasure. The impulse came slow, even though he was fucking me frantically, shaking my entire body with his rattling hips.

A minute later, I was bouncing on his cock. He shoved me up and down, back and forth, side to side like an honest-to-God ragdoll built for jerking off his dick.

He took his pleasure rough, without apology, and my pussy loved every second of it.

I tried to hold back as long as I could. When I closed my eyes there was nothing but the *thud-thud-thud* of the headboard slapping the wall behind us, his jagged breaths, my own heartbeat slowly bleeding into my ears.

Then the explosion came.

Raw heat blossomed inside me, a dozen points at once, coalescing around the inferno in my womb. My pussy clenched tight around his dick and convulsed. I lost it. He was still jerking my hips around like he owned them, grinding my clit on his short, rough hair, digging so deep and sharp inside me that I thought he'd rip me in two.

Rabid grunted, snarled, and added his masculine fury to mine a second later. Hot seed shot inside me, pouring more molten goodness into the foundry my body had become, wrecked on this lust.

We rocked. We panted. We came so hard I almost went blind.

You can laugh at me wilting on his dick, coming completely undone, unhinged, unchained. I would've done the same thing if anyone else told me about this sex.

Difference is, I *lived* it.

I came on his dick so hard it defied belief. Fireworks exploded in my head and in my pussy too, spreading heat and shrapnel to every nerve, every inch of me. Everything had to burn fused to this man before I could finally settle down.

His dick was still pulsing as I started to come down. Low, rhythmic growls slurred out his lips, the primal sound a man makes when he's fully mated to his woman.

He slipped out reluctantly. I rolled, crashed back on the bed, pulling my phone off the nightstand. I checked the time and almost did a flip.

"Shit! We've got to get going, Rabid. We're going to be late!"

"Aw, baby, are you fucking with me? You know I can't get enough of you in the morning…" His words melted in a growl.

He was on top of me again, kissing and pawing at me, rabid and wild as his name. I laughed and batted him away. I used the bear on his chest as a target and slapped it hard with my palms.

"Come on. We need to run through the shower and gulp some coffee. Dad's lost his sense of time, but the nursing home sure hasn't for Sunday visiting hours."

Snarling, Rabid pulled himself away. "Fuck. All right."

He slid off the bed and stuck a hand out to help me. I caught a dangerous glimpse of his strong ass before he turned. God, I think I loved that ass more than he loved mine.

"We'll take our shower together," he growled, dragging me into the bathroom. "We'll be on time. I'm fucking you again – fast and hard. Don't keep my dick waiting."

I shook my head. He was crude and insatiable, but damn it, he made me smile. Soon, the water was running, bathing us the same way it did on the night we narrowly escaped our deaths. His dick jerked taut against my belly, ready to go less than five minutes after we'd finished in bed.

"You're such an animal!" He reinforced what I said with a growl, flipping me over and pinning me to the wall.

My eyes sizzled with mad heat as he pushed into me. "Fucking right, babe. You know I gotta do something to blow some steam before I meet the old man who raised you."

We rode like hell through town. The sex set us back a few minutes longer than I would've liked. Not that it wasn't totally worth it.

So was taking this furious ride on Rabid's bike. My

hands pinched tight to him as he weaved around corners, blowing through the green lights before they showed a hint of yellow. To anyone who didn't know him, it would've looked like showing off, but I'd been around him long enough to know it was all natural.

This was my man, shamelessly brash down to his fingertips.

We pulled up to the nursing home with a couple minutes to spare, a little more than an hour before the visitor's cutoff. Knots pulled at my stomach, anxious and melancholy. I'd waited for this day since I was a little girl, the day I'd introduce my dad to the man I'd fallen in love with.

I just wished he still had the mental capacity to understand it. Whatever. Wishes weren't in the cards. The best I could hope for was a flash of lucidity, just enough to talk to us and take us in. Maybe on some level, he'd understand what was happening, even if it came later when I wasn't there to see it flash in his eyes.

"You need a minute, baby?" Rabid asked, noticing the slowness in my step when we got to the door.

"No, I'll be fine. This was my idea." I gave him a quick peck on the cheek. "I need this, and I'm glad you're here. It means a lot to me."

He grinned. "Family's everything. I'm down with meeting your daddy today. It's a lot easier with him in town than driving you up to Washington to meet my ma. Don't worry. That day's gonna come too."

The sincerity in his voice reminded me he really

wanted the whole package. This old lady thing was like being engaged in an outlaw biker's world.

My new tattoo burned, our new lives inscribed in ink. There was no looking back with my hand in his.

Just forward, forward.

I knocked on the door to dad's room – an old habit that didn't really matter here. He rarely answered.

He was at his spot by the window, gazing out. Dad didn't turn his head until I put my hand on his shoulder. I sighed, knowing it wasn't a good sign for a lucid day.

"You again, baby?" He looked, surprised to see me. "Weren't you by for breakfast an hour ago?"

I shook my head. "No, dad. That was someone else. I'm here to introduce you to someone today."

He nodded, let me help him turn his wheelchair. Rabid gave a respectful nod when he saw my dad for the first time. The old man's eyes went wide.

Suddenly, he reached for my hand, gave it a tighter squeeze than anything I'd felt in years. "Fuck me backwards. You've finally decided to come out of your shell! That's cause for…celebration. Yeah, come on. Wheel me the hell out of here."

I started to wheel him forward, but he signaled me to stop when we were next to the door with Rabid. "What's the boy's name?"

"Charlie, sir." Rabid stuck his hand out. "Road name's Rabid."

"Jim. They used to call me Strum back when I could ride."

They shook hands. Rabid's eyes widened, like he was surprised at the strength in the grip. For some stupid reason, that made me smile.

We all headed for the cafeteria, a little more room for us to sit down and chat. I got us all some coffee while dad fixed himself at the table. When I came back, the two men were talking about bikes, some stuff I didn't quite understand about how the old hogs were different.

"Grizzlies, huh?" Dad reached out and thumbed the small patch on the left flap of Rabid's cut. "I knew a few of those. The club was good in the old days, back before that fucker Fang started using 'em to run the nasty stuff."

"Fang's gone," Rabid said. "The club's cleaning up its act. I'm proud to say I'm a part of that. You don't need to worry about this patch being anywhere around your daughter, Strum."

Dad's eyes narrowed. "Daughter? Huh, I had a funny feeling she'd end up heading back to her roots. I tried to send her out into the world on a different path. But you know they say – you can't pick the way your kids grow up. You can only shape them while they do."

My heart stuck in my throat. I didn't dare hope he recognized me, but I reached out and gave his hand a squeeze just the same. "You shaped me just fine, dad. I wouldn't be here with this wonderful man if it were any other way."

Dad looked at me. Like, stopped, put the whole world on pause, and *really* looked.

"You did well for yourself, baby, if this boy's as honest

as he looks. Take care of him. Keep him from getting into the crazy shit and you'll have a love that would make your mama proud."

I gasped. Almost fell completely out of my chair. No kidding.

Rabid put his hand on my shoulder and looked at the old man. "My old lady's already doing a fine job making everybody proud. Mostly me. You raised a keeper, buddy. I'm gonna make sure she stays happy and safe."

"Damned right, she will." He gave Rabid a severe look. "You give her the love I can't. My mind's too far gone. The days like this are getting less and less…you got no idea how long I've been waiting for this. I've been waiting to see my girl with somebody strong, somebody she can trust…"

He trailed off. The bright spark shining in his eyes like beautiful stars slowly faded. When dad looked at me again, it was the vacant stare that always stabbed me in the heart.

I looked at Rabid, heading off the painful transformation, grateful for the moment, however brief.

"You did it, Charlie. He hasn't addressed me as his daughter since…" I couldn't even remember.

I leaned over and gave him a quick kiss. Dad asked me about another razor. I laughed and apologized, told him I still owed him a few. I'd get it taken care of before next week.

After another half hour, we were wheeling him to his room. I tried to hold in the tears.

Dad was right about one thing – there wouldn't be too

many days left where he'd recognize me as a human being standing in front of him, much less his daughter. One black day would come where he wouldn't be breathing.

I'd always dreaded it before, a bitter lining to the rare beautiful days like today. Before Rabid, there was nothing but a gaping void when I imagined any future without my father.

Today, for the first time ever, I saw that one was possible. And that meant even more to me than wearing his name on my skin and my shoulders. When dad was safely back in his room and we were ready to get on his bike, I stopped him, threw my arms around him, and pulled him close.

I managed to land a long, warm kiss on his lips without either of us turning into sex crazed maniacs. Rabid helped me onto his bike, his eyes wide, searching.

"What was that for, baby?"

"For being my rock. I know how sappy it sounds, but it's true." I blushed. It was so hard to say these kinds of things, but it was getting easier with him. "You bring out the best in everybody, Rabid. You bring out the best in *me*."

He handed me my helmet with a new grin on his face. "Babe, I think you're wrong about one thing. You haven't even imagined the best. Not yet. We've got a little while longer 'til my ring's on your finger and you've got my kids in your arms. But damn, you'd better believe I'm gonna work like a fucking dog bringing you all that and more. You're loving what I've brought out now? Just wait."

He didn't say another word as he climbed on and started the engine. Tears rolled down my scarred cheeks, but they slid right off the stupid wide smile I was wearing.

I only hoped I could make my old man half as happy as all the incredible promises he'd made. I had my work cut out for me because I knew he'd deliver.

X: End of the Line (Rabid)

The big bash at the clubhouse was perfect timing. When I came by to pick up Christa, my dick nearly punched me in the chin. Her new jacket looked fucking beautiful.

It was the first time I'd seen her wear it. I stopped her next to the curb, told her to turn around.

PROPERTY OF RABID was etched on the back perfectly, a brand matching what she already had on her skin. The girl was a proper old lady now, and she was mine – *all mine.*

Christ.

"Fuck, you're beautiful. You sure you don't wanna skip the hog roast and hop in bed right now?"

She grinned and folded her arms. "Rabid – come on. You know your friends are waiting."

Damn it. She was as right as she was fucking hot. I helped tuck the helmet on her head and sat her sweet ass behind me. I'd have to settle for a quick blow in my old room at the clubhouse if I got her drunk enough.

Her little hands clung tight to me as we rode. It was our first time visiting the clubhouse as a real couple, and my last as a man living there. The deposit I'd put down on renovating the old family ranch was going through next week.

It was the place I'd brought her when we had our first serious talk, our first kiss. Grandpa gave it up years ago before he died, and ma didn't have any interest in all that work. I liked to visit the place when I needed to think, really sort shit out.

Never expected it'd help me sort out my whole damned future by landing me this girl. I couldn't wait to fucking surprise her when it was all fixed up. It was just a matter of days 'til we had ourselves a quiet, private place to settle down and figure out the rest of our lives.

The work was the hard part, but it was mostly being done by the crew I'd hired. My shit would be easy to move out, seeing how I'd never had much time for a buncha shit except my bike and a few trinkets.

Christa's move later in the month would be tougher, but I was game. Anything to get her in my bed permanently. Not to mention a nice big place where she could set up a room for her tutoring gig – assuming we were gonna hold off a few more years on starting a family.

Roaring down the road, I couldn't stop thinking about it. The fire in my blood said this girl was gonna have a ring on her finger by the end of the year. And when that happened, I was planting my seed deep, unprotected, carving out a future and claiming her the last and greatest way I could.

She leaned in and kissed me in the cheek when we

rolled into the garage. "Try to be good. You know I'll put out later. I just want to have a little fun first."

I shrugged, trying to tame the lust rippling in my blood. The girl had a point. Straining dick aside, it was a special night for the club, and that made it a special night for me too.

We'd been through some serious shit the last few months. This was our chance to cut loose and fuck around like brothers, temporarily free from worrying about whose machete might be swinging at our necks.

The music was thumping something fierce by the time we got inside. Classic rock blasted out the new speaker system Brass had installed, throbbing so loud you couldn't have heard an engine snort inside the place.

Hang arounds, whores, and brothers stood around drinking in big groups. I pulled my girl forward, giving the evil eye to any of the fuckers who tasted her with their looks before they saw the brand on her back. They wouldn't have tried shit, especially because I was a full patch member, but my psycho jealousy didn't know any better. When they caught what either of us had on our leather, they slunk away like dogs with their tails between their legs.

I'd been around guys in the past who shared their girls. I couldn't imagine that shit no matter how hard I tried. It was bad enough thinking about putting my dick in anything less perfect than her – but giving this pussy to another man?

Fuck. That.

Gray haired Southpaw served us some beers with Jack generously splashed into the bottles. I laughed when Christa took her first swig and coughed. The chick had been away from this shit for too long.

"What's wrong, baby? You need something sweeter, maybe a little weaker?"

Her brow furrowed. "Nope. Just getting my taste buds used to this life again."

"Come on. I saw the way you slammed it at the resort. Lemme see you channel that shit again."

She nodded, gave me a mischievous wink. I watched her tip the bottle straight up. She guzzled the whole fucking thing almost as fast as one of the guys. Hmmm, maybe it wouldn't take much to get her back in the lifestyle after all.

"Impressive. You'd better slow the fuck down, babe. The night's young, and I've got a couple things to do with my brothers before they're too busy getting their dicks wet."

"Christa! Oh my God! You're finally wearing his patch!"

As if on cue, Missy came strutting over, Brass at her side. She flicked her chestnut hair over her jacket and gave my girl a sloppy hug, laughing the entire time. Brass and I grinned. The two girls squealed, flapping their hands and swaying like sisters who hadn't seen each other for years.

The sweetest girls went to pieces at these things when they got some liquor in their bellies and a little excitement. We knew we'd both have to keep an eye on our chicks to keep 'em in line. These club gatherings were about more now than slamming as much Jack as we could into our guts and dragging the closest whore off to our rooms to fuck.

"You ready for that rematch with Asphalt, brother? I saw him an hour ago. He's already pretty sauced. I think you'll have the edge this time."

"Good. I'll beat his ass if he fucks up and puts his dart through the club standard this time."

Brass laughed. "Whatever, dude. Just make sure neither Blackjack or me see that shit."

He waved his hand and our prospect, Stryker, came over to meet us.

"Make sure our girls stay safe and don't trip on anybody's dicks," the Veep growled. "I've seen guys at these things who are dumb enough to try to get their hands on a brother's old lady. You let us know right away if it's going that way so we can beat the fucker blind."

Stryker nodded and took off, running after the two gabbing old ladies. My blood surged, same as Brass', judging by the look in his eyes. Our girls could be trusted, but some of the other fucks who attended these giant club parties couldn't. And if anybody laid a finger on our women, we'd be in a fucking race to break the asshole's nose.

"Come on. We'll let 'em have their fun. It's been a rough few weeks. Everybody needs to blow off some steam." Wise words from my closest brother.

We headed for the dart board, where Asphalt was

already waiting, his bald head flecked with sweat from the Jack burning in his veins. "Fucking finally. I've been waiting for you guys."

Brass went to retrieve the darts. When he returned, Asphalt hiccuped. We both laughed. This was gonna be easier than I thought.

Or maybe not.

The first few tosses had us about equal. The digital score counter always tried to fade the fuck out while it was counting, so I walked over and gave the machine a good whack.

When I came back to my spot, Blackjack was lined up next to the wall, a drink in his hand, watching us. Oh, fuck.

Having the Prez playing spectator wasn't in the plans. Why couldn't he just skip off to the shadows? Did this guy ever fuck? Whores were everywhere tonight, ready to hop on any cock attached to a full Grizzlies patch – not that I could blame anyone for laying off the whores after what happened with Red.

The heat was on. Asphalt felt it too. He fucked up his next two throws, swore as I took the lead. I was just a couple good hits away from finishing his ass off.

I didn't even realize the crowd was growing larger 'til the end. When we were down to the final stretch, Missy and Christa were next to Brass, looking on and laughing with excitement in their eyes.

"Asphalt! Asphalt!" a couple guys screamed, local loudmouths trying to suck up to get their prospect patches faster.

The girls started to cheer me on. I was about to throw my dart when I paused and looked at the big guy standing in the corner. Roman kept his distance from everybody, a big pool cue in his hand like a spear. He gave me a silent, dark nod.

Fuckin' fancy that. Never thought I'd see the sleeping volcano of a man giving me his endorsement.

By my last throw, I was starting to match Asphalt's drunkenness with the Jack fogging up my brain. But something magic was in the air that night. I jerked forward, watched it cruise like a missile toward the very center. Perfect strike.

Growling, Asphalt punched the machine as it struggled to display the score. It came back a perfect zero.

Christa squealed and collided with me. Brothers circled, slapping me on the back. I couldn't say no to smashing my lips on hers. I smelled and tasted pure whiskey. Fucking shit, how much had my girl had?

Still, it was good to see her come unraveled. My hands roamed her back, wishing they could rip everything off except her new leather jacket.

Whatever, we'd be fucking later with nothing but her brand draped around her. Guaranteed.

I let go of her and spun. Came face to face with Asphalt, looking like a pissed off bull. I thought the crazy asshole was going to hit me for a second, but his hand shot out instead.

"Good game, brother."

I took it, gave him a ferocious squeeze. "You know it, bro."

Behind him, Blackjack was smiling. The old man might be a savage SOB, but he obviously enjoyed the times when we solved shit with brotherly handshakes rather than bloody fists.

Next thing I knew, Christa was tugging on me, dragging me through the crowd. We grabbed some food and more drinks. We hit the tables, carving out a little place for ourselves. Just in time for the real rowdy shit to start.

Christa's eyes popped out when she saw the whores coming in a big conga line, wearing the skimpiest shit this side of nothing over their tits and pussies. They found brothers, prospects, and local hang arounds, sometimes three girls to one man.

Mouths sucked. Tongues whirled. Hands grabbed asses everywhere.

It didn't do shit for my dick 'til I looked at the woman in front of me. Brass must've had a similar reaction, because him and Missy were behind her, laughing and sharing a bottle.

"Do you ever miss those days, Rabid?" Christa asked.

"Fuck no. Not since I got you. You really think I haven't learned my lesson about who I'd better sink my dick into after a bitch I used to fuck tried to kill us?"

She laughed and shook her head. "Well, if you ever start to feel nostalgic, you need to let me know…"

"Baby, you can be my slut any time. That's part of

being my old lady. Long as I've got that pussy on demand, any way I want it, leaving you absolutely fucking breathless, we're gold."

Fuck, my dick was about to pop. I flexed my fists on the table, then reached for her hand. She was so warm, so hot with all that whiskey in her veins. My cock jerked, wondering if her pussy would feel that much hotter wrapped around me tonight.

Shit, shit. I wanted to drink more to numb the lust building in my blood, but that would mean we'd have to wait longer to blow this place. The fun was mostly over with all the brothers about to become real scarce, disappearing to a quiet corners with their girls or their bunk rooms.

"Come the fuck here." I walked over to the table and grabbed Christa off her chair, sat her on my lap, one hand squeezing her thigh the way I used to do to my whores.

We kissed. Long. Hard. Deep.

Yeah, there was no doubt or longing about the past. *This* was right. This made me feel better than anything else I'd enjoyed in my life.

A few tables over, Brass and his old lady were getting down to it too. Missy suppressed a moan. I saw his hand slide down her pants. I had to look away – seeing that kinda shit fed the beast inside me, and he was already on a short chain.

"We gotta walk, baby. Right now. Or else I'm gonna rip your pants off and fuck you on this table."

Shit! Something about my warning only made her kiss

me harder. Tease. I had to push her away and keep a gap between us as we got up and walked. Otherwise, I'd have done exactly what I threatened, and I wouldn't have given a shit who the fuck saw it.

We walked through the bacchanal as the clubhouse got crazier. Had to step over half naked, totally drunk couples rolling on the floor in a few places. Drunk or not, the guys who weren't full patch brothers cleared the way when they saw me coming through with my bottom rocker.

"Rabid? Are we ready yet?" I smiled at her purring the question into my ear. The girl was cute as fuck when she was drunk, but damn if I'd put too much away without realizing it.

"Another hour or two, babe. I'm not risking us on my bike 'til I shake this shit outta my system." We took the long route back by the bar. I downed some water and passed her a cup too. "Drink it, or you're gonna feel like shit tomorrow."

She giggled. I watched her suck long sips down her throat, and nodded when she did. Good.

We headed for the game room, a quiet place where I figured we could cool our heels 'til I was good to drive – assuming nobody else was in there fucking. I opened the door and heard a slap like a gunshot.

Roman was the only man in there, standing next to the pool table, watching the balls he'd smacked rolling toward their slots. He never even looked at me.

I guided Christa over to a chair and told her to chill. Maybe she'd be over the giggle phase by the time we were ready to go. Last thing I needed was her falling all over the place without me to hold her up.

"Thanks for your support during the dart game, bro." I slapped Roman on the back.

The giant stiffened, stood up tall, and looked me right in the eye. "Better you than Asphalt."

Nice.

Why the fuck did this guy set everybody on edge? I seriously wondered what would ever knock the chip off his bison shoulders.

"Hey, Roman," I said, making sure to keep my distance with the table between us. "I know about the blonde. Is she the reason you're not out there taking shots and having Twinkie suck you off?"

The pool cue whipped up. He slapped the blunt end on the floor and gave me another dead-eyed stare. "That's nobody's business, brother. Not even mine. I'm sorry you were the only one who had to sneak a peek at that fucking sideshow. Told you already – we're nothing."

Right. Where the fuck have I heard that before?

I looked at Christa in the corner. She was struggling so hard to hold her head up without laughing or falling asleep. I'd driven all the resistance outta her, and the love bug embedded itself underneath our skin, even when it looked like it was a million miles away. I had a crazy feeling Roman and the mystery chick were next on the list.

"If you say so, bro. If you decide to change your mind, I'm here for you. Just shout any time you need a favor. I owe you one." His eyes were back on the table. He didn't say anything. "I'm not talking about the darts neither. You saved my ass and helped whip me in line. I fucking hated your ass at the time, but now I appreciate it. Without you, I might not have an old lady at all."

He grunted, all I'd get from him acknowledging I'd said a damned thing. I shrugged and started to walk, leaving him to his solitary, moody bullshit.

There was an old deer hunter arcade ame in the corner. I was still feeling the fucked up buzz in my veins, and I sure as shit wanted to give the bastard at the pool table his space. I grabbed Christa and walked her over. Drew out a few quarters and pushed the plastic rifle into her hands.

"Come on, baby. Let's shoot some fucking animals."

We played for an hour. It was strange to put so much effort into hitting make believe shit on screen after I'd put more bullets into human heads than I wanted to count. I did my best, hit a few targets through the drunkenness, growling when I found my mark. I thought about Big Ed, Rip, and all the other motherfuckers I'd sent to hell each time I pulled the trigger.

Christa laughed her way through it. She missed most of the deer, but bagged a grizzly bear instead.

Why the fuck do we got a game where we're killing our club's symbol? I wondered.

Some things were meant to be mysteries. It wasn't important – seeing my old lady happy was. She didn't show a bit of trauma in her eyes when she pulled the trigger. I worried killing Red would fuck her up, especially when it was up close and personal.

But that bitch deserved to die. We both knew it, and there was nothing to regret.

By night, the buzz wasn't pulling at my brain anymore. I was ready to get the fuck on my bike and leave. Didn't think I could take another round of listening to Roman growl while he smashed the billiard balls together.

"You feeling better, baby?" I asked, helping her stand up.

She nodded, and so did I. "Good. Let's get the fuck outta here."

She'd gotten the giddiness outta her system. We were roaring down the highway, heading back into Redding proper, and I'd chosen to take the long way underneath the wide summer sky.

The full moon didn't help the crazy shit I had surging in my blood. I wanted nothing better than to jerk this bike to the curb, throw it in park, and fuck her right here on the ground. My balls churned each time she rubbed her soft hands up my abs, hugging me tight, close enough to feel my pulse.

Fuck it.

Tonight was too damned perfect. Nights like were rare in any man's lifetime. I turned down a service road and growled at her to hold on tight. I'd find us the perfect spot.

It was right there in a clearing by the trees. I slowed my bike. The wheels only chugged a little when I guided it off road, kicking up grass and dirt in its wake.

Christa's squeeze on me tightened. I grinned, but it wasn't half as tight as the pull jerking at my dick, turning it into a fucking pike.

"Rabid? What's up? Why're we –"

I killed the engine and jumped off, turning to face her. "We're here because I can't wait ten more minutes to get to your place. I *need* you, babe. Right fucking now."

A dozen more questions rippled in her cheeks. Too damned bad. I ripped her up by the hand and flipped her around. She yelped when I unfastened her belt, grinding her ass on my dick. I had it down to her ankles and her panties followed, exposing her slit to the open air.

I dropped to my knees and inhaled. Pushed two fingers into her silk. Sopping wet, just like I thought.

Fuck me.

No, fuck her. That's what I was gonna do as soon as I got her to calm the fuck down by pulling her clit into my mouth.

My tongue flicked across her pussy. She squirmed and gasped.

"Rabid –"

"Don't you Rabid me, baby girl. Keep your little lips together and just hold lay across my bike. We're fucking outdoors tonight."

Outside. Uninhibited. I told her to keep it down, but I didn't blame her when she started to moan, fighting the urge to buck her pussy against my mouth.

Good. I loved a challenge. I sucked her clit deep, running my tongue across it in fast moving waves. My fingers fucked her where my mouth couldn't. Meanwhile, my cock thundered something wicked in my pants, soaking my boxers with a steady trickle of pre-come.

Having her pressed up against my bike while I ate her pussy was the hottest thing I'd ever seen in my fucking life.

I licked long and hard. She started squirming faster, making those little hisses that always came out before she tightened up and screamed.

Just fuck my tongue, I thought. *Let it all out, baby. I wanna taste what I'm gonna be fucking in a couple minutes.*

I hoped she'd come fast and hard, perfect for warming her up and settling her into the cool night. My dick was gonna go nuclear if there were any interruptions.

Fuck. I used that lust to suck and tongue and needle her tender flesh with my teeth. One more gasp and her walls constricted around my fingers. Heat, wetness, and pleasure flowed like Jack back at the clubhouse.

Slick sweet cream bathed my face. I lapped it up, never taking my attention off her clit. I'd never get sick of making this girl squirt.

I normally gave her a minute to breathe after I tongue fucked her to heaven. Not tonight.

I'd suppressed my cock for far too long, and he was in control now. Christa whined when I fisted her hair and jerked her head up, planting my lips on hers. She tasted the lingering traces left on my lips. I fucked her tongue with mine as I undid my belt. One quick shove and my pants and boxers were gone.

Growling, I plunged into her while our tongues were still twined. The moan she pushed into my mouth was almost as sweet as everything her about her pussy.

My hips wouldn't let me savor the moment too long. I had to fuck. Had to make her come on my dick while I spent myself inside her. My balls seethed, bulging to capacity, ready to fire in her tight cunt.

I didn't hold a damned thing back. My hips rocked into hers hard enough to bruise. The moaning, sighing mess she became told me I could get even rougher. You'd better believe I fucking did.

Jerking her hair in one hand, I brought my coarse palm down on her ass. She yelped, she moaned, and then she hooked her legs around me as her pussy folded to the fire.

"Rabid!" her voice hitched right before she let go. "Don't. Fucking. Stop."

Like I needed any encouragement. I grinned, gave her another whack on the ass, and plowed right through her convulsing velvet. I had to hold onto her to make sure she didn't go over my bike headfirst.

The Harley held up well with the ride we were giving it. My first love on wheels damned well better get used to it too, because I knew right then there was no way we were stopping. This shit was addictive. This shit was hot.

This sex was the kind a man remembers on his fucking deathbed.

I fucked right through her orgasm. It was good to give her a freebie to loosen up. Then my hips really began to throttle her hard. Swung my ass backward so far I nearly pulled out before I shot forward again, pressing my tip to her womb, stroking her entire pussy with my length.

I saw her fingernails dig into the Harley's seat and she tipped her head up. "Rabid! Fuck!"

"Keep screaming my name, baby. I want every creature in this forest to hear who's breaking you, putting you back together with this dick."

The hellfire in my balls was rising, growing more insistent with every stroke. I knew I wouldn't be able to hold it anymore the next time she clenched on my cock.

Time to bring it home.

I jerked her head up and reached for her tits. My hands dove up her shirt, cupped them through her bra, and squeezed. Her nipples were so fucking hard it felt like she had rocks stuffed in there.

Fuck!

Clenching my ass, I whipped into her so hard I heard my skin crashing against her butt like lightning. She jerked her head in my hands while I held those beautiful red locks like reigns. She was trying to escape, trying to get away from the pleasure about to overwhelm us.

And that really pissed me off. I hate fucked her harder, rough and fast as I could go, snorting as I smelled our sweat mixed with motor oil. My sac was tightening by the second. She needed to come.

I dragged her off the bike with my next thrusts, and our knees were on the ground. Her eyelids fluttered as she kept her nails raking the bike, trying to keep the grip, trying to keep her mind intact.

Not what I wanted. And I always got my way.

"Fucking let go," I growled into her ear. "I need you to come hard and suck my dick dry."

She responded with a hiss. Her whole body tensed up, coiling like a spring about to leap up to the sky. Her pussy got so tight around me I thought I'd get stuck. Only encouraged me to fuck faster, harder, taking us both over the ledge.

My eyes caught the patch on her back and the brand above her jiggling ass. PROPERTY OF RABID.

Mine. All mine. Mine, mine, mine for fucking ever!

I lost it. I roared, drowning out her screams, wondering if I was coming apart at the seams. This was fucking ecstasy. This was perfection – the fuck of a lifetime.

Her pussy sucked everything my cock spat, taking it good and deep. I shook her ass, letting her jerk every drop outta my body, giving her everything I had. I wasn't a believer in full body orgasms before, but damn if I wasn't converted.

We collapsed against the bike together when I pulled out, panting in the fresh summer air, listening to the soft sounds of night. I pulled her onto my lap and we sat curled up for a good long while. Felt like it took more than an hour to muster up the energy to find the bottoms I'd ripped off her.

I watched her dress the entire time. Of course my dick stirred, hungry to get her back to a place with a floor. Maybe we'd clean up first and I'd fuck her in the shower before I laid her out, screwing 'til dawn.

I sat on my bike and tucked her helmet down over her head. She pursed her lips for one more kiss before I started my bike.

We locked lips. It was hard as hell to let go, but finally I did. She reached up and squeezed my shoulders.

"I'm sad," she whispered. "It can't get much better than this. You know we've just had the best night of our lives, right? It's been too good lately. How long before the world decides to punch us in the face?"

I snorted. Couldn't help but smile at her glass half empty shit. Luckily, I was up for the challenge, and in less than a year I'd have her singing a different tune.

"You won't be sad when we get back to your place," I said. "You're gonna realize it just gets better from here. I don't give a shit about the ups and downs. You're my old lady, baby, and if you think I'm ever gonna lay down when you're the least bit unhappy, think again. If you can't, I'll make you. All this fucking's gotta do something to the brain with the way we shake, right?"

She laughed and gave me a playful punch. My cue to ride. We were on the highway again, and home in about fifteen minutes, taking the scenic route through Redding. I wanted a few more minutes beneath those stars.

They confirmed this half-empty crap was pure, unadulterated bullshit. Our lives were gonna be overflowing 'til my last breath, bright and beautiful and immortal as the view overhead.

There'd be a lot more nights like this. I didn't doubt it for a second.

By the time I parked at her place and we were walking toward her door, the light in her eyes was different. The melancholy faded just like her scars. Yeah – that's what I thought – she was starting to believe what I said.

I grabbed her one more time, pulling her lips to mine with that furious determination burning in my blood, hotter and brighter than ever.

Thanks!

Want more Nicole Snow? Sign up for my newsletter to hear about new releases, subscriber only goodies, and other fun stuff!

JOIN THE NICOLE SNOW NEWSLETTER! - http://eepurl.com/HwFW1

Thank you so much for buying this book. I hope my romances will brighten your mornings and darken your evenings with total pleasure. Sensuality makes everything more vivid, doesn't it?

If you liked this book, please consider leaving a review and checking out my other erotic romance tales.

Got a comment on my work? Email me at nicolesnowerotica@gmail.com. I love hearing from my fans!

Kisses,
Nicole Snow

More Erotic Romance by Nicole Snow

KEPT WOMEN: TWO FERTILE SUBMISSIVE STORIES

SUBMISSIVE'S FOLLY (SEDUCED AND RAVAGED)

SUBMISSIVE'S EDUCATION

SUBMISSIVE'S HARD DISCOVERY

HER STRICT NEIGHBOR

SOLDIER'S STRICT ORDERS

COWBOY'S STRICT COMMANDS

RUSTLING UP A BRIDE: RANCHER'S PREGNANT CURVES

FIGHT FOR HER HEART

BIG BAD DARE: TATTOOS AND SUBMISSION

MERCILESS LOVE: A DARK ROMANCE

LOVE SCARS: BAD BOY'S BRIDE

Outlaw Love/Prairie Devils MC Books

OUTLAW KIND OF LOVE

NOMAD KIND OF LOVE

SAVAGE KIND OF LOVE

WICKED KIND OF LOVE

BITTER KIND OF LOVE

Outlaw Love/ Grizzlies MC Books

OUTLAW'S KISS

SEXY SAMPLES: OUTLAW'S KISS

I: Cursed Bones (Missy)

"It won't be long now," the nurse said, checking dad's IV bag. "Breathing getting shallower…pulse is slowing…don't worry, girls. He won't feel a thing. That's what the morphine's for."

I had to squeeze his hand to make sure he wasn't dead yet. Jesus, he was so cold. I swore there was a ten degree difference between dad's fingers in one hand, and my little sister's in the other. I blinked back tears, trying to be brave for Jackie, who watched helplessly, trembling and shaking at my side.

We'd already said our goodbyes. We'd been doing that for the last hour, right before he slipped into unconsciousness for what I guessed was the last time.

I turned to my sister. "It'll be okay. He's going to a better place. No more suffering. The cancer, all the pain…it dies with him. Dad's finally getting better."

"Missy…" Jackie squeaked, ripping her hand away from me and covering her face.

The nurse gave me a sympathetic look. It took so much effort to push down the lump in my throat without cracking up. I choked on my grief, holding it in, cold and sharp as death looming large.

I threw an arm around my sister, pulling her close.

Lying like this was a bitch.

I wasn't really sure what I believed anymore, but I had to say something. Jackie was the one who needed all my support now. Dad's long, painful dying days were about to be over.

Not that it made anything easy. But I was grown up, and I could handle it. Losing him at twenty-one was hard, but if I was fourteen, like the small trembling girl next to me?

"Melissa." Thin, weak fingers tightened on my wrist with surprising strength.

I jumped, drawing my arm off Jackie, looking at the sick man in the bed. His eyes were wide open and his lips were moving. The sickly sheen on his forehead glowed, one last light before it burned out forever.

"Daddy? What is it?" I leaned in close, wondering if I'd imagined him saying my name.

"Forgive me," he hissed. "I...I fucked up bad. But I did it for a good reason. I just wish I could've done it different, baby..."

His eyelids fluttered. I squeezed his fingers as tight as I could, moving closer to his gray lips. What the hell was he saying? Was this about Mom again?

She'd been gone for ten years in a car accident, waiting for him on the other side. "Daddy? Hey!"

I grabbed his bony shoulder and gently shook him. He was still there, fighting the black wave pulling him lower, insistent and overpowering.

"It's the only way...I couldn't do it with hard work.

Honest work. That never paid shit." He blinked, running his tongue over his lips. "Just look in the basement, baby. There's a palate...roofing tiles. Everything I ever wanted to leave my girls is there. It was worth it...I promised her I'd do anything for you and Jackie...and I did. I did it, Carol. Our girls are set. I'm ready to burn if I need to..."

Hearing him say mom's name, and then talk about burning? I blinked back tears and shook my head.

What the hell was this? Some kinda death fever making him talk nonsense?

Dad started to slump into the mattress, a harsh rattle in his throat, the tiny splash of color left in his face becoming pale ash. I backed away as the machines howled. The nurse looked at me and nodded. She rushed to his free side, intently watching his heartbeat jerk on the monitor.

The machine released an earsplitting wail as the line went flat.

Jackie completely lost it. I grabbed her tight, holding onto her, turning away until the mechanical screaming stopped. I wanted to cover my ears, but I wanted hers closed more.

I held my little sister and rocked her to my chest. We didn't move until the nurse finally touched my shoulder, nudging us into the waiting room outside.

We sat and waited for all the official business of death to finish up. My brain couldn't stop going back to his last words, the best distraction I had to keep my sanity.

What was he talking about? His last words sounded so strange, so sure. So repentant, and that truly frightened me.

I didn't dare get my hopes up, as much as I wanted to believe we wouldn't lose everything and end up living in the car next week. The medical bills snatched up the last few pennies left over from his pension and disability – the same fate waiting for our house as soon as his funeral was done.

Delirious, I thought. *His dying wish was for us, hoping and praying we'd be okay. He went out selflessly, just like a good father should.*

That was it. Had to be.

He was dying, after all...pumped full of drugs, driven crazy in his last moments. But I couldn't let go of what he said about the basement.

We'd have to scour the house anyway before the state kicked us out. If there was anything more to his words besides crazy talk, we'd find out soon enough, right?

I looked at Jackie, biting my lip. I tried not to hope off a dead man's words. But damn it, I did.

If he'd tucked away some spare cash or some silver to pawn, I wouldn't turn it down. Anything would help us live another day without facing the gaping void left by his brutal end.

My sister was tipped back in her chair, one tissue pressed tight to her eyes. I reached for her hand and squeezed, careful not to set her off all over again.

"We're going to figure this out," I promised. "Don't worry about anything except mourning him, Jackie. You're not going anywhere. I'm going to do my damnedest to find us a place and pay the bills while you stay in school."

She straightened up, clearing her throat, shooting me a nasty look. "Stop talking to me like I'm a stupid kid!"

I blinked. Jackie leaned in, showing me her bloodshot eyes. "I'm not as old as you, sis, but I'm not retarded. We're out of money. I get that. I know you won't find a job in this shitty town with half a degree and no experience...we'll end up homeless, and then the state'll get involved. They'll take me away from you, stick me with some freaky foster parents. But I won't forget you, Missy. I'll be okay. I'll survive."

Rage shot through me. Rage against the world, myself, maybe even dad's ghost for putting us in this fucked up position.

I clenched my jaw. "That's *not* going to happen, Jackie. Don't even go there. I won't let –"

"Whatever. It's not like it matters. I just hope there's a way for us to keep in touch when the hammer falls." She was quiet for a couple minutes before she finally looked up, her eyes redder than before. "I heard what he said while I was crying. Daddy didn't have crap after he got sick and left the force – nothing but those measly checks. He didn't earn a dime while he was sick. He died the same way he lived, Missy – sorry, and completely full of shit."

Anger howled through me. I wanted to grab her, shake her, tell her to get a fucking grip and stop obsessing on disaster. But I knew she didn't mean it.

Lashing out wouldn't do any good. Rage was all part of

grief, wasn't it? I kept waiting for mine to bubble to the surface, toxic as the crap they'd pumped into our father to prolong his life by a few weeks towards the end.

I settled back in my chair and closed my eyes. I'd find some way to keep my promise to Jackie, whether there was a lucky break waiting for us in the basement or just more junk, more wreckage from our lives.

Daddy wasn't ready to be a single father when Mom got killed, but he'd managed. He did the best he could before he had to deal with the shit hand dealt to him by this merciless life. I closed my eyes, vowing I'd do the same.

No demons waiting for us on the road ahead would stop me. Making sure neither of us died with dad was my new religion, and I swore I'd never, ever lose my faith.

A week passed. A lonely, bitter week in late winter with a meager funeral. Daddy's estranged brother sent us some money to have him cremated and buried with a bare bones headstone.

I wouldn't ask Uncle Ken for a nickel more, even if he'd been man enough to show his face at the funeral. Thankfully, it wasn't something to worry about. He kept his distance several states away, the same 'ostrich asshole' daddy always said he was since they'd fallen out over my grandparent's miniscule inheritance.

All it did was confirm the whole family was fucked. I had no one now except Jackie, and it was her and I against the world, the last of the Thomas girls against the curse turning our lives to pure hell over the last decade.

A short trip to the attorney's office told me what I already knew about dad's assets. What little he had was going into state hands. Medicare was determined to claw back a tiny fraction of what they'd spent on his care. And because I was now Jackie's legal guardian, his pension and disability was as good as buried with him.

The older lawyer asked me if I'd made arrangements with extended family, almost as an afterthought. Of course I had, I lied. I made sure to straighten up and smile real big when I said it.

I was a responsible adult. I could make money sprout from weeds. What did the truth matter in a world that wasn't wired to give us an ounce of help?

Whatever shit was waiting for us up ahead needed to be fed, nourished with lies if I wanted to keep it from burying us. I was ready for that, ready to throw on as many fake smiles and twisted truths as I needed to keep Jackie safe and happy.

Whatever wiggle room we'd had for innocent mistakes slammed shut the instant daddy's heart stopped in the sharp white room.

I was so busy dealing with sadness and red tape that I'd nearly forgotten about his last words. Finishing up his affairs and making sure Jackie still got some sleep and decent food in her belly took all week, stealing away the meager energy I had left.

It was late one night after she'd gone to bed when I finally remembered. It hit me while I was watching a bad spy movie on late night TV, halfway paying attention to the story as my stomach twisted in knots, steeling itself for the frantic job hunt I had to start tomorrow.

I got up from my chair and padded over to the basement door. Dust teased my nose, dead little flecks suspended in the dim light. The basement stank like mildew, tinged with rubbing alcohol and all the spare medicine we'd stored down here while dad suffered at home.

I held my breath descending the stairs, knowing it would only get worse when I finally had to inhale. Our small basement was dark and creepy as any. I looked around, trying not to fixate on his old work bench. Seeing the old husks of half-finished RC planes he used to build in better times would definitely bring tears.

Roofing tiles, he'd said. Okay, but where?

It took more than a minute just scanning back and forth before I noticed the big blue tarp. It was wedged in the narrow slit between the furnace and the hot water tank.

My heart ticked faster. So, he wasn't totally delusional on his death bed. There really were roofing tiles there – and what else?

It was even stranger because the thing hadn't been here when I was down in the basement last week – and daddy had been in hospice for three weeks. He couldn't have crawled back and hidden the unknown package here. Jackie definitely couldn't have done it and kept her mouth shut.

That left one disturbing possibility – someone had broken into our house and left it here.

Ice ran through my veins. I shook off wild thoughts about intruders, kneeling down next to the blue plastic and running my hands over it.

Yup, it felt like a roofing palate. Not that I'd handled many to know, but whatever was beneath it was jagged, sandy, and square.

Screw it. Let's see what's really in here, I thought.

Clenching my teeth, I dragged the stack out. It was lighter than I expected, and it didn't take long to find the ropey ties holding it together. One pull and it came off easy. A thick slab of shingles slid out and thudded on the beaten concrete, kicking up more dust lodged in the utilities.

I covered my mouth and coughed. Disappointment settled in my stomach, heavy as the construction crap in front of me. I prepared myself for a big fat nothing hidden in the cracks.

"Damn it," I whispered, shaking my head. My hands dove for the shingles and started to tug, desperate to get this shit over with and say goodbye to the last hope humming in my stomach.

The shingles didn't come up easy. Planting my feet on both sides and tugging didn't pull the stack apart like I expected. Grunting, I pulled harder, taking my rage and frustration out on this joke at my feet.

There was a ripping sound much different than I expected. I tumbled backward and hit the dryer, looking at the square block in my hands. When I turned it over, I saw the back was a mess of glue and cardboard.

Hope beat in my chest again, however faint. This was no ordinary stack of shingles. My arms were shaking as I dropped the flap and walked back to the pile, looking down at the torn cardboard center hidden by the layer I'd peeled off. Someone went through some serious trouble camouflaging the box underneath.

I walked to dad's old bench for a box cutter, too stunned with the weird discovery to dwell on his mementos. The blade went in and tore through in a neat slice. I quickly carved out an opening, totally unprepared for the thick leafy pile that came falling out.

My jaw dropped along with the box cutter. I hit the ground, resting my knees on the piles of cash, and tore into the rest of the box.

Hundreds – no, thousands – came out in huge piles. I tore through the package and turned it upside down, showering myself in more cash than I'd seen in my life, hundreds bound together in crisp rolls with red rubber bands.

Had to cover my mouth to stifle the insane laughter tearing at my lungs. I couldn't let Jackie hear me and come running downstairs. If I was all alone, I would've laughed like a psycho, mad with the unexpected light streaking to life in our darkness.

Jesus, I barely knew how to handle the mystery fortune myself, let alone involve my little sis. I collapsed on the floor, feeling hot tears running down my cheeks. The stupid grin pulling at my face lingered.

Somehow, someway, he'd done it. Daddy had really done it.

He'd left us everything we'd need to survive. Hell, all we'd need to *thrive*. Feeling the cool million crunching underneath my jeans like leaves proved it.

"Shit!" I swore, realizing I was rolling around in the money like a demented celebrity.

Panicking, I kicked my legs, careful to check every nook around me for anything I'd kicked away in shock. When I saw it was all there, I grabbed an old laundry basket and started piling the stacks in it. I pulled one out and took off the rubber band. Rifling my fingers through several fistfuls of cash told me everything was separated in neat bundles of twenty-five hundred dollars.

I piled them in, feverishly counting. I had to stop around the half million mark. There was at least double that on the floor. Eventually, I'd settle down and inventory it to the dime, but for now I was looking at somewhere between one to two million, easy.

It was magnitudes greater than anything this family had seen in its best years, before everything went to shit. I smoothed my fingers over my face, loving the unmistakable money scent clinging to my hands.

No shock – sweet freedom smelled exactly like cold hard cash.

An hour later, I'd stuffed it into an old black suitcase, something discreet I could keep with me. My stomach gurgled. One burden lifted, and another one landed on my shoulders.

I wasn't stupid. I'd heard plenty about what daddy did for the Redding PD's investigations to know spending too much mystery money at once brought serious consequences. Wherever this money came from, it sure as hell wasn't clean.

I'd have to keep one eye glued to the cash for...months? Years?

Shit. Grim responsibility burned in my brain, and it made my bones hurt like they were locked in quicksand. Dirty money wasn't easy to spend.

I'd have to risk a few bigger chunks up front on groceries, a tune-up for our ancient Ford LTD, and then a down payment on a new place for Jackie and I.

It wouldn't buy us a luxury condo – not if we wanted to save ourselves a Federal investigation. But this cash was plenty to make a greedy landlord's eyes light up and take a few months' worth of rent without any uncomfortable questions. It was more than enough to give us food plus a roof over our heads while I figured out the rest.

Survival was still the name of the game, even if it had gotten unexpectedly easier.

Once our needs were secure, then I could figure out the rest. Maybe I'd find a way to finagle my way back into school so I could finish the accounting program I'd been forced to drop when dad's cancer went terminal.

It felt like hours passed while I finished filling up the suitcase and triple checked the basement for runaway money. When I was finally satisfied I'd secured everything,

I grabbed the suitcases and marched upstairs, turning out the light behind me. I switched off the TV and headed straight for bed.

I sighed, knowing I was in for a long, restless night, even with the miracle cash safe beneath my bed. Or maybe because of it.

I couldn't tell if my heart or my head was more drained. They'd both been absolutely ripped out and shot to the moon these past two weeks.

I closed my eyes and tried to sleep. Tomorrow, I'd be hunting for a brand new place instead of a job while Jackie caught up on schoolwork. That happy fact alone should've made it easier to sleep.

But nothing about this was simple or joyful. It wasn't a lottery win.

Dwelling on the gaping canyon left in our lives by both our dead parents was a constant brutal temptation, especially when it was dark, cold, and quiet. So was avoiding the question that kept boiling in my head – how had he gotten it?

What the *fuck* had daddy done to make this much money from nothing? Life insurance payouts and stock dividends didn't get dropped off in mysterious packages downstairs.

He'd asked for forgiveness before his body gave out. My lips trembled and I pinched my eyes shut, praying he hadn't done something terrible – not directly, anyway. He was too sick for too long to kill anyone. He'd been off the force for a few years too.

I lost minutes – maybe hours – thinking about how he'd earned the dirty little secret underneath my bed. Whatever he'd done, it was bad. But at the end of the day, how much did I care?

And no matter how much blood the cash was soaked in, we needed it. I wasn't about to latch onto fantasy ethics and flush his dying legacy down the toilet. Blood money or not, we *needed* it. No fucking way was I going to burn the one thing that would keep us fed, clothed, sheltered, and sane.

Jackie never had to know where our miracle came from. Neither did I. Maybe years from now I'd have time for soul searching, time to worry about what kind of sick sins I'd branded onto my conscience by profiting off this freak inheritance.

Fretting about murder and corruption right now wouldn't keep the state from taking Jackie away when we were homeless. I had to keep my mouth shut and my mind more closed than ever. I had to treat it like a lottery win I could never tell anyone about.

Besides, it was all just temporary. I'd use the fortune to pay the rent and put food in our fridge until I finished school and got myself a job. Then I'd slowly feed the rest into something useful for Jackie's college – something that wouldn't get us busted.

It must've been after three o'clock when I finally fell asleep. If only I had a crystal ball, or stayed awake just an hour or two longer.

I would've seen the hurricane coming, the pitch black

storm that always comes in when a girl takes the hand the devil's offered.

An earsplitting scream woke me first, but it was really the door slamming a second later that convinced me I wasn't dreaming.

Jackie!

I threw my blanket off and sat up, reaching for my phone on the nightstand. My hand slid across the smooth wood, and adrenaline dumped in my blood when I realized there was nothing there.

Too dark. I didn't realize the stranger was standing right over me until I tried to bolt up, slamming into his vice-like grip instead. Before I could even scream, his hand was over my mouth. Scratchy stubble prickled my cheek as his lips parted against my ear.

"Don't. You fucking scream, I'll have to put a bullet in your spine." Cold metal pushed up beneath my shirt, a gun barrel, proof he wasn't making an empty threat.

Not that I'd have doubted it. His tight, sinister embrace stayed locked around my waist as he turned me around and nudged his legs against mine, forcing me to move toward the hall.

"Just go where I tell you, and this'll all be over nice and quick. Nobody has to get hurt."

I listened. When we got to the basement door, he flung it open and lightened his grip, knowing it was a one way trip downstairs with no hope for escape.

Jackie was already down there against the wall, and so

were four more large, brutal men like the one who'd held me. I blinked when I got to the foot of the stairs and took in the bizarre scene. They all wore matching leather vests with GRIZZLIES MC, CALIFORNIA emblazoned up their sides and on their backs.

I'd seen bikers traveling the roads for years, but never anything like these guys. Their jackets looked a lot like the ones veterans wore when they went out riding, but the symbols were all different. Bloody, strange, and very dangerous looking.

The men themselves matched the snarling bears on their leather. Four of them were younger, tattooed, spanning the spectrum from lean and wiry to pure muscle. The guy who'd walked me down the stairs moved where I could see him. He might've been the youngest, but I wasn't really sure.

Scary didn't begin to describe him. He looked at me with his arms folded, piercing green eyes going right through my soul, set in a stern cold face. He exuded a strength and severity that only came naturally – a born badass. A predator completely fixed on me.

An older man with long gray hair seemed to be in charge. He looked at the man holding my sister, another hard faced man with barbed wire ropes tattooed across his face. Jackie's eyes were bulging, shimmering like wide, frantic pools, pulling me in.

I'm sorry, I hissed in my head, breaking eye contact. One more second and I might've lost it. The only thing worse than being down here at their mercy was showing them I was already weak, broken, helpless.

They had my little sister, my whole world, everything I'd sworn to protect. No, this wasn't the time to freak out and cry. I had to keep it together if we were going to get out of this alive.

"Well? Any sign of the haul upstairs, or do we need to make these bitches sing?" Gray hair reached into his pocket, retrieving a cigarette and a lighter, as casually as if he was at work on a smoke break.

Shit, for all I knew, he probably was.

"Nothing up there, Blackjack." The man who'd taken me downstairs stepped forward, leaving the basement echoing with his smoky voice, older and more commanding than I'd expected. It hadn't just been the rough whisper flowing into my ear.

"Fuck," the psycho holding Jackie growled. "I like it the fun way, but I'm not a fan when these bitches scream. Makes my ears ring for days. Can't we gag these cunts first?"

Nobody answered him. The older man narrowed his eyes, looking at his goon, taking a long pull on the cigarette. My head was spinning, making it feel like the ground had softened up, ready to suck me under and bury me alive.

Oh, God. I knew this had to be about the mystery money the moment those rough hands went around me, but I hadn't really thought we were about to die until he said that.

Gray hair turned to face me, scowling. "You heard the

man, love. We can do this the easy way or the hard way. I, for one, don't like spilling blood when there's no good reason, but some of the brothers feel differently. Now, we know your loot's not where it was supposed to be – found this shit all torn up myself."

Blowing his smoke, he pointed at the mess on the ground. I could've choked myself for being too stupid to clean up the mess earlier.

"You've got it somewhere. It couldn't have gotten far," he said, striding forward. "Look we both know me and my boys are gonna find it. Only question left is – are you gonna make this scavenger hunt easy-peasy-punkin-squeezy? Or are you gonna make all our fucking ears ring while we choke it out of you?"

I didn't answer. My eyes floated above his shoulder, fixing on the man across from me, stoic green eyes.

"Well?" The older asshole was getting impatient.

Strange. If Green Eyes wasn't so busy hanging out with these creeps and taking hostages, he would've been handsome. No, downright sexy was a better word.

My weeping, broken brain was still fixed on the stupid idea when Gray Hair grunted, pulled the light out of his mouth, and reached for my throat...

Look for Outlaw's Kiss at your favorite retailer!